BADMAN'S BULLET

"Who the hell is that?" Odell asked, startled. His forearm stung from tiny particles of chipped rock that had pelted him.

"Damn it! It's Cray Dawson!" Tapp said to Odell. "How did he get around behind us? He'll pick our eyes out from there!"

"Oh no, he won't!" Odell said with confidence. "Hold your Gawdamned fire, Sheriff! I wager you'd never forgive yourself if something bad happens to this little woman!" He waved Turner up from behind the rock. Turner was holding Carmelita against his chest, his pistol pointed at her head.

Dawson froze at the sight of Carmelita; his rifle fell silent.

Odell grinned and relaxed a bit, unaffected by the wild rifle shots coming up from the trail below. "I thought that would get your interest, Sheriff," he called out. "I'm Odell Clarkson, and I'm here to ruin your whole day if you don't play the cards I'm dealing you!"

THE LAW IN SOMOS SANTOS

Ralph Cotton

A SIGNET BOOK

SIGNET
Published by New American Library, a division of
Penguin Group (USA) Inc., 375 Hudson Street,
New York, New York 10014, USA
Penguin Group (Canada), 10 Alcorn Avenue, Toronto,
Ontario M4V 3B2, Canada (a division of Pearson Penguin Canada Inc.)
Penguin Books Ltd., 80 Strand, London WC2R 0RL, England
Penguin Ireland, 25 St. Stephen's Green, Dublin 2,
Ireland (a division of Penguin Books Ltd.)
Penguin Group (Australia), 250 Camberwell Road, Camberwell, Victoria 3124,
Australia (a division of Pearson Australia Group Pty. Ltd.)
Penguin Books India Pvt. Ltd., 11 Community Centre, Panchsheel Park,
New Delhi - 110 017, India
Penguin Group (NZ), Cnr Airborne and Rosedale Roads, Albany,
Auckland 1310, New Zealand (a division of Pearson New Zealand Ltd.)
Penguin Books (South Africa) (Pty.) Ltd., 24 Sturdee Avenue,
Rosebank, Johannesburg 2196, South Africa

Penguin Books Ltd., Registered Offices:
80 Strand, London WC2R 0RL, England

First published by Signet, an imprint of New American Library,
a division of Penguin Group (USA) Inc.

First Printing, July 2005
10 9 8 7 6 5 4 3 2 1

Printed in the United States of America

PUBLISHER'S NOTE
This is a work of fiction. Names, characters, places, and incidents either are the product of the author's imagination or are used fictitiously, and any resemblance to actual persons, living or dead, business establishments, events, or locales is entirely coincidental.

For Mary Lynn . . . *of course*

PART 1

Chapter 1

Cray Dawson had pinned a tin sheriff's badge on his chest three months after he'd ridden into his hometown of Somos Santos, Texas, and killed Martin Lematte, a crooked sheriff who, with the help of his gunmen, had turned the small town into a haven for thugs, thieves and murderers. But even after killing Lematte and cleaning up the town, Dawson had been reluctant to take on the *official* role as sheriff.

Only under the urging of Carmelita, the young woman he lived with, had Dawson agreed to keep order in Somos Santos until such time as the town board found an interested party willing to run for the duly elected position.

But after three months, with no takers coming forward, Dawson had resigned himself to the fact that he was stuck with the job, in spite of what the town board members had assured him.

"Nobody's fool enough to come sniffing around after *your* job, Sheriff Dawson?" One of the Tinsley boys had commented one night on his way to jail. With a broken-toothed grin Benson Tinsley had added, "Hell, I'm drunk as a hoot owl and *I've* got enough sense to see that!"

"You don't know what you're talking about, Benson," Dawson had replied grudgingly, giving the staggering cowboy a slight shove toward the jail. "And don't call me *Sheriff.*"

"Whatever you say, *Sheriff,*" Benson Tinsley laughed drunkenly.

Dawson had only frowned to himself, knowing the Tinsley boy spoke the truth. Whether he wanted to admit it or not, Cray Dawson had gained himself a reputation with a gun. It seemed nothing he did would ever change that. The townsfolk weren't about to forget how he'd cleaned up Somos Santos; nor were they going to forget how, before cleaning up the town, Dawson had ridden with Lawrence "Fast Larry" Shaw, another hometown boy who'd become known as the fastest gun alive.

Together Dawson and Shaw had hunted down and killed the men who had murdered Shaw's wife. Shaw had warned Dawson at the outset that his life would never be the same. Shaw had been right. Like it or not, Cray Dawson had become a noted gunman. He had to accept it. So he did.

"Carmelita," he'd said, sitting her on the porch step beside him in the paling red sunset, "I'm doing it. What do you think?"

She sighed, knowing what *doing it* referred to. "I think if you are going to be known as a gunman, it is better that you become a lawman. Perhaps men will think twice before they try to kill you if they know you represent the law."

"Yes, maybe so," Dawson replied, knowing better, but not wanting to go into it right then.

So, at the end of three months, he'd stepped forward before a circuit judge who presided over such matters, sworn an oath with his right hand on the judge's battered leather-bound Bible and accepted the tin badge that the town blacksmith, Lou Prior, had fashioned out of the top of a tin can.

Pinning the shiny new badge onto Dawson's chest, Judge Addison Moore had cursed and said in a lowered tone of voice, "Damned if he didn't spell *Sheriff* wrong." He started to remove the badge, but Dawson stopped him. "Dawson, you can't wear this! I'll take it and have Lou correct it," the judge growled under his breath, trying to keep the spelling error between the two of them.

"Let's get on with it, Your Honor. I'll have it fixed later," Dawson replied in the same lowered tone.

"It's not dignified!" the judge protested. He started to grasp the badge again, but Dawson closed his hand over the judge's fingers, firm enough to make his point. "Dignified or not, Your Honor, if we put this off another minute I'm apt to back out altogether."

Three weeks later, that ceremony is what came to Sheriff Crayton Dawson's mind as he stood in the dirt street, a curl of gray gunsmoke rising from the barrel of his big single-action .45 caliber Colt.

"Deputy," Dawson said quietly, the sound of both his gunshot and the gunshot from Teddy Bryce's pistol ringing inside his head, "watch the windows. He had another hardcase named Tony Weaver riding with him."

"I've got you covered, Sheriff," said Hooney Carter, his voice sounding a bit shaky but under control. Twenty yards away, Carter had left a young gunman named Jimmy Shaggs lying knocked cold at the edge of a boardwalk. Now Carter waved a double-barreled ten gauge back and forth slowly along the roof line, the windows, the shadowed doorways along the boardwalk.

"I know all about Tony Weaver," Carter called out. He'd raised his voice deliberately, making sure Weaver would hear him, should the gunman be listening. "I wish that sumbitch *would* show his face here about now. I'd like to count how many nailheads this scattergun can put into his chest."

Upon hearing the deputy's threats, townsfolk who had started to venture out of stores and offices stopped in their tracks and stepped cautiously back inside their sanctuaries. "That's right, all you folks," said Hooney Carter. "Everybody sit tight till the sheriff says otherwise."

Both sheriff and deputy stood in silence for a moment until, as if on cue, the sound of pounding hooves arose from deep within an alley alongside the town mercantile store and beat a hasty path of retreat toward the distant hill line. A moment later, the two lawmen watched Tony Weaver grow smaller and smaller at the head of a rising trail of dust. Only then did Dawson let out a tight breath, drop the spent cartridge from his Colt and replace it with a fresh one.

"Looks like that's it, Sheriff," the deputy said, for some reason still scanning the rooftops.

"Yes, for now," said Dawson. He stepped forward and stopped a few feet from Teddy Bryce, lying dead on the ground. He stooped, picked up the dead gunman's pistol, which had fallen to the dirt, and shoved it down behind his gun belt. Behind him, Hooney Carter had hurried over, jerked Jimmy Shaggs to his feet and shoved him forward with the tip of the shotgun.

Shaggs staggered forward like a drunkard and fell at Dawson's feet. Rolling his dazed eyes upward at Dawson, Shaggs said in defiance, "Go on and shoot me. I ain't telling you a Gawdamned thing!"

"I didn't ask you anything," Dawson replied.

"About what?" Shaggs asked, seeming puzzled and still not fully alert.

Dawson and his deputy gave each other a look. "Why did you come here backing a snake like Bryce against the sheriff, Shaggs?" Carter asked, reaching down and poking him roughly with his shotgun barrel.

"Take it easy, Deputy," Dawson said, seeing that Carter had gotten a bit carried away with himself.

"Yeah, Deputy," Shaggs repeated, "take it easy! I never done anything anyway." His hand cupped the long swollen welt along the side of his head.

"You tried to kill this man, you son of a bitch!" said Carter, holding himself back from poking Shaggs again. "We'd be within our rights to blow your damned empty head off. Wouldn't we, Sheriff?"

"I wouldn't go that far, Deputy," said Dawson, concerned with what agreeing with Carter might bring about. "But you've sure bought yourself a year or two in prison, if I decide to press charges against you."

"That wouldn't be very sporting of you, Sheriff," said Shaggs. "Not to mention how it would look, a big-name gunman like yourself taking up a grudge over something like this."

Dawson reached down and dragged Jimmy Shaggs to

his feet. "This is no sporting event, Shaggs!" he said harshly, shaking the still dazed gunman. "That's what I want idiots like you, Weaver and Bryce to get through your thick skulls. I'm no big name gunman, and coming here wanting to kill me is not a damn sporting event!" He shook Shaggs harder. "Do you think you can remember that after a few weeks in jail?" He gave Shaggs a shove toward the jail. "Or should I turn this into a couple of years of prison time, let you break rock until you start to understand?"

Staggering forward, Shaggs looked over his shoulder, still cupping the welt alongside his head. "No call to get upset about it, Sheriff! I'm just exercising my freedom to speak as I damned well please!"

"That's it. I'm cracking his skull!" said Hooney Carter, stepping closer and drawing back the butt of his shotgun.

"Hold it, Deputy!" Dawson shouted, stepping in between the two.

Shaggs cowered behind Dawson and threw his arms up to protect his already sore and swollen head. "He's crazy, Sheriff! Look at him! He's the one ought to be behind bars! Look what he did to me. And I didn't do a damned thing!"

"Keep moving, Shaggs," said Dawson, giving him another shove. To Carter, he said, "Deputy, go round up a couple of men to help you get Bryce's body out of the street. Take him to the barber for some undertaking. Get Jessup Stinnett to take a photograph or two so we can send them around, see if he's wanted anywhere else in Texas."

"Will I get part of any bounty if there is any?" Carter asked shamelessly.

"You won't be overlooked," said Dawson. "Now hurry up so we can get on Weaver's trail. He's as guilty as Shaggs."

"All right!" Carter grinned. His grin went away quickly as he frowned and jerked his head toward Jimmy Shaggs. "What about him?" Hooney Carter asked, glaring hard at Shaggs. "What if he makes a break for it before I get back?"

"I've got him under control, Deputy," Dawson said firmly.

"Not one damned thing did I do!" Shaggs said, still chastising the deputy for knocking him cold. "I hadn't broken no damned law or nothing else!"

"You're a lying son of a bitch!" shouted Carter, after turning away. He stopped and pointed a finger back toward Shaggs. "You came here to help kill our sheriff!"

"I never fired a shot!" Shaggs protested. "You can't arrest a man for doing *nothing*! You've got to have some kind of charge against him!"

"We'll charge you with intent, Shaggs," said Dawson, walking along behind him, nodding the deputy away toward the body in the street. Carter left grumbling under his breath.

"Intent?" Shaggs gave Dawson a look of disbelief. "How can you arrest a man just because he *might* have been *intending* to do something? I never got a chance to show what I intended to do!"

"I know," said Dawson. "But if Carter had waited until he did see your intentions, I might be laying dead out there instead of Bryce. Now shut up and keep walking."

"I got to get myself a lawyer. I can see that," said Shaggs, shaking his head as he staggered on toward the jail. "Law in this country has gone straight to hell, when a man can't even *think* about breaking a law without getting his head busted." He pointed a shaky finger at some onlookers along the boardwalk in front of the bank across the street and said, taunting Dawson, "Quick, Sheriff! Look over there. Those fellows look like they *might* be *intending* to rob the bank! Better go arrest them just to be safe!" He raised his voice toward the onlookers, shouting, "We know you're *intending* to rob the bank, you bunch of low-down—"

"Pipe down, Shaggs!" Dawson cut him off, seeing that Shaggs' words had caused a bit of a restless stir on the boardwalk. Directing him up onto the boardwalk beneath a large wooden sign in the shape of a badge that read SHERIFF'S OFFICE & SOMOS SANTOS TOWN JAIL, Dawson added, "Unless you want me to tack on a charge of disturbing the peace."

"Disturbing the peace. I'll be double dog damned," Shaggs said shaking his lowered head with a look of dejection. "I used to love this country, back before all these damned *laws* started taking over everything. I've turned despondent and hopeless of late."

Opening the door to his office, Dawson said in mock sympathy, "We'll see what we can do to cheer you up while you're here, Shaggs."

Stepping inside the sheriff's office and looking at the row of cells along the far wall, Shaggs said, "I hope you will at least keep that crazy sumbitch Carter from killing me in my sleep."

"Carter and you will get along, Shaggs," said Dawson. "You just see to it you mind your business and not give him a hard time doing his job. Everybody will be just fine."

"Yeah, he'll do his damned job all right," said Shaggs, walking over to the nearest cell with its door open in grim invitation. "Trouble with men like Hooney Carter is that the badge makes them go plumb loco. They want to do *too* good of a job."

Dawson smiled slightly to himself. "All the more reason you'd do well to keep your mouth shut and do as you're told," he said. He closed the barred door to the cell, turning the key in the lock as he spoke.

Inside the cell, Shaggs turned to face Dawson through the bars. "Did you mean what you said about me spending some time here and not having to go to prison?"

"It depends," said Dawson, stepping away from the cell.

"Depends on what?" Shaggs grasped the bars and shook them a bit as if testing them.

"On whether or not you're wanted anywhere else," said Dawson. "We'll telegraph your name around and see if anybody has any charges against you. If they don't, and you can keep your nose clean a few weeks, maybe I'll drop charges against you and we'll turn you loose. Fair enough?"

Shaggs grimaced and said, "Well, you see, there might just be a small charge or two, somewhere."

"Oh, really?" Dawson stared at him.

"Nothing serious mind you," said Shaggs. He

shrugged. "But you know how it is with rowdy ole boys like me. We're always up to something—getting into mischief, you might say."

"I see," said Dawson. "Anything you want to tell me about beforehand?"

"Naw, nothing worth mentioning," said Shaggs. "I wouldn't go to the trouble of telegraphing everybody, getting them all worked up over nothing."

Before Dawson could comment, Deputy Carter rushed in from the boardwalk, his shotgun still in hand. "Ready when you are, Sheriff!" he called out, his voice still sharp and excited.

Dawson looked him up and down. "I want you to settle down some, Deputy. We could be on the trail all night chasing Weaver."

"I am settled down," said Carter. He cut a dark glance toward Jimmy Shaggs and said to Dawson, "What's this sonsabitch been saying about me anyway?"

"Nothing, Deputy," said Dawson. "I just want you to ease down a little before we get started after Weaver. Will you do that for me?"

"Sheriff, if I'm not doing my job—"

"Deputy, you're doing a good job," Dawson cut in. "I just want you to settle down."

"I told you, Sheriff, I am settled down," said Carter.

Dawson let out a breath, giving up on the excited deputy. "All right." He pitched the cell key to him, saying, "Take this over to Bently's. Tell Ned to look after the prisoner while we're gone. Stop by the livery barn and ask Fosse to send his son out to the hacienda and tell Carmelita I might not make it home tonight."

"Yes, sir, Sheriff." Carter grinned in excitement, but

stopped abruptly before he turned to leave. "Are we bringing him back dead or alive, Sheriff?"

Dawson looked at the deputy for a moment, then said, "Alive, of course."

"What if he puts up too much of a fight?" Carter asked, looking disappointed at the prospect of bringing the third gunman in alive.

"We'll have to deal with that when the time comes," said Dawson, not wanting to commit easily to the taking of a man's life.

"Good enough for me." Carter grinned, as if hearing some sort of permission in Dawson's words. He turned and rushed away toward Bently's Mercantile Store with the cell keys in his hand.

"See what I mean, Sheriff?" Jimmy Shaggs said from his cell. "He's crazier than a june bug.

"Shut up and make yourself comfortable, Shaggs," Dawson said over his shoulder as he walked over and pulled a Winchester repeating rifle from a gun rack. "We'll bring Tony Weaver back here to keep you company."

"Ha!" said Shaggs. "Weaver is good as dead if you let Carter get a shot at him."

Chapter 2

Pushing his horse harder than he should across the rocky trail, Tony Weaver had made it three miles from Somos Santos before looking back at the two fresh plumes of dust rising on the trail behind him. "Damn it," he said aloud to himself, "here they come!" Slapping his reins back and forth wildly, he pushed the horse even harder. But before he'd gone another mile, he looked back again and saw that the two riders had gained on him.

"Okay, lawdog," Weaver growled aloud as if Sheriff Dawson could hear him, "if it's a bloodbath you're after, you've found it!" Jerking his tired horse to a halt, he snatched his rifle from his saddle boot and jumped to the ground. "Maybe you ain't as handy in fighting a man out here like this as you are in the middle of a street."

Weaver slapped his horse on the rump and sent it trotting away. "Either way, one of us ain't leaving this place alive." He studied the dust for a moment longer, then moved back and upward into the shelter of a loose pile of rocks. He lay as still as the stones themselves for the next half hour, sweat streaming down his cheeks and the middle of his back. With his finger on the rifle's trigger he waited tensely the last few moments until two horses topped a low rise and came into sight, the afternoon sun blazing behind them.

The first shot from Weaver's rifle fell short by a yard, but kicked up enough sand at the horses' hooves to cause both animals to rear up and try to bolt away. Weaver's second shot whistled past the riders as the two struggled to settle their horses and gig them back below the crest of the low rise. "Come back up and fight, you rotten sons-abitches! I ain't afraid of yas!" Weaver bellowed, sending another shot whistling through the air above them.

Ducking down, Weaver waited for a tense second as one rifle shot ricocheted off a rock near his shoulder. Realizing that he had a good safe position, he rose quickly, sent a shot down onto the crest of the low rise, then ducked down, grinning and calling out, "There, you bastards! You ain't near as tough when a man's holding the high ground on yas!"

"Come down out of those rocks you dry-gulching son of a bitch," an irate voice called out in reply. "I'll show you where *tough* got started!"

Weaver laughed aloud. "I've got the best of you now, don't I, Sheriff?" Feeling more confident, he rose higher than he had before and leaned a bit forward, taking closer aim at the brim of a tall tan Stetson showing above the crest of the rise. "This one is for Bryce," he said in a low growl as he squeezed the trigger.

His shot caused a high puff of dust to explode in the dirt near the exposed hatbrim. The hat dropped quickly out of sight. But a shot resounded from the low rise and the bullet struck a rock beneath Weaver's knee, unseating him. With a loud, startled cry, Weaver fell forward over the edge of the loose pile of rocks. His rifle flew from his hands; rocks spilled down behind him. He rolled and bounced and slid amid rocks both large and small until he came to an abrupt halt against the side of a deeply implanted boulder at the edge of the trail.

"The stupid son of a bitch!" a voice cried out from beneath the low rise. "He's fell and busted his damned brains out!"

Weaver lay sprawled facedown in the dirt, the top of his bloody head still pressed against the large boulder.

"He's got to be dead," a voice said quietly after five silent minutes had passed with Weaver showing no signs of life. "Let's go over there and check him out."

But the fall had only knocked Weaver out, leaving a deep cut and a rising knot on the very top of his head. Hearing boots crunching toward him through the rocky dirt, he moaned and tried to raise his head. His right hand felt around slowly in the dirt for his rifle right up until one of the dusty boots reached out and kicked the rifle farther away from his grasp.

Unable to raise his face from the dirt, Weaver said through dust-caked lips, "Sheriff, you are . . . one lucky bastard. . . ."

"Sheriff?" said Lonnie Freed, turning a bemused stare to his partner, Dick Hohn, who stood with a cocked pistol pointed down at the back to Weaver's bloody head.

"Yeah," Hohn replied, "that's what the idiot called us a while ago." He thought for a moment, then shrugged, as if to say he'd put as much thinking into it as he intended to. "Oh well," he sighed, placing a flat hand behind his pistol to protect himself from exploding bone and brain matter.

"Wait up, Dick!" said Lonnie Freed, reaching out and nudging Hohn's arm sideway away from Weaver's head. "I want to know more about this."

"What is there to know?" Hohn said. "He got out in the sun too long, saw us and started thinking we're a couple of lawmen out to kill him." He started to ready his hand again for a shot.

But again Freed nudged his arm away. "I said wait, damn it, Dick."

Hohn lowered his gunhand a bit and gave Lonnie a harsh gaze. "I realize you and me haven't worked together long, but I'm not a man who'll take a lot of shoving," he warned Freed, coolly but firmly. "You probably ought to know that about me."

"Aren't you just a little bit curious if what he said has anything to do with what happened to us in Somos Santos?" Freed asked.

Hohn's expression turned contemplative for a moment. Finally he said, "Yeah, come to think of it, I wonder if there is any connection in all this."

"Then let's not kill the one sonsabitch who might be able to tell us," said Lonnie Freed, trying not to make Hohn look foolish.

"Good thinking," said Hohn, not seeing the incredulous look Freed gave him. He stooped and shook Weaver back and forth by his dusty shoulder. "Hey, wake up!" he demanded.

Weaver moaned and tried to roll over onto his back. "I—I can't make anything work," he rasped.

"You stupid bastard, you're lucky you're breathing."

Hohn grinned at Freed as he spoke to Weaver. “I never seen a man fall that hard *that far* and live to talk about it.” He snatched the dazed gunman by his shoulder and yanked him upward.

“I ain’t going back . . . to jail,” Weaver murmured. “You might as well . . . kill me here.”

Holding him up on his wobbly feet, Hohn shook him harder and demanded, “Look at me, you knocked-out sonsabitch! Do I look like a lawman to you?”

“I—I don’t know,” Weaver said, his mind still in a muddle of falling, shooting and running.

“Hang on to him while I go get his horse,” Freed said. He turned and walked away toward Weaver’s sweat-streaked dun, which stood watching from thirty yards away.

“What—what are you going to do to me?” Weaver asked in a weak voice.

“We just had a strange thing happen in Somos Santos. You’re going to tell us what the hell is going on there,” said Hohn, staring coldly into his unsteady eyes.

“I’ll tell you . . . anything I can,” said Weaver, staggering a bit in place, not having the slightest idea what Hohn was talking about.

“Damn right you will,” said Hohn, “less you want a pistol barrel shoved all the way up your nose.”

Walking Weaver’s horse back toward the two men, Freed saw Hohn raise his pistol and jam the tip of it beneath the half-conscious man’s nose. “Ease up, Dick!” he called out, not knowing what Hohn might do next. “I’ve got his horse! Let’s mount up and get out of here. We’ll go meet the boss and the others.” He spoke quickly, hoping to distract Hohn from whatever dark intentions he had in mind.

Hohn turned to face Freed, still keeping the pistol barrel firmly under Weaver's nose. "Don't worry, Lonnie, I'm just making a point here."

Freed grumbled under his breath and brought the dun up to where the two men stood. To Weaver he said, "Get up in that saddle."

"I—I'll try," said Weaver.

"Try *damned* hard," Lonnie said gruffly. "We ain't forgot that you laid up there waiting to pick our eyes out."

"I thought . . . you two were lawmen coming to get me," Weaver offered in his own defense. His voice took on a nasal twang with Hohn's pistol jamming the middle of his lip upward, giving him the look of a rabbit.

"Call us lawmen again," Hohn warned, "and see if I don't start taking pieces off you and discarding them in the dirt."

"I—I'm sorry," said Weaver, wide-eyed. "I was on the run. The sheriff in Somos Santos just shot my friends down like dogs! I reckon I lost my head!"

"Take your pistol down, Dick," said Freed, "so's we can understand this fool."

Hohn removed his pistol grudgingly. "There," he said, "now answer the man."

"Th-thanks," Weaver gulped. "I went to Somos Santos with a couple of pards. One of them was Teddy Bryce. He was going to call down the sheriff one on one. Me and the other man hid out to ambush the sheriff. But that damned lawdog wouldn't trust it to be a fair fight. The cheating sonsabitch sent a deputy sneaking around to flush out me and my other pard whilst we waited to back Bryce's play."

Lonnie Freed offered a trace of a wry smile. "Damn lawmen, never trust one," he said.

"That's what I always say." Weaver took a breath, his sense coming back quickly now, in spite of a hard throbbing deep inside his bloody head. "Anyway. Seeing they was dead, I lit out—you know, hoping to fight another day. I saw your dust and figured it was the sheriff and his deputy on my trail."

"That's some story, mister," said Hohn, giving him a shove toward his horse. "Now get up there and let's get moving."

"Weaver took ahold of his saddle horn, but stalled for a moment, saying, "All things being as they are . . . what say we all just go our separate ways? Look back on this some day and even have ourselves a good laugh about it?"

"Not a chance in hell," said Freed. "I want you to tell that story to our boss. I think he'll be real interested in hearing it."

Dawson and Hooney Carter rode their horse at a steady pace, keeping an eye on the three fresh sets of tracks leaving Somos Santos at a dead run. Dust from the horses still loomed above the trail. "You suppose Bryce brought more than just Weaver and Shaggs with him?" Carter asked, seeming anxious to hurry ahead and catch up with Tony Weaver and whoever else might be riding with him.

"I doubt it," said Dawson, keeping an uneasy feeling in his chest. "There's something more going on here than we know about." He gave a searching glance along the hills ahead of them.

"Is that why we're dragging back so much?" Carter asked pointedly, unable to keep his impatience from showing.

"No, Deputy," said Dawson. "We're doing this at *our* pace, not theirs." He nodded toward the hills. "I've learned that when it comes to manhunting, the more rules I keep under my control, the better."

Carter let out a tense breath. "You're right, Sheriff. No offense intended."

"None taken, Deputy," Dawson replied.

"Who do you reckon those two other sets of prints belong to?" Carter asked, changing the subject.

"I don't know," said Dawson, "but I'd sure feel better if I did. Whoever it is, they want to get away from Somos Santos as bad as Weaver. But that doesn't mean they're even connected to him."

"I see what you mean," said Carter, studying the hill line himself. There were things to be considered before charging ahead blindly. "But who could they be?" he asked.

Dawson only shrugged.

"Bounty hunters," Carter said, answering his own question.

"Could be," Dawson replied quietly. "Tony Weaver has been running outside the law for a long time. Shaggs and Bryce are no better."

"With Bryce's reputation as a gunman, it could be somebody trailing him for vengeance," Carter added.

"That's right. It could," said Dawson, feeling Carter

look him up and down, knowing the deputy wanted to hear his take on the situation as a former gunman.

"Like you and Lawrence Shaw riding vengeance on the men who killed his wife?" Carter asked quietly, hoping to initiate a conversation about something Dawson always avoided discussing.

"Maybe" was all Dawson commented. He stepped up his horse's pace a little, and the two rode on in silence until they topped the low rise in the trail, where Hohn's and Freed's horses had stopped abruptly when Tony Weaver fired down on them.

"Now what?" Carter said, the two of them studying the ground, seeing empty rifle cartridges strewn about in the dirt.

"Now we know the three weren't together," said Dawson, studying each piece of the puzzle that lay in the dirt beneath them. He nudged Stony forward, following the other two horses' prints, and stopped again at the boulder where Weaver had knocked himself cold. Stepping down from his saddle with his reins in his hand, Dawson touched his finger to the wide dark spot on the rocky ground. "Blood," he said. He wiped his finger in the dirt, and his eyes followed the long slide marks up the steep hillside.

Studying right along with him, Carter commented, "These two down here shot that one off his perch, wouldn't you say?"

"Yep, so it looks," said Dawson. He stood and stepped into his saddle.

"Do you figure Weaver's dead?" Carter asked.

Dawson followed the tracks of three horses away from the spot back onto the trail. "I don't know. They rode off together . . . but Weaver might have rode away draped over his saddle instead of sitting in it." He looked off along the long trail that circled the foot of the hills and disappeared out into the curve of the earth. He sighed at the vast endless land and said with resolve, "Either way, we're not putting much more time into him. We'll give the rest of the day, then make camp and give these horses a full night's rest. Unless we can make more of it come morning, we're headed back."

"What? Headed back?" said Carter. "Sheriff this man tried to kill you, siding with Bryce that way!"

"But he didn't kill me, Deputy," Dawson replied, "and trying to kill me isn't the worst he could have done. Every day that we're out here, the town is without a sheriff. I can't leave the town at risk while I chase a man that might already be dead or captured."

"But we've come this far," said Carter.

"And this far is going to have to be *far enough,*" said Dawson. Without another word on the matter he nudged his horse forward and followed the tracks along the foot of the hills.

Chapter 3

Odell Clarkson and his men sat sprawled around a blackened circle in the middle of a rocky clearing halfway up the side of a hill facing south, in the direction of Somos Santos. In the west the sun had turned red and begun its slow descent. Beside the blackened circle, Paco O'Mally Rojero had broken up small branches of mesquite, sun-dried cottonwood and pine and set them ablaze, fanning the low flames with his battered sombrero.

"Three riders coming, boss!" Eddie Rings called out from his lookout position along the edge of their high cliff perch. "Two of them looks like Lonnie and Hohn. Can't make out the third."

Chewing a mouthful of dried elk jerky, Odell Clarkson stood up, dusted his trousers and walked over to the cliff edge, his rifle in hand. Harvey Blue Walker stood up and followed a foot behind him. The other six men just watched without bothering to go take a look for themselves.

Odell and Harvey Blue stopped at the edge of the cliff and looked down at the three horses approaching on the trail below. "Yeah, that's our two," Odell said, raising his rifle and waving it slowly back and forth above his head.

"But who's that third man?" Harvey Blue asked warily.

"Relax, Blue," said Odell. "Whoever it is, my men wouldn't be bringing him to us 'less they knew he's all right."

Harvey Blue's cautious expression didn't change as he stared out and saw Lonnie Freed raise a gloved hand and wave in response. "I only relax when I know it's time to relax," Blue said flatly. His eyes searched the darkening land behind the three riders. "The way you boys are waving back and forth, every eye in this country knows we're up here now."

"You worry too much, Harvey," said Odell, a bit of a snap in his tone.

"I don't *worry,*" Harvey Blue snapped in reply. "I plan and stay on guard—that way I don't have to *worry*. This is your job we're on. I've turned all the *leading* over to you."

"That's a wise decision," said Odell, staring him in the eyes. "You're not going to be disappointed."

"I better not be," said Harvey Blue, returning the stare.

Odell shrugged and let the warning pass. He knew that Harvey Blue was not a man to take lightly. To change the subject he turned to Paco, who had stood up and placed his sombrero back atop his head now that the campfire crackled in flames. "Paco, get some coffee boiling. We'll stay the night, now that Lonnie and Dick are back."

Paco gave Odell a sharp stare, but then caught himself

and turned his eyes away and looked down at the empty coffeepot sitting on the rocky ground.

"Yeah, Paco," said the muffled voice of Buck Turner, who was sitting near him, "you best get us some coffee boiling, and make sure it's just the way we like it." He chuckled under his breath.

Paco gave Turner an even harder stare. The other men saw it. Marshal Campbell commented to Turner, "Careful, hoss, I don't think he appreciates your gringo humor."

"Aw," said Turner, passing it off, "Paco knows I'm funning with him. Me and him goes back a long ways, right, Paco?"

"That is so, Turner," said the Mexican. "But you know that I am getting a bellyful of this tell-the-Mexican-to-do-it bullshit."

"I know it, Paco," said Turner. He took a bite of jerky and chewed it. He said to Campbell, as Paco picked up the pot and turned away, "See, Paco is only half Mexican. His pa was a straight-up Irishman."

"Yeah?" Campbell studied Paco closely, watching him hold out the coffeepot to each man in turn for a share of water from their canteens. "I reckon I don't see it."

"Well, see it or not, it's true," said Turner. "Me and Paco just threw in with Odell a week before you and your pals came along. No sooner had we started riding with Odell than he started calling on Paco to be his errand boy. Paco don't like it."

"I wouldn't either," Campbell commented. He gave a glance toward Odell and Harvey Blue, then asked in a lowered voice, "Is any of yas here a part of the *old* Odell Clarkson gang?"

Chewing his jerky, Buck Turner looked around at the faces of the other men. "Only a couple," he said. "Old Freddie Tapp over there is one of the old Clarkson gang, so is Lonnie Freed. But that's about it." He looked from the face of one outlaw to the next, then over to Eddie Rings, standing beside Odell at the cliff's edge. "Eddie Rings and Earl Duggins have only been riding with him a few weeks now. You, Hohn and Curtis Miggs all rode in with Harvey Blue."

"I reckon that covers everybody," said Campbell.

"Yep, I reckon it does," said Turner.

Campbell's expression turned grim as he said, "So this whole bunch has never done a bank job together."

Turner chuckled a bit. "No, not yet. Somos Santos will be our first. It'll be sort of a get-acquainted bank job, you might say." He grinned. "Sounds shaky, don't it?"

"Shaky as hell," said Campbell. "I'd feel better if somebody besides Clarkson was leading it, to tell you the truth."

"Better not let *him* ever hear you say something like that," said Turner. "He can get pretty damn fierce."

"Everybody I know can get pretty damn fierce," said Campbell, "including me." He eyed Turner and added, "So I ain't expecting you to mention what's been said between us."

"That's understood," said Turner. "Fact is, I've been thinking along those same lines myself. I ain't saying this just because you rode in here with Harvey Blue. But I'd feel a little better if he was the man in charge."

"Me too," said Campbell, still eyeing Turner closely for any sign of treachery. "I'm wondering about maybe asking his opinion on the matter. How would that sound to you and Paco?"

"I can't speak for Paco," said Turner. "But as you can see, he ain't real happy with how Odell has gotten his name stuck in his mouth every time he wants a fire built or a pot of coffee."

From the edge of the cliff, Odell Clarkson called out to the others, "They're coming up, boys. Paco, how's that coffee coming?"

Paco grumbled bitterly under his breath, but called out, "It's coming, boss." He gave Turner a dark look that said he wasn't going to be able to take such treatment much longer.

"There's your answer, Campbell," Turner said quietly.

"Yeah," said Campbell. "First chance I get, I'll feel Harvey Blue out, see what he thinks of the idea."

Odell Clarkson waited impatiently while the three horsemen rode out of sight long enough to climb the winding trail upward to the clearing. As soon as the tired horses came back into sight, Clarkson stood waiting, saying to Lonnie Freed, "What the hell took you so long?"

Stepping down from his horse, Lonnie replied, "Odell, we are damned lucky we made it back at all!" Beside him, Dick Hohn stepped down from his saddle and pulled Tony Weaver down. Weaver landed on the ground with a thud and struggled to his feet.

"Who's this?" Odell asked, eyeing Weaver.

"This is some fool who tried to ambush us on our way back," Lonnie answered, pulling Weaver forward as if to give Odell a better look at him. "I'm telling you, Odell, this has been one strange trip we've been on." His eyes went to Harvey Blue. "But it was a damn good idea Harvey had about scouting out Somos Santos before we all went charging in there."

"Yeah, I suppose it was," Odell said grudgingly. "Now what the hell happened? Are we ready to rob that bank or not?"

"Hell no, we're not," said Lonnie. "We'd be riding right into a trap."

"A trap?" Odell looked curious.

"Yeah, boss," said Lonnie. "We weren't in town five minutes, some fellow jackpotted us right off. Put his finger straight at us and announced clear as day that we were there to rob the bank!"

"How the hell could he have known that?" Odell asked. "Nobody knew that outside of all us here."

"It was eerie, boss," said Lonnie. "It was like he'd read our minds or something!"

"Ah, horseshit!" Harvey Blue barked. Looking past Lonnie at Dick Hohn, he asked, "What the hell is he talking about?"

Hohn hesitated, but only for a second. "I don't know," he replied, "but it was damn sure odd that the man singled us out and put the finger on us." He looked all around at the other men, then said, "I ain't blaming nobody for nothing, but damn, he must've been tipped off."

Odell and Harvey Blue both looked all around at the others, then back to Hohn. "Nobody has left camp since we decided to pull the job, except you two."

"That's why I'm saying it was damned *eerie*, boss," said Lonnie.

"Don't say *eerie* again, Lonnie," Odell warned him, pointing a finger at him for emphasis. "Do you hear me?"

"Yes, sorry, boss," said Lonnie. "I just couldn't think of no other to say it. We about jumped out of our boots, walking along, thinking about robbing that bank, and all of a sudden here's some fellow shouting his fool head off, saying, 'They're going to rob the bank! They're going to rob the bank!' It was plumb eer— I mean, *peculiar!*"

"Gawdamn it!" Odell grumbled. He jerked his head toward Tony Weaver. "What about the ambush?"

"That was peculiar too," Hohn cut in, directing his words to Harvey instead of Odell. "He thought we were lawmen after him, so he commenced firing on us. Turns out, he was on the run. Him and two others had just got themselves shot out of Somos Santos by none other than Crayton Dawson."

"Dawson? You mean the gunfighter?" Odell looked surprised. "The one who rode with Lawrence Shaw?"

"Yep," Hohn said. "That's what this one says, and I believe it. We both heard a big shooting ruckus as we rode in through an alley south of town. Soon as we go to the main street there was a body stretched out deader than an oak plank."

Odell looked at Lonnie as if in disbelief. "It's the truth," said Lonnie. "We hadn't made it more than a few yards along the boardwalk before we got fingered."

"Jesus," said Odell. He scratched his chin, thinking. "Damn, I thought Cray Dawson got himself shot and died of a gut wound."

"I heard that too a few months back," said Lonnie.

"But I reckon it could have just been incorrect gossip." He too rubbed his chin.

Dick Hohn gave Harvey Blue a look that showed disdain for Lonnie and Odell.

Harvey Blue nodded slightly. He'd stood watching and listening with slimly veiled contempt. Finally he said to Odell, "How do you know this bummer didn't make the whole thing up?" He grabbed Weaver by his shoulder and shook him roughly. "Huh? Ain't that right? You ambushed a couple of riders, figured you'd take everything they had and leave them laying dead in the sun. But when they got the best of you, you had yourself a story all made up and waiting."

Weaver's head still throbbed mercilessly with pain. "I ain't lying, mister," said Weaver. He'd looked around at the men and heard enough to know that he had landed amid his own lawless element. "I'm a thieving, lying, no-good sonsabitch. But when I tell you Cray Dawson is sheriffing in Somos Santos, you can call it the gospel."

Harvey turned the other man's shoulder loose. "What the hell's your name? Or do you just go by *Theiving, Lying No-Good Sonsabitch*?"

Weaver managed a slight grin, just enough to test his standing with Harvey Blue. "I'll answer to it. But my real name is Tippan . . . Howard Tippan," he lied.

"And he is one *lying sonsabitch,*" Eddie Rings called out, stepping forward from over beside the campfire. The men's eyes turned to him as he continued, saying, "His name is Tony Weaver. Used to be known as *Anything for a Dollar*, owing to him once agreeing to kill a schoolteacher up in Arizona Territory for a dollar."

"Is that you, Eddie Rings?" Weaver's voice turned

shaky. "Damn ole hoss, it's good to see you." He eagerly stuck out his hand as if greeting a long-lost friend.

"Don't stick your greasy paw in my direction," said Rings. "I'll cut it off to the elbow, you worthless pile of sheep shit."

Weaver dropped his hand quickly, but held his ground enough to say, "You always could work up a mouthful of tough talk to an unarmed man, Rings."

"Somebody *arm* this bastard," shouted Rings, "so I can send him home to hell!"

Odell's eyes glistened in excitement. "Give him a gun, Lonnie! We've got ourselves a sporting event."

Lonnie pulled out the pistol he'd taken from Weaver's holster. But before he could give it to Weaver, Harvey Blue stepped in and intercepted it.

"Just a damn minute, Odell," said Harvey. "Don't we want to find out everything we can from this owlhoot?"

"Excuse the hell out of me, Harvey," Odell said with more than a little sarcasm in his tone, "but I thought we already *had.*"

"Oh?" Harvey turned to Dick Hohn and asked, "Dick, can you think of anything we might want to know from this man?"

"Yeah, I believe I can," said Hohn. His eyes went first to Odell, then to Tony Weaver. "I'm curious as hell about what might make a big gun like Crayton Dawson want to work as sheriff in a town like Somos Santos."

"Hey!" said Odell in mock surprise. "Now there's a dandy question we might want to ponder!" He held up a gloved finger. "Somos Santos couldn't afford a big gun like Dawson"—he let the thought trail for a moment, then said as if he'd been stricken by a revelation—"unless of course there is something so valuable there that someone else is footing the bill for it." He stared at Odell long enough to let the idea sink in.

"A railroad company?" Odell offered.

"Or a mining company," said Harvey. "There's all sorts of possibilities, once a man let's himself work on it."

Odell felt embarrassed. "I wasn't going to let these two shoot it out," he said, jerking a nod toward Weaver and Eddie Rings. "I just wanted to see which one had the guts to take it up."

"I'm glad to hear that, Odell," said Harvey Blue. "If I thought otherwise, I'd feel like I was riding with a Gaw-damned fool."

Odell felt the sting of Harvey's words, even though the insult was given in a roundabout way. His hackles rising, Odell poised his hand near his gun butt and said, "Anybody who thinks he's riding with a Gawdamn fool is welcome to leave . . . or fill his hand."

"Easy, Odell," said Harvey without seeming disturbed by either the other man's words or his threatening position, "I didn't call you a fool."

"That's a good thing, Harvey," said Odell. "Otherwise I'd be obliged to blow a hole the size of Kansas in your gullet." The two stared at each other, Odell still fuming, Harvey Blue staying cool, giving everybody a look at who was the hothead and who was the one in control.

Finally Harvey shrugged slightly. Dismissing the matter he said, "And you'd be justified in doing it. Now back to business. What other banks do you have in mind as a backup plan?"

"Backup plan . . . ?" Odell stalled for a moment, searching his mind for something to say.

"Yeah," said Odell, "because I know you're not about to go riding into Somos Santos until we know more about what we're facing there, right?"

"Right," said Odell, taking up Harvey's suggestion. Turning his gaze to the men he said, "If there's something big in the works in Somos Santos, we're going to get it. But not until we know more about it."

"Than where are we headed now, boss?" asked Lonnie Freed.

"That's for me to know!" Odell lashed out at him.

"I'm just asking," Freed said meekly, spreading his hands in a show of submission.

"And I'll tell you when it damn well suits me!" Odell shouted. "There's been too much loose talk around here already! From now on only Harvey Blue and me are going to know where this bunch is headed, right, Harvey?"

Harvey gave the men a knowing look, then said to Odell Clarkson, "Suits me, *boss*. We can't be too careful."

Listening, and hoping to find a way to stay alive, Tony Weaver said, "If you could use another hand, I'd sure be glad to ride with you fellows."

Odell didn't answer. Instead he looked at Lonnie and Hohn. The two shrugged as one. "He ain't afraid to ambush and pull a trigger," Lonnie offered.

Odell looked at Eddie Rings. "What about you, Rings? What kind of trouble is there between you two?"

Eddie Rings said grudgingly, "He stole a woman from me."

Odell chuckled and replied flatly, "A woman—is that all?"

"She was a whore at that," said Weaver, offering a trace of a good-natured grin. "Nothing worth shooting each other over."

"Is that true, Rings?" Odell asked.

Rings looked embarrassed. "Sort of, I reckon."

"Well damn, boys," said Odell, "I'm just going to put you two together and see if you can't work this all out between yas. How does that suit you, Mr. *Anything for a Dollar* Weaver?"

"I'm always one to seek a peaceable solution," said Weaver, feeling great relief at having landed on his feet.

"What about you, Rings?" Odell asked. "Are you going to be all right with this?"

"If I'm not, I know how to settle it," said Rings, casting a hard stare at Weaver.

"Paco!" Odell called out. "You stick close to these two and see to it they don't kill one another."

Paco gave Odell a disgruntled look, but managed to say in a level tone of voice, "*Sí,* Odell, I will try."

"All right then," said Odell without giving Paco another glance, "everybody be ready to ride tomorrow. We're headed northwest to Schalene Pass."

Chapter 4

No sooner had Sheriff Dawson and Deputy Carter left Somos Santos on the trail of Tony Weaver than young Thomas Fosse, the livery tender's son, hopped onto a big bay mare from the corral and rode her bareback out toward the Shaw hacienda, where Dawson and Carmelita lived. But before he arrived there, he saw Carmelita sitting in a one-horse buggy at the fork of the Old Comanche Trail. Reining the big mare down to halt a few yards away to keep from stirring dust around the buggy, Thomas nudged the animal forward with his bare feet.

"What is it, Thomas?" Carmelita already sensed that the boy had ridden out to deliver a message to her, and at the first sight of him, she'd felt a dark sense of dread sweep instantly through her. But just as quickly the dread lifted some as she reminded herself that had something terrible happened to Cray Dawson the word of it would not have been delivered to her by the livery owner's son.

"There's been a shoot-out in town, ma'am," the boy answered in a rushed tone. "Sheriff Dawson and his deputy is gone off chasing one of the men who got away.

He had Pa send me to tell you he might not be coming home this evening."

"I see," said Carmelita. "Was anyone injured?"

"No, ma'am," said Thomas. "But one man is shot dead—the main one who tried to shoot the sheriff, of course!"

"Of course," she responded in a barely audible tone. This was the first time such a thing had happened since Dawson agreed to officially become the law in Somos Santos, but it was something that she had gone over in her mind a hundred times during the past few weeks. She kept herself composed, her hands folded in her lap, holding the buggy reins in her gloved hands. "*Gracias,* Thomas, for coming to tell me."

Thomas eyed the leather suitcase and carpetbag sitting in the buggy beside her and asked, "Are you going on a trip somewhere, ma'am?"

Carmelita sighed and said, "No, Thomas." She gazed off in the direction the stage would be coming from at any time. Then she said to the boy, "You ride back to town now. Tell your father I received the message, and that everything is all right here."

"Are you sure, ma'am?" Thomas asked, his eyes again going to the big leather suitcase. "Pa said not to say anything that might worry you." He winced slightly. "I might not should have told you about the shooting, huh?"

"You did fine, Thomas," said Carmelita. "Now go back to Somos Santos. Tell your father that I am all right."

"Yes, ma'am," said Thomas, turning the big mare without another word and riding away at an easy gallop.

Carmelita sat watching him ride away until he gradually seemed to sink down into the wavering heat, then farther down into the earth itself. And she sat staring even longer at the long, empty trail and the swirl of dust that now lay higher up, drifting along on a hot breeze. A tear welled up in her eye, and she left it unattended until it spilled in a thin trickle down her cheek.

She took a small handkerchief from the sleeve of her black dress and pressed it to her cheek. On the distant horizon, from the other direction of the fork in the wide trail, she saw the first sign of dust coming from the stagecoach's large wooden wheels. With no change in her expression, she tucked the handkerchief back into her sleeve, took up the reins, turned the buggy around and sent the horse back toward the hacienda at a slow walk.

She carried the suitcase and carpetbag into the hacienda and set them at the bedroom door. She picked up the envelope that contained a letter she'd written and left on a small table for Dawson to find. She put the envelope away, changed out of her traveling clothes into a loose cotton dress and spent the rest of the day alone. That evening, after a silent dinner, she turned back the covers on the large bed, climbed in and spent the night alone. She fell asleep reminding herself that what had happened in town today had not changed anything. She was still leaving, for his sake as well as for her own. She would think no more about it.

Yet thinking about it was all she did throughout the following day into the late afternoon. At dusk she walked out onto the front porch and seated herself on the soft buffalo hide and colorful serapes that lay draped over a large porch swing Dawson had made from the rough-hewn limbs of a white oak. Darkness had set in when she heard the soft drop of Stony's hooves turn in off the main trail and walk up into the wide yard.

"Carmelita?" she heard Dawson say softly. The sound of the horse's hooves stopped at the hitch rail. Without looking at him, Carmelita heard the soft creak of saddle leather as Dawson swung down, hitched his reins and walked up to the edge of the porch. "Are you all right?" he asked.

She turned her gaze down to where he stood in the yard and replied, "*Sí,* I am all right."

Seeing her eyes glisten with tears, he said, "Fosse told me what his son, Thomas, said. . . ."

"And what *did* he say?" Carmelita asked, her voice sounding a bit tight in spite of her effort to keep it level and steady.

"He said that you were waiting for the stage, that you had bags packed," Dawson said, her voice and demeanor already letting him know that Thomas Fosse had not been mistaken.

"*Sí,*" she said, "I was waiting for the stagecoach to arrive."

"You were leaving me?" Dawson asked softly, sounding hurt. "Just like that?"

"I was going to leave you a letter," Carmelita replied.

"A letter?" said Dawson. "After all we've—"

"Please do not tell me that you haven't been expecting this, Cray," Carmelita said.

Dawson could hear her tears in her voice. He stood silent for a moment, then said, "Yes, I suppose I have been expecting this."

"I'm sorry that I was going to leave without telling you," she said. "I knew that was wrong. Perhaps I would have turned back even if Thomas hadn't arrived when he did." She looked away and touched her handkerchief to her eyes. "When he told me what had happened, I knew I could not leave you at such a time. I also knew he would tell his father that I had been waiting for the stage." She shrugged in resignation. "So now it is out in the open. I am leaving. Next week when the stage comes again, I will be waiting for it. I will leave the buggy at the trail. You can come for it when you return from town that evening."

Dawson shook his head slowly. "Have I done something wrong? Because if I have, I will make it up to you, I promise, Carmelita."

"No, you have done nothing wrong, Cray," Carmelita said softly. "You are a good man—the best man I know. A far better man than Lawrence Shaw could ever hope to be."

"But?" Dawson stared at her.

"But I do not love you, and I know that you do not love me."

Dawson started to object, but before he could say anything, Carmelita cut him off. "I know you care for me very much, and I care for you the same way. But we must not deceive ourselves any longer into thinking that we love one another, at least not the way two people should love one another." Her voice softened. "At least, not the way I *want* to love a man and to *be* loved by him."

"You're right." Dawson sighed, realizing that the simple truth had been so close to the surface and had taken only a few words from her to make him admit it. "I know people who would give anything to feel the way we do toward each other. They spend their entire lives together, but deep down it's not love that keeps them holding on. And if it's something deeper that you and I need, I'm sorry to say, it's not here for us." He looked down and shook his head. "I had that kind of feeling for Rosa, even though she was a married woman. I thought I would have it for you, given some time. I told myself that I must be crazy to *not* feel that way for you. But I don't."

"I am glad that you do not," said Carmelita, "because I could not return that feeling to you. I must be *crazier* than you. I still love Lawrence Shaw, the husband of my poor dead sister. And God forgive me, I believe I loved him since long before her death."

"I suppose we have no say over who we fall in love with, Carmelita. That's what Rosa always said, those nights when she and I were together while Shaw traipsed all over the country building himself a gunman's reputation. I believe that is also what Rosa would have to say about you being in love with her husband."

"Gracias," Carmelita said softly. After a silence had passed, she said, "There is no more for us to say. We both know what we must do."

"We could try one more time," said Dawson. "I'll do that for you—for *us* I mean. I know it's going to hurt something awful, seeing you get on that stage. Maybe we do love one another. Maybe we just need to—"

"Don't, Cray, *por favor,*" she said, stopping him. "You came to me wounded, needing a place to heal. And now you are healed. I too needed someone, to help me get over Shaw. You came at the right time. You were so in love with my sister, Rosa, that you would have grieved yourself to death over her. To save yourself, you convinced yourself that you love me, but it is only because I reminded you so much of her."

"I can get over her, Carmeilta," Dawson said. "I know I will never forget her, but I swear to you, I believe I have gotten over her some."

"*Sí,* you have gotten over her *some*," said Carmelita, as gently as she could. "But as you get over her, so will you get over me. To you, my sister and I have been one and the same."

Dawson surprised himself, talking this way after only moments ago realizing and admitting that Carmelita was right. But he suddenly felt the return of all the misery and the deep loneliness he'd come to know before Carmelita took him in. It caused him to speak in a bitter tone, and he said before he could stop himself, "I could say the same thing about me and Lawrence Shaw, and that you never really gave me a chance. I rode with him and fought side-by-side with him. But when the killing was over, I was the one who came back to Somos Santos. Would you have taken up with me if I hadn't been the one who rode with—"

"Stop it, Cray," Carmelita said, cutting him off. "This is what I promised we must not do. We both love people we can never have. We have been together because of them. But now I must go. If I stay, soon we will regret it."

Dawson walked away and stood in silence for a moment, staring off into the wide Texas sky, to where black shadows of distant hills stood jagged against a purple starlit sky. He considered Carmelita's words and realized that she was right. After a while he started to turn and walk back to the porch, but before he could, he felt Carmelita at his side. Lifting his arm he placed it around her as she put her arm around his waist and nestled against him in the darkness. "For two people *not in love,* we sure have loved each other well," Dawson whispered.

"And if we end it this way," Carmelita whispered, "we will always have the very best feelings for one another."

"We're fools, the two of us, aren't we?" Dawson whispered.

But before Carmelita could answer, his lips were upon hers, softly, gently. *Kisses of goodbye,* she told herself.

When the kiss ended, they stood in the moonlight in an embrace, and she wished that she could love this man the way she knew she would always love her dead sister's husband. "Do you feel like talking about what happened in town?" she asked, ending their embrace slowly and looking into his eyes.

"Some crazy young outlaw named Teddy Bryce got it in his mind that he had to take me down." Dawson stepped back and took her hand in his. Arm in arm, they turned and walked back to the hacienda.

"Did you know this man?" Carmelita asked. "Did he have a grudge against you?"

"No," Dawson said flatly. "He just figured he'd build himself a reputation, I reckon."

"They will never stop coming, will they?" Carmelita asked.

"No, I suppose not," said Dawson, "not as long as I'm still alive." He looked at her in the moonlight and asked quietly, "Is that why you didn't leave today?"

"Partly," said Carmelita. "I could not leave here thinking you would ride home to an empty house after facing men who intended to kill you."

"Thanks," said Dawson. "I can't tell you how much that means to me." At the porch steps they stopped again and stood for a moment. "You said that was *partly* why," Dawson said.

"*Sí,* that was partly why I turned back," said Carmelita. She looked up at Dawson, who saw her eyes glisten with tears again. "But the truth is, you are not an easy man to leave, Cray Dawson."

Dawson offered a sad smile and said, "Thanks again." He drew her against him and said, "I'm going to miss you something fierce."

Chapter 5

Paco O'Mally Rojero, Buck Turner and Odell Clarkson rode into Schalene Pass from the north and reined their horses in front of an apothecary shop, three doors down from the bank. They blended easily into the foot traffic along the busy boardwalk and at length crossed the rutted dirt street and drifted back to Appleton's Roi-Tan Saloon. Turner and Odell went inside, but Paco stood in front just off the boardwalk at the corner of an alley. In a moment Turner came through the bat-wing doors, carrying a shot glass of whiskey and a foaming mug of beer.

"*Gracias,*" Paco said. He took the shot glass, downed the liquor in a gulp, took the beer, sipped long and slow and let out a breath of pleasure. Wiping a leather cuff across his lips, he nodded at Freddie Tapp and Eddie Rings, who came riding into town from the south, weaving their way through buckboards, buggies and saddle horses on the crowded street.

"I see them," Turner said quietly. Glancing east, he saw Dick Hohn, Lonnie Freed and Harvey Blue Walker riding in slowly. "It won't be long now," he said. Searching along the boardwalk across the dirt street, he saw a familiar-looking young man stop at the door of a gunsmith's shop and glance all around. For a second their eyes met. But then the young man slipped inside the shop and closed the door behind himself.

"Bennie?" Turner murmured aloud to himself.

"What?" asked Paco.

"Nothing," said Turner. "I just saw a fellow I used to know from over around Bentonville—some dumb cattle drover, like I used to be."

Across the street, in the back room of the gunsmith's shop, beneath a cloud of cigar smoke, Joe Christi dropped six poker chips onto the scarred wooden tabletop and said, to the hard-looking face across the table from him, "I see your three, and I raise you three."

"Hey, Joe," said the returning Bennie Betts upon entering the small room, "guess who I just saw across the street?"

"Not now, Bennie," said Carl Morris, the owner of the shop. He pulled Bennie aside and whispered, "Joe and Turley Whitt are horn-locked. This might be the big game!"

Bennie Betts fell silent and backed away with Carl Morris to stand against the wall. The men watched intently.

After a long silent pause, Joe said respectfully, "It's up to you, Mr. Whitt."

Facing him across a pile of chips and cash, Turley Whitt picked up the shot glass sitting next to a nearly empty bottle of rye. He tossed back the drink and set the empty glass down with a solid thud. "I know when it's my Gawdamned turn, boy."

"No offense intended, Mr. Whitt," Joe said calmly.

"None taken," Turley growled under his breath, studying his cards again, then staring into Joe's eyes, trying to decide if this young man in his ragged range clothes was trying to bluff him. Turley smoothed down the front of his shiny brocade vest and composed himself.

The small room waited tense and silent.

Joe saw the spot Turley Whitt had placed himself in. Turley had gotten more and more drunk throughout the preceding night, as if drinking would make up for his constant losing. His luck had not changed with the coming of a new day. It was midmorning, and young Joe Christi knew that in the next few minutes he would be the man who gutted Turley Whitt at poker. He could feel it coming, and without thinking he let out a low breath in relief.

He caught himself and stopped abruptly, hoping no one had noticed. At first it appeared no one had. But then Turley Whitt calmly laid his cards down on the tabletop and stared coldly at Joe. "Am I boring you, boy?"

"No, sir," Joe replied quickly. "It's just that it's been a long night and a longer morning. I apologize if I've given any—"

"You seem to spend lots of time apologizing for your shortcomings," said Turley, interrupting him. "I'm wondering if you were never taught any manners at all. Isn't that right, Black Ed?"

Beside the rear door, standing where he had stood most of the morning and all of the night before, Black Ed Stiles answered in a low level tone, "Yes, Mr. Turley, that is right."

Two other players slid their chairs back away from the

table. One of them, a traveling stove peddler, bolted from his chair, saying, "My, my! But how time has flown! I should have been on the trail to Cedar Wells hours ago!" He grabbed his bowler hat from a peg and stepped quickly toward the rear door. But the tall black gunman blocking the doorway nudged him aside with his forearm, saying firmly, "Sit down somewhere, peddler."

The stove peddler stepped backward into the other player, an elderly man with a long silver beard, who'd already flattened himself against the wall.

Joe Christi remained calm. But he also laid his cards down and, in doing so, slumped a bit in his chair, letting his right hand slide as close to the table edge as he dared. His fingertips paused on the edge.

"Wouldn't it be just as easy to accuse me of cheating, Mr. Whitt?" Joe said quietly.

From his spot against the wall, Morris the gunsmith said, "I don't want any trouble in here!" But everybody ignored him.

Whitt's face reddened. "I don't know what you're talking about, boy!" He stood up from his chair and leaned forward, his left hand supporting him on the tabletop, his right hand poised near the big bone-handled Colt standing in a tied-down slim-jim holster on his hip.

"I can't have trouble here," Morris said. Still his words were ignored.

Christi gave a slight shrug, deciding not to say what he'd started to about the way Whitt was acting. This was not the first time he'd seen a player act this way when he'd lost too much and embarrassed himself; but this wasn't the kind of behavior he'd expected from a big-named shootist like Turley Whitt.

It was already clear to Christi that Whitt wasn't going to listen to anything he had to say. "All right, Whitt," said Joe, "what is it I need to do to keep from having trouble with you?"

Whitt didn't reply right away. Instead he stared cold and hard into Christi's eyes, able to read no more in them now than he had throughout the game. Finally a trace of a cruel grin showed beneath his drooping mustache. "You mean what do you need to do to keep me from *killing you?*"

The silence in the room grew even more tense. But Joe Christi seemed unaffected by it. He also took his time before answering. "Yes, that's what I mean: to keep you from killing me."

Behind Whitt, Black noted the lack of fear in Christi's voice. He kept his hand poised, but he cocked his head slightly to the side, curious to see how Whitt handled this young man. Whitt was clearly in the wrong. *All this over a damn card game*, Stiles said to himself. As far as he was concerned, the fading gunman was on his own.

Whitt nodded slowly, saying to Joe Christi, "What you do, *boy*, is you get up from that chair. Real polite-like, you thank me for the game. Then you leave here, walk your ragged ass out that door and leave the money on the table."

That's what I thought, Christi thought. But he said nothing to Whitt until he stood up slowly, backed away from the table a step and said, "Obliged for the game, Mr. Whitt." With a half step he started to turn and head for the door.

"Wait a damn minute, Joe!" Bennie Betts cut in. He said to Turley Whitt, "He had you gutted this game, and you know it!"

"Stay out of it, Bennie," Joe Christi warned. He reached to grab Bennie by his arm and pull him toward the door. But Bennie would have none of it. He shook free of Christi's hand and said, "Damn it, this ain't right! This is thievery!"

"Are you calling me a thief?" Whitt demanded, his nostrils flaring.

"He didn't mean it," Joe said quickly. As he spoke, he shoved Bennie toward the door.

"*Thief* ain't even the worst thing I'm calling you, you tin-horn son of a bitch!" shouted Bennie, pushing back against Christi.

"He apologizes for saying that, Mr. Whitt!" Christi shouted, pulling the door open and giving Bennie a hard shove.

"He's too damn late!" shouted Whitt in reply. His hand went for his Colt. Instinctively, so did Joe Christi's. Black Ed watched the shooting erupt. In that instant he decided not to make a move for his gun unless he had to.

Both Whitt's and Christi's shots exploded as one in the small room. But the bullet from Whitt's shiny bone-handled Colt only nipped at Christi's shirtsleeve as it sliced past him. The bullet from Christi's battered old range pistol nailed Whitt dead center in his chest, leaving in its wake a thick stream of dark smoke.

"My God!" cried the stove peddler, his face turning ashen in terror.

Whitt stood stone still for a moment, staring at Christi in disbelief, stunned at being bested by the young cowboy in his ragged drover's clothes. "Sonsa—" he muttered, unable to complete his words. Blood pumped out of the bullet wound in his chest and splattered down onto the tabletop and its contents in front of him. His big Colt slumped on his finger, then fell heavily to the floor. Whitt followed it, like a bundle of loose rags.

The second that Christi saw his shot had hit its target, he'd jerked his smoking range pistol in Black Ed's direction, cocked and ready.

But the black gunman only shook his head slowly back and forth, his hands half spread in a manner that told Christi he wanted none of it. "He called it. You shot him fair, kid," Black Ed said in a calm voice.

"I've got no trouble with you then?" Christi asked, his gun poised, ready to explode at the flicker of an eyelid.

"Not at this point," Black Ed replied. He nodded at Christi's gun. "But that old smoker of yours doesn't look too stable to me."

Christi got the message and eased the gun down a bit and to the side. The room seemed stuck in a stunned silence for a moment until Christi said over his shoulder, "Bennie, gather up my money!"

Carl Morris fanned his wool cap back and forth against the dark cloud of burned gunpowder and made a low nervous chuckling sound that caused Christi's eyes to snap toward him. "Easy, Joe," said Morris, his fanning stopping abruptly. "You're worried about your money—don't you realize what you've just done?"

"It was self-defense," Christi said quickly. "You all saw it."

"Hell, yes, it was self-defense," said Morris, "but

that's small potatoes. You just killed Turley Whitt in a straight-up shoot-out."

"I suppose I did," Joe Christi said flatly to the gunsmith, not looking at all proud of what he'd done. To Bennie he said, "Are you going to get my money?"

Bennie suddenly snapped to life. He rushed forward, sweeping his hat from his head, and began raking the bloody chips and piles of dollar bills and gold coins into it. "Joe, this is a mess," he said, blood dripping from the upturned brim of his hat and from his fingertips.

"It'll have to do," said Christi, still covering the room loosely with the battered range pistol. To the rest of the men in the room he said, "If anybody asks, I want you all to say this was self-defense. I'm obliged if you'll all do that. I wish to God nobody had to ever know this happened."

"If you mean that, Joe," said Morris, "I'll go you one better than self-defense." He looked at the two players standing against the wall. "If these two will keep their mouths shut, we'll get rid of Whitt's body and forget this whole thing ever happened." He saw the look of inquiry on Christi's face and explained, "Hell, I'm running a gunsmith shop, not a saloon. I'm not supposed to allow gambling to go on here."

"What about the gunshots?" Joe asked, trying to decide whether or not this was a good idea.

"Like I said, Joe, this is a gunsmith shop," Morris repeated. "I worked on a gun with a bullet stuck in it. It went off, simple as that, if anybody comes asking. It wouldn't be the first time it happened."

Christi looked at Black Ed, who shrugged. He turned his eyes to the two other players. The stove peddler said,

"I need to be on about my business. I'd just as soon not have to wait around here to explain what I saw."

"I don't like explaining nothing either," said the old man with the silver beard. "I'm headed for El Paso on the afternoon stage. I never saw a thing."

"He owes me twenty dollars," said Black Ed Stiles. He stepped forward slowly and gestured toward the money in Bennie's hat.

"Give him twenty, Bennie," said Christi.

"And I'm keeping his horse and personals," said Black Ed.

"All right," said Christi. "Take everything he's got. Make sure there's no trace left of him."

"Done," said Black Ed. He took a bloody twenty-dollar gold piece that Bennie fished from his upturned hat and handed to him. Grinning, Black Ed looked down at his former employer lying in a bloody heap. "Damn, boss. You ain't been dead five minutes, and already it's looking like you never was born." He started to stoop down and pick up Turley's bone-handled Colt.

"Leave it," said Joe Christi, with no idea why he'd said it.

"Oh?" Stiles stared at him curiously.

"Yes. I'm keeping the gun," said Christi, still not sure what his intentions were.

Ed Stiles scrutinized him for a moment, then shrugged and said, "Sure enough. Hell, you *are* the one who killed him. I reckon you ought to get something off him."

"Obliged," Christi said out of force of habit before he could stop himself.

"Obliged?" Black Ed looked bemused. "Mister, you

don't have to thank anybody for anything anymore if you don't want to. Like the man just said, you killed Turley Whitt straight up. You took all his respect. Now it all belongs to you." His smile widened as he added in a wry tone, "You've become the man to be respected."

"Huh-uh," said Christi, shaking his head. "All I did was shoot a man to keep him from shooting me. I told you, I don't want nobody to even *know* about it."

"I understand, kid," said Black Ed. "But that's today, while the smoke is still circling your gun barrel." He paused long enough to kick Turley Whitt's bone-handled gun across the floor. It stopped at Joe Christi's scuffed-up boot toes. "How's all this going feel to you tomorrow, once you've had time to mull it over?"

Chapter 6

Although muffled by the walls of Morris' gunsmith shop, the two pistol shots exploding at the same time in the back room caused heads to turn inside the bank, which stood across the street and a few yards down the boardwalk. Upon hearing the sound, Odell Clarkson's hand pulled back from the side of his riding duster to get to his pistol.

Beside him, standing just inside the front doors, Harvey Blue said under his breath, "Not yet, Odell! That wasn't our boys starting a commotion!"

"It wasn't? Then what's that about?" Odell stared at him, while in front of them an elderly woman wearing a wide flowered hat gave a glance in the direction of the gunshots, then stepped up to the counter to transact her business.

"I don't know what *that's* about," said Harvey Blue, "but it's not our boys. I told them to wait until Hohn jerked the door blinds up and down twice."

"Oh," said Odell, glancing toward Dick Hohn. "Then he best get to doing it. This rout is about to commence!

I want plenty of shooting and confusion in the streets when we come running out."

"You'll get plenty of action out front, soon as Hohn gives the signal," said Harvey Blue, reassuringly patting his dusty back. "I've got it all covered. This is going to go smoother than anything you've ever seen."

"It better," said Odell, getting impatient, his gunhand falling back into place.

From his seat behind a wall of ornate yet sturdy iron bars, the bank president, Arvin Potts, saw five rough, unfamiliar faces in his bank lobby. Two of the men stood in line, saddlebags over their shoulders, behind Irma Wix, the town's schoolmarm. The other three had drifted off, two standing near the teller entrance at the far end of the counter, one standing at the front door, gazing out as if enjoying the sight of traffic back and forth along the street.

"Gentlemen, good morning!" said Potts in a pleasant but robust voice. He arose from his chair, tugged down on the edges of his vest and stepped forward toward the barred door separating him from the public. "May I help you?"

"You sure as hell can," said Odell, his eyes shining with excitement.

Looking closely at these men, Potts decided he wanted to get them waited on and out of the building. He was used to dusty, hard-jawed cattlemen swaggering into his facility carrying saddlebags filled with cash and gold coins. While their business was always welcome, Potts knew that their dress and demeanor often caused anxiety among his other, more civilized clients.

"Please step this way then," said Potts. As he spoke,

he took a key from under his vest, unlocked the door and held it open a foot. Odell and Harvey Blue gave one another a quick glance of disbelief and immediately stepped over toward the unsuspecting bank president without a word. As they did so, Dick Hohn, tipped his hat and held the front door open for Irma Wix, who gave him a courteous nod as she walked out.

"I take it you men are some of the first returning from the trail drives to Abilene?" Potts beamed and extended his right hand toward Odell. "Here today to deposit that cattle money?"

"No, you stupid son of a bitch, we're *here today* to rob you!" Odell Clarkson hissed, his gun coming up quickly from under his duster as Hohn closed the front door and jerked a sign around from OPENED to CLOSED with the flick of his wrist.

"Oh dear!" said Potts, his expression turning from sunshine to mud as Odell's pistol jammed into his belly.

Harvey Blue gave the other men a nod, then said to Potts, "Tell your clerk to get his hands down and get that other door open or else we'll blow his brains out!"

"Jeffrey!" Potts called out to the frightened young teller, who, seeing what was going on, threw his hands in the air in terror. "Lower your hands and let them in. If we cooperate, they won't harm us!" His eyes pleaded with Odell. "Right, gentlemen?" he asked in a shaky voice.

"We'll see how it goes," said Odell, motioning the teller toward him, then shoving the frightened men toward a large safe built into the back wall. "Get that safe open, pronto, banker!" Cutting a glance toward the front door, Odell said to Harvey Blue, "What's wrong out there? How come our boys ain't raising no hell yet."

"It's coming, Odell," said Harvey. "Trust me. Let's keep down the shooting and razzing until we get all the money out of the safe."

"I always feel better hearing our backup men out there scaring the hell out of the townsfolk," said Odell.

"I told you, don't worry about it, they'll start shooting as soon as Hohn gives them the signal. I've got it covered."

At the safe, Potts nervously unlocked two locks, then turned the safe dial back and forth from number to number until the big tumblers released. Beside him the teller stood wide-eyed in fear.

Giving the bank president a shove, Harvey Blue swung the large door open and made a sweeping gesture with his gun toward the interior of the safe, saying jokingly to Odell, "After you, my good man."

"Don't mind if I do, sir," Odell chuckled walking inside and looking around at boxes of ore, stacks of gold coins and stacks of bills in large denomination all in a neat row along wooden shelves.

Hurrying into the large safe behind Odell, Lonnie Freed and Eddie Rings gasped at the sight of the money. "Lord God almighty!" said Freed. "We have hit the motherlode this time!"

Standing at the open safe door, Harvey grinned, then pushed Potts and the teller inside and toward a rear corner. "All right," he said to his awestruck men, "we can admire it later. Get it bagged and get it out of here!"

"We ain't got enough saddlebags to hold all this!" said Lonnie Freed.

On the safe's floor, against the rear wall, three large leather express bags lay slumped and empty. "Use these,

Gawdamn it!" Odell said, sounding irritated and harried. He shot a glance at Harvey Blue and said, "Good thing they didn't start shooting up the town just yet. It'll take some time to get all this bagged up and ready."

Harvey grinned. "I know. That's why I wanted to wait as long as we could before having Hohn give the signal."

Odell returned the grin. "You and me are going to go far together, Harvey Blue! I see that right now."

Lonnie Freed and Eddie Rings hurriedly stuffed the leather express bags full of cash. Finishing a few seconds before Lonnie, Rings turned and hurried out of the safe, getting past Harvey Blue and Odell, who stood emptying the wooden boxes of gold coins into their saddlebags. But as Lonnie turned with the leather express bag bulging with cash, Dick Hohn appeared at the open safe door and held out a large canvas bag, saying, "Here, take this and start filling it. Give me the express bag."

Lonnie Freed started to protest, but before he could speak, Odell saw Hohn and said, "Damn it, you're suppose to stay at the door and be ready to signal the men!"

"I'll take care of it, Odell," said Hohn. "Stop acting like some scared old woman about it!"

All movement stopped inside the safe. Lonnie Freed almost gasped aloud as he got out from between the two men, expecting trouble at any second.

"What did you just say to me?" Odell asked in a menacing tone. His hand was poised an inch from his holstered pistol.

"Come on, Odell," said Harvey Blue. "He didn't mean nothing by it. Let's keep stuffing!"

But Odell's and Hohn's eyes had locked. Dick Hohn

said low and evenly, "Yeah, Odell, I meant nothing by it."

Odell eased up, letting his hand move an inch away from his gun butt. "We're not stopping now," he said to Hohn, "but as soon as we're out of here and get our loot sorted out, you and me are stepping off and settling up with one another. That's a promise."

"Make sure you really do want a piece of me before you go *promising* anything, Odell," said Hohn, "because I'll hold you to it."

"Cut it out, Dick!" Harvey warned. "You ain't doing nothing that might foul up this job." His eyes shot back and forth between the two men. "We're all on the same side here, men! Damn it, let's not foul things up over a mouthful of bad talk."

Lonnie Freed cut in, saying cautiously to Odell, "He's right, boss. There's too much at stake here to risk it over a gunfight."

"We'll talk about it later," said Odell, already cooled out and wanting to get on with the business of robbing the bank.

"Yeah, later," Hohn agreed, wearing a trace of a knowing smile. "Right now I best get out there and get ready to give the men a signal."

No sooner was Hohn out of sight than Odell grumbled but went back to stuffing gold coins into his already bulging saddlebags. Eddie Rings reappeared with two more empty canvas bags. "Here, Lonnie, keep it going!" he said, handing the empties to Lonnie Freed and taking a full one.

Harvey Blue saw Odell fastening the flaps on his saddlebags. "Wait a minute, Odell. I'll lend you a hand." He hurried out of the safe, dropped his heavy saddlebags onto Potts' desk and stepped back inside. Pulling another folded canvas bag from inside his duster, Harvey handed it to Odell and said, as he reached and slipped his hand under Odell's saddlebags, "Damned if this ain't turning into hard work, pard."

"Yeah!" said Odell, beaming once again with greed and excitement. "But it's the kind of hard work I was born to do!" He shot a glance around at Lonnie Freed. "How much is left over there, Lon?"

"Not much," Lonnie replied, a bit out of breath. "I believe we've just about got it all."

"We sure can work fast when we have to, eh, men?" said Odell, making a visual sweep of the empty shelves and scattered wooden boxes that held the coins. "Are you sure that just about cleans this place out?" he asked in a half-joking tone. "We don't want this fellow holding out on us." He gestured toward Potts and the teller, who lay huddled in the corner, watching with sick and frightened expressions on their sweaty faces.

Feeling good about how well the job was going, Odell passed the last bag of money to Harvey Blue and stepped over to the bank president. "You're not holding out anything, are you, banker? Because if you are . . ."

"N–no, sir," Potts stammered in a trembling voice, "this is everything. I swear it!"

"Hear that?" Odell chuckled over his shoulder to Harvey Blue. "We've got it all."

But Harvey Blue didn't answer. All Odell heard behind him was a slight metal creaking sound as darkness began to engulf him. "Harvey? *Harvey!*" he cried out, hearing the tumblers of the safe make a clucking sound in the darkness behind him.

"Boss!" shouted Lonnie Freed, a few feet away and invisible now in the pitch-darkness. "Boss, he's forgot and locked us in here!" Odell heard Lonnie stumble forward and land against the safe door, slapping on it with both hands, shouting, "Harvey! Harvey! Come back! You've locked us in! Damn it, don't forget about us!"

"Shut up, Lon!" Odell raged loudly in the pitch-blackness. "He's *jackpotting us*, you damn fool!" Odell stumbled around blindly among wooden coin boxes, one hand holding his pistol, the other reaching out, searching for something to grab on to. "Banker! Get over here, you sonsabitch! Open this damn door! Let us out!"

From his spot on the floor, Potts hesitated for a moment before answering in a meek voice, "Sir, I'm afraid the door cannot be opened from inside."

"What?" Odell turned around quickly toward the sound of Potts' voice. "Don't you lie to me, you little turd! I'll blow your Gawdamned head off!"

"He's telling the truth, sir!" said the teller, his voice sounding a bit more stable than Potts'. "The only way the door can be opened is from the outside, and then only by someone who knows the correct combination."

"Jesus! That's the stupidest damn thing I ever heard of!" Odell shouted. "There has to be a way out of here!" He stumbled back to the door and slapped it again as if the big door would suddenly swing open. "All right," he shouted at the teller, "who else knows it?"

"In this case, only the safe company in Chicago," the teller replied sharply. "Once they give the combination to the pres—"

"That will be all, Jeffrey," said Potts, cutting the teller off and taking on the authority befitting his title as bank president. "Sir," he continued to Odell, "although it is highly irregular to do so, I gave the combination to my wife."

Jeffrey gasped aloud in the darkness.

"It's true," said Potts. "I gave her the combination in preparation for just such an event as this." He paused, then said, "But how on earth will we manage to get anyone's attention from in here?"

"Lonnie," said Odell, "get over here and start pounding your gun butt against this door!"

"But what about the law?" Lonnie inquired.

"To hell with them," said Odell. "We'll shoot our way through them. I just want to get out of here and kill the dirty snake who did this to us."

PART 2

Chapter 7

Harvey Blue grinned and patted the large iron door, saying quietly, "Adios, ole pard." He and the rest of the men gathered at the front door and left the bank. Standing guard at a nearby hitch rail, Paco and Buck Turner watched each of them carry either an express bag or one of the bulky canvas bags into the crowded street. When the men had blended quietly into the passing foot traffic and moved away toward their horses without incident, Paco let out a breath of relief and said to Turner under his breath, "This is the *only* way to rob a bank, eh?"

Turner gave a tight wry grin. "I feel almost guilty, getting paid for my part in this."

"*Sí,* but I think I will take it all the same." Paco chuckled. He watched the bank door for a moment longer, then asked, "Where are Odell and Lonnie? They have not come out yet."

"Nobody talked to you beforehand, Paco?" Turner asked, looking surprised.

"Talked to me about what?" Paco shrugged.

"Never mind," said Turner, not wanting to get into it

right there. "Odell and Lonnie left through the rear door," he added matter-of-factly. "Let's go."

But Paco would have none of it. "Where are they?" he asked bluntly. "I do not leave a man behind."

"Paco, this ain't the time or place to go into it," said Turner, "but take my word for it, Odell and Lonnie are in a safe place. Now let's ride before we wear out our welcome here."

"I don't know what you mean by a safe place," said Paco, making no attempt at walking away with Turner. "What kind of answer is that?"

A few minutes earlier the two had watched the town sheriff walk into the gunsmith to investigate the sound of gunfire they'd heard. Now Turner spotted the sheriff stepping out of the blacksmith shop and back onto the boardwalk. "I'll explain it all to you later, Paco," said Turner. "Trust me. You'll get a kick out of it. Right now we best get our knees in the wind. We're supposed to stick close behind the gang until we get away from here to make sure they ain't being tailed." He nodded toward the sheriff, who stood looking back and forth along the busy street. "Are you coming with me or not?"

"*Sí,* I am with you," said Paco. "But I want you to know that I do not like riding with men who use trickery on one another. Men who ride together must stick together. This has always been my belief."

Turner shook his head slightly, saying, "All right, Paco, I get your message. Let's ride."

The two stepped down to the hitch rail, mounted their horses and backed away from the rail slowly, taking their time without drawing attention to themselves. The sheriff stood looking the town over without casting them a second glance as they rode past him.

"Are you still here, Sheriff Edwards?" asked Carl Morris, stepping out of his gunsmith shop.

"Yeah, I'm still here," the sheriff replied, his eyes still watching the busy street. "I'm not sure I believe what you told me happened in there."

Carl Morris shrugged. "Sheriff, why would I lie about it? I was trying to free up a lodged bullet, and the gun went off. It's happened before. What's the big deal about it this time?"

"I ain't the smartest man in the world," Sheriff Edwards said, still searching back and forth along the street as he spoke, "but I can tell the sound of *one* gunshot from *two* most any day of the week, even if they are awful close together."

"What can I say, Sheriff? You're wrong," said the gunsmith. "If it'll make you feel any better, let's go search my whole shop, back room and all." He had a poker face as he looked at the sheriff.

The sheriff turned a piercing gaze to the gunsmith, saying, "Careful what you say. I might just take you up on it, Morris. I know you run a poker game in that back room now and then. Maybe we ought to go back there and see if there's any lingering smell of gunsmoke, since I didn't smell any around your workbench."

"Be my guest," Morris said, hoping the shallow turn in his voice didn't betray his bluff. After Bennie Betts, Joe Christi and the others had slipped out the rear door, Bennie and Joe carrying Turley Whitt's body between them, Carl Morris had quickly left the room, hastily closed its door and laid an old Starr pistol on his workbench. Sheriff Edwards had arrived moments later to find him busily at work on the jammed gun. But now Morris needed to get rid of the lawman so he could clean up the bloody mess and put things back to normal.

"I just might," said the sheriff, turning his eyes back to the street without seeing the sick expression sweep across the gunsmith's face. But instead of following through, Sheriff Edwards' eyes stopped at the door to the bank, noting the CLOSED sign in the glass door. "Have you seen Potts this morning?" he asked Morris.

"I saw him come from Mavis Reno's restaurant this morning and open the bank, same as usual," said Morris, grateful that something else might have caught the sheriff's attention. "Why?"

"Because the closed sign is on the bank door but I haven't seen Potts or Jeffrey out and about," the sheriff remarked.

"Oh? Maybe you ought to go check things out over there."

"You know what strikes me?" the sheriff murmured, getting more and more interested in the bank as he stared at it.

"What, Sheriff?" Morris asked, wishing Edwards would go on over there, but not wanting to appear too eager to get rid of him.

"When Potts closes down for a few minutes, he always pulls down the door blinds behind the sign so no one can see inside," Sheriff Edwards said, his voice taking on a suspicious tone.

"Uh-oh," said Morris, actually getting a little concerned himself in spite of the mess awaiting him in his back room. "Maybe you *really should* get over there and check it out."

"Yeah, I believe so," said Edwards. He turned to walk back toward the gunsmith shop.

Morris' eyes widened. "Whoa, Sheriff, hold on. I thought you were going to check on the bank!"

"I am," said Edwards. "But I want to carry that sawed-off you keep in the back room. I'm not going all the way to my office to get mine."

"I'll get it for you, Sheriff!" said Morris. "Get on over there. I'll be right behind you. I can't let you go alone anyway, if there might be a robbery going on."

"Well, I'm obliged to you for your help, Morris," said Edwards, "but don't take all day. This could turn dangerous real fast." Adjusting his gun belt on his hips, Sheriff Edwards stepped down off the boardwalk and walked across the street to the bank.

"Jesus!" Morris hissed to himself. He hurried inside his shop, into the bloody back room, grabbed the shotgun from its pegs on the wall and checked it as he ran from the shop to catch up with the sheriff.

Across the street, Sheriff Edwards had already stepped inside the door to the bank and stood with his Colt drawn, looking all around. Easing into the open door behind him, Morris said quietly, "It's me back here, Sheriff. Don't get spooked and start shooting at me."

"Be still, Morris," Edwards replied in a harsh whisper, his eyes scanning the empty back. "There's something amiss here, I can feel it same as I feel like something's amiss about that gunshot at your place."

Morris ignored the remark about the gunshot and nodded at the open barred door between the lobby and Potts' office area. "I've never seen that door standing open," he said, lowering his tone of voice, gripping the shotgun in his hands.

"Nor have I," said the sheriff, stepping forward with caution. Glancing back at the gunsmith, he said, "Get to one side or the other, Morris. I don't want you shooting me in the back if something breaks out."

The two eased forward through the open door, seeing nothing out of the ordinary. "This gives me the willies," the gunsmith whispered, seeing a deeply concentrated look on the sheriff's weathered face. "It reminds me of men creeping around inside a tomb or—"

"Shh," said Sheriff Edwards, cutting him off. "Be quiet and listen to that."

"To what?" Morris whispered, his hands tightening around the shotgun.

"That tapping sound. Hear it?" The sheriff cocked his head slightly toward the vault. The two listened intently, hearing first the muffled tapping sound of metal on metal. Then, upon closer scrutiny, they heard the faint sound of Potts' and his teller's voices, sounding as if the two were shouting for help from a distance away.

Sheriff Edwards gave the gunsmith a surprised look, saying, "Well, I'll be hammered. They're inside that big ole safe!"

Morris listened long enough to realize the sheriff was right. Shaking his head in disbelief he said, "Potts has sure made a damned fool of himself. He's locked himself and Jeffrey in the safe. Wait until everybody at the saloon hears about this, the poor, stupid man."

Sheriff Edwards just stared at Morris for a moment.

"Is that all you see here, Morris? You think a banker like Potts locked himself and his teller in a vault?"

Morris shrugged. "Yeah, it sure looks like it."

"Potts is no idiot, but you are," Edwards growled. As he spoke, he walked toward a canvas bag lying crumpled on the floor. "How the hell could they lock themselves in a vault? You have to lock the door from out here!" He reached with his boot toe and kicked the canvas bag over at the gunsmith. "Look at this, and tell me what's going on."

Morris looked down at the bag as realization set in. "Aw hell," he said, "the bank has been robbed! And without a shot being fired."

Edwards grumbled, cursing under his breath as he stepped over to the big iron door, and began tapping soundly on it with the butt of his Colt. "Potts, it's me, Sheriff Edwards," he bellowed loudly into the thick iron slab. "Can you hear me in there?"

After a pause, Morris asked Edwards from a few feet away, "What he'd say, Sheriff?"

"Damn it," said Edwards, "I was right. He says him and Jeffrey have been robbed. Two of the thieves are locked in there with them."

Four miles out of town, where the trail led up into a stretch of low rocky hillside, Bennie Betts rode along beside Joe Christi and struggled with the lead rope to the small donkey he led behind them. Across the donkey's back lay Turley Whitt's body wrapped in a bloodstained riding duster, his arms dangling from beneath it. A small shovel lay wrapped against him.

"Come on, you ornery son of a bitch!" Bennie

shouted at the stubborn animal. But the donkey only stepped along grudgingly, letting out a loud bray in defiance. Wiping a shirt cuff across his face, Bennie said to Joe, "When Morris said *we'll get rid of the body,* I should have known that the *we* he was talking about would be you and me!"

"It still beats sticking around trying to explain everything," said Christi. "You never know how the law is going to look at a shooting. Besides, there's nothing we can do about it now." He looked back over his shoulder toward town, at the cloud of rising trail dust closing in on them. "We best get off the trail up here and see who this is coming upon us."

"The sheriff?" Bennie asked, looking back himself.

"I don't know," said Christi, "but I'm not going to be sitting here with Turley's body when I find out." The two nudged their horses upward off the trail and into the cover of rock, the donkey braying and resisting every step of the way. "Can you shut that donkey up?" Christi asked.

"Not unless I shoot him," said Bennie, jerking again on the lead rope, "and that would make him louder than he is."

But by the time the riders rounded into sight, the donkey had settled and stood twitching its ears. Watching the horsemen pass by single file on the trail beneath them, the pair noted the large bags, both canvas and leather, as well as the two pairs of bulging saddlebags draped behind Harvey Blue's saddle.

"Jesus!" said Bennie, as the riders moved away from them along the trail, riding at the same brisk steady gallop. "Do you know who that is?"

"Who?" Christi asked, keeping his eyes on the riders as trail dust began to obscure them from view.

"The mean-looking one in the lead is Harvey Blue Walker, that's who!" Bennie said. "I've seen him before. Like as not, I'd say they just robbed the bank back in town."

"No," said Christi, "if they'd robbed the bank, we were close enough we'd have heard some shooting earlier. Anyway, look at them. They're moving right along, but they ain't in that big a hurry."

Bennie looked puzzled and scratched his beard-stubbled chin. "Well, you got me there," he said. "There weren't no noise and they ain't in no rush—"

"Where do you know Harvey Blue from?" asked Christi. "Or was you just blowing off?"

"I wasn't *just* blowing off," said Bennie, sounding indignant.

"Then where do you know him from?" Christi asked, nudging his horse back down to the trail now that the riders were out of sight and the trail dust began to settle.

"Never you mind where I know him from," said Bennie, nudging his horse along behind, pulling the donkey by its rope.

"All right then, forget I asked," said Chisti, meaning it. He looked out across a stretch of flatlands to the south and said, "We best get off this trail."

Bennie sighed and said, "How far are we going to tote him anyway. He's going to start getting ripe real quick."

"Not far," said Christi. "A mile, maybe two."

"I don't see why we can't roll him off into the rocks somewhere and forget about him. It's as good as most gunfighters ever get."

"I wish Morris would have taken care of this like I thought he was going to," said Christi. "Then I wouldn't have to worry about it." He nudged his horse off the trail onto the flat rocky ground. "But since I have to get rid of his body, at least I'm going to get him into the ground proper-like."

"Hell, you killed him, Joe!" said Bennie. "Nobody expects you to throw him a *funeral.*"

"That's how it is," said Christi with finality on the matter. He rode on. Bennie coaxed his horse up beside Christi, struggling with the lead rope, and said, "You still don't understand what it is you've done, do you?"

"Yep," said Christi, staring straight ahead. "I killed a man, plain and simple."

"But not just any man, Joe!" Bennie insisted. "That's Turley Whitt! He's known all over the country for his skill with a gun. They used to call him a shootist back years ago."

"I know it," said Christi. Ignoring the subject, he nodded at another stretch of cliffs and low hills in the distance. "There's a creek runs through a stand of cedars over there. I believe that would be a good place to plant a man."

"Damn it, Joe!" Bennie cursed, heeling his horse crossways in front of Christi's and stopping suddenly. "You ain't listened to a word I've said! You've outshot one of the all-time fastest, meanest gunman who ever lived. Why can't you understand what that means?"

Christi stopped his horse and stared at Bennie. Behind Bennie the donkey began to pull back and forth on the rope.

"It means no more dirty bunkhouses and bed ticks,"

said Bennie. "It means no more beans heated in airtights and et with a flat stick! It means walking into a saloon and not seeing the better whiskey shoved under the bar when they see you!"

"Yeah," said Christi. "It means some other gunmen wanting to shoot me first chance they get so they can take that away from me." He shook his head. "Obliged, but no, thank you. None of that means anything to me."

"Not at all?" Bennie asked.

"That's right. Not at all," said Christi.

Bennie nodded at Turley's big Colt shoved down in Joe Christi's belt. "Then why'd you keep his gun?" Bennie asked.

"I don't know," said Christi. "But killing Whitt was just a fluke of fate. I'm lucky he didn't kill me."

"A *fluke*?" said Bennie, shaking his head at Christi's words. "I'll tell you something, Joe. I've always known how fast you are. So have all the drovers we've worked with in this part of the country. I'm not surprised you beat Turley Whitt."

"Well, it's over and done with," said Joe. "Now we've got to—"

"Lift your hand away from that gun real easy-like," said a voice behind them.

Christi's first instinct was to raise the Colt, as he turned, and start firing. But he resisted the urge, raised his hand and turned halfway around in his saddle.

Bennie raised both hands, still holding the lead rope. Leaning slightly sideways in his saddle he looked at the two men holding rifles aimed at them from less than fifty feet away and said as recognition came upon him, "Turner? Buck Turner?"

"Yeah, it's me, Bennie," said Turner. He and Paco were sitting at ease in their saddles, but with their rifles cocked and ready. "What are you two cowhands doing carrying a dead man around out here?"

Bennie stalled on answering and looked at Christi for help. Christi turned his horse with a soft tap of his knees and sat facing the two riflemen. "Who's asking?" Christi said in a calm, quiet voice, his hand had moved a few inches from the Colt in his belt, but was still poised near the old range pistol holstered on his hip.

"Whoa!" said Bennie, feeling he needed to say something to keep down any trouble. "Buck, this here is my pard, Joe Christi. Him and me work the drives all around these parts. He's a-okay and a top hand to boot."

Buck Turner grinned flatly, keeping his eyes leveled on Christi. "Hear that, Paco? This man is *a-okay and a top hand to boot.* That means he gets along good with cows."

"*Sí,* I hear it," Paco said with no trace of a grin. "I am impressed."

Turner nodded at the body on the donkey but kept his stare fixed on Christi as he asked, "Was this the shot we heard in town, Bennie?"

"You heard it?" Bennie asked in response.

"You boys just don't seem to want to answer anything I ask," said Turner.

"No, Buck. That ain't the case at all," Bennie said quickly. "I'll answer anything you ask—you ought to know that." He shrugged and continued. "Yep, that must have been the shot you heard. We was playing cards in back of the gunsmith shop and—"

"That's enough, Bennie," said Christi, cutting him off.

"I'll tell him when it's enough," said Turner.

"I already did," said Christi.

Seeing trouble coming, Bennie spoke fast, saying to Turner, "Joe here killed Turley Whitt. That's the shot you heard in town."

Turner fell silent for a second. He heeled his horse forward while Paco kept his rifle on the two drovers. At the donkey, Turner leaned in his saddle, pushed a corner of the duster aside and grabbed a handful of Turley Whitt's disheveled hair. He raised the dead blue face for a look.

"I'll be damn," Turner said, dropping Whitt's head and backing his horse away. Paco eased his horse forward and looked for himself.

"This one shot Turley Whitt?" Paco asked as if in awe.

"Deader than hell," said Bennie. "Joe here fought him straight up, one on one."

"One on one," Turner repeated almost to himself. His and Paco's rifle barrels sagged a bit. Turner tried to maintain his same hard expression, but Bennie noticed a difference. Something in Turner's attitude had weakened and changed. Joe Christi saw it too.

"What say you two ride with us? We'll help you bury ole Turley later on. I'd like for Harvey Blue to see this with his own eyes."

"Is that a *friendly* invite?" Christi asked flatly.

"Nothing but," said Turner, lowering his rifle and laying it across his lap. "Any man who kills a big gun like Turley is a friend of mine from the get-go."

Chapter 8

In the darkness inside the big vault, Odell slapped Lonnie Freed's hands away from his shoulder. "Damn it, Lonnie! This is *me*! Get the teller, like I told you to! I just heard something click inside the door."

"All right, boss. I'm sorry," said Lonnie fumbling with his gun in the darkness. "If I could just see something in this damn dark . . . "

"Banker, don't you dare try to balk on us!" Odell growled. "If you and that plug flunky of yours don't get over here, we'll just turn and start shooting. Take *Pott* luck, so to speak."

"Please don't shoot, sir!" said Potts. "In all this iron, the bullets will ricochet in every direction!"

"Then you best cooperate and not give us a hard time, unless you never want to see that wife of yours again." As he spoke, Odell put out a hand in the direction of Potts' voice, grabbed him and jerked him closer. "What did you say her name is, Clara?"

"Sa-Sarah, sir," Potts answered quietly. Moments earlier Potts had shouted loudly into the iron door, telling Sheriff Edwards to send someone to his home and bring back his wife, the only other person who knew the combination to the vault.

"Yeah, Sarah," said Odell. "You better hope to hell *Sarah's* got a good memory. If this door don't swing open pretty soon, you and junior banker here are dead." He poked the tip of his gun barrel to the side of Potts' head and turned it as if boring a hole with it.

"I da-daresay, sir," Potts offered in a meek shaky voice, "if this door isn't opened before much longer we'll all be dead."

"What are you talking about, banker?" Odell asked, rounding the gun barrel some more.

"We'll run out of air, sir," Potts replied.

"Bull," said Odell. "That's the craziest thing I ever heard of."

"No, it's not," said Lonnie. "I've heard the same thing myself! After a while the air wears out."

"The air wears out? If you believe that, you're as crazy as he is," said Odell. "Air never *wears* out. Air is air. It's everywhere, you idiot." He chuckled. "It ain't like a pair of boots or a saddle."

"No, really, Odell," said Lonnie. "Air wears out. It's what they call a *scientific* fact!"

"Scientific fact, my ass!" Odell bellowed, his voice ringing inside the iron walls. "We could hold out in here the rest of our natural lives if we had plenty of food and water!"

"I'm afraid you are wrong, sir," the young teller interjected from the darkness.

"Jeffrey, stay out of this," Potts warned, but he was too late.

"What did you say?" Odell shouted, turning toward

the sound of the teller's voice. "Nobody says I'm *wrong*, you son of a bitch! Especially not some bank teller I'm robbing!"

In the darkness, Jeffrey found the courage to stand up against the back wall and shout defiantly back at Odell, *"You are wrong! You are wrong! Wrong, wrong, wrong!"*

Outside the vault, Sarah Potts jumped away from the door as if it had turned red-hot. She turned a frightened gaze to Sheriff Edwards, who was standing a foot behind her.

"Uh-oh!" said Edwards. "That was a gunshot. No mistake about that." He motioned over his shoulder for the crowd of townsmen carrying shotguns to move in closer. "You men get ready. It sounds like they're getting really spooked in there." He looked back into Sarah Potts' clear green eyes, seeing anticipation, and said, "Go right ahead, ma'am. Turn that last number. Then step aside. I'll open the door myself." As he spoke he lifted his Colt from his holster and cocked it.

Inside the vault, Odell Clarkson wiped warm blood from his forehead and tightened his arm around Potts' neck from behind. He watched slanted light creep into the blackness and spread slowly as the big door opened slowly. "Hang on to that flunky. Here they come," he whispered to Lonnie, who stood beside him, using Jeffrey as a shield.

Squinting as their eyes adjusted to the light, the two outlaws saw over a dozen cocked shotguns, rifles and pistols pointed in their direction. In the center of the armed townsmen stood Sheriff Edwards, his Colt out at arm's length and aimed at Potts and Odell. "It's all over for you thieves! Lay down your guns!" he demanded.

"Ain't nothing over, lawdog!" Odell shouted, not giving an inch. "Lay down *your* guns, unless you want to spend the day picking these fools' brains out of your whiskers! Ain't that right, banker?" He rounded the tip of his Colt into Potts' ear. "Now tell these *good folks* what I told you to."

"Ple-please, Sheriff!" Potts stammered. "Do what they say. Don't gamble with our lives!" His words sounded hastily rehearsed.

"If you think you're riding out of here free, outlaw," said Edwards, "you're crazy."

"Then start shooting, all of yas!" Odell bellowed, blood running freely down into his eyes as he blinked and stared from one townsman to the next. "This is what one ricochet did to me! All them guns start going off, you'll carry these two out of here in water buckets! Now fire them or drop them!"

Behind the safety of the thick door, Sarah Potts gasped and shrieked, "My God, Sheriff! Do something!"

"Easy, ma'am," said Morris the gunsmith, standing near her. "Our sheriff knows what he's doing."

Sheriff Edwards kept his head and took his time, wanting to let the charged air settle. But looking all around the looted vault, he grumbled, "Rotten sunsabitches," under his breath. "Where's all the Gawdamned money?"

"I'd have to speculate that it's well on its way to Mexico by now," said Odell. "Now drop the guns! Somebody bring four horses to the front door and get out of our way!"

"You're Odell Clarkson, ain't you?" Edwards asked,

ignoring the outlaw's demands, recomposing himself with a deep breath.

"That's right, Sheriff," Odell replied, "and this is Lonnie Freed, my right-hand man. You've heard of both of us. You know what we'll do."

"Who's the others?" Edwards asked.

"Go to hell, Sheriff," said Odell. "I never jackpotted a man in my life!"

"They sure jackpotted you right enough," said Sheriff Edwards, his eyes going to Lonnie Freed and his hostage, then back to Odell.

"That they have," said Odell. "But they'll soon be wishing to hell they hadn't."

"Then you know where to find them?" Edwards asked pointedly.

"That's right. I do," said Odell. "But you don't, and there's nothing you'll do to make me tell you. Now drop them guns. Don't make me say it again."

"Don't let them out of here, Sheriff," Morris warned, leaning and whispering from around the edge of the thick vault door.

"Shut up, Morris," Edwards whispered in reply. To Odell he said, "I'm not letting you take these men out of town with you."

"Oh, yeah, you are, Sheriff," said Odell. "Now the question is, what kind of attitude do you want me and Lonnie to leave here with? Send us away from here cross about how long it took you to do like you're told, and you can bet we'll leave them nailed to a tree and killed Comanche-style."

Again Sarah Potts gasped. This time she swooned.

Morris stepped in, slipped his arm around her waist and caught her before she toppled forward.

"And if we get you some horses and get you out of here, then what?" asked Edwards.

"Then you and these two fellows can talk about all this over a nice hot meal, soon as they come riding back in," said Odell, sounding sincere.

Sheriff Edwards studied the outlaw's face for a moment, then said over his shoulder to one of the townsmen, "Bert, go get four of your best horses and get them ready for the trail. Hurry back here with them."

"And don't try sticking us with some livery plugs," said Odell, "unless you like riding into the smell of fried eyeballs."

"You heard him, Bert," said Edwards, still staring at Odell as he spoke over his shoulder to Bert Collins, the livery man. "And be sure and bring only the best horses you've got. Mr. Potts and Jeffrey's lives depend on it."

Riding up a tight, rocky trail, Turner, Paco, Bennie Betts and Joe Christi heard Harvey Blue's laughter resound across a wall of boulders and cliffs and echo along the hillside.

"Sounds like our new boss is real happy about something," Turner said, giving Paco a grin. He still carried his rifle across his lap, as did Paco.

"What do you mean?" Paco asked, looking suspicious.

"Relax," said Turner. "I'll let Harvey explain it. I think you'll get a kick out it, if you've got any sense of humor at all." Looking up at the top of a large boulder embedded in the rocky hillside, Turner added, "You do have a sense of humor, don't you?"

"Si," said Paco, "just as much as the next man. But I do not like surprises."

"None of us do, Paco," Turner said, still grinning as he waved.

Hearing Turner, Joe Christi and Bennie gave each other short glances and rode on in silence.

Atop the large boulder, Freddie Tapp saw Turner's wave and stepped into sight. He watched the four riders and the donkey carrying Turley Whitt's body approach; and he waited until Turner gave him a signal, letting him know the two new faces were no threat to anyone. Then Tapp waved them in with his rifle barrel.

By the time the four had ridden around a steep turn in the trail, Tapp had sent word of their arrival down the other side of the boulder to Harvey Blue and the rest of the gang. The laughter had stopped and a wide circle of men stood up slowly and faced the new arrivals, Harvey Blue and Dick Hohn at the center, Harvey dusting his seat and holding a tall bottle of whisky.

"Well, well," said Harvey Blue, eyeing the body on the donkey and the two new faces, "what have we here? Looks like our two rear guards have met themselves a couple of new playmates." He chuckled and cut himself a long swig of whiskey.

"What the hell are they doing bringing strangers in here like this?" Dick Hohn asked just between himself and Harvey Blue. "I don't like this."

"Take it easy, Dick," said Harvey. "You're a rich man now. You'll have to learn to be more tolerant of others and appreciate new things."

"Yeah, right, I will," Dick Hohn grumbled.

Harvey Blue called out as the four men drew to a halt a few yards away, "I hope you two have kept a good eye on our backside."

"Yes, sir, boss," said Turner, waiting a moment before stepping down. "All's clear behind us, right up to the town limits." He grinned and added, "I expect the sheriff and the townsfolk had things to keep them occupied."

Paco gave both Turner and Harvey Blue a questioning look, then looked all around at the gathered outlaws. To Harvey Blue he said, "What is going on, Harvey? Where are Odell and Lonnie Freed?"

Harvey Blue raised a hand toward the Mexican, putting him off. "First things first, Paco," he said. Looking at Bennie and Joe Christi, he said, "Who are these two? What are they doing here?"

"I brought them here to show you something you ain't going to believe, Harvey," said Buck Turner. As he spoke, he and Paco swung down from their saddles. Bennie Betts started to follow suit, but Joe Christi gave him a look, stopping him. The two remained mounted and quiet, Joe keeping his eyes on Harvey Blue.

"We found these two out on the flats about to bury this body," said Turner, as he stepped around and grabbed the corner of the duster covering Whitt's head. "Their names are Joe Christi and Bennie something-or-other," he continued. "Joe here shot this one dead as hell."

"That's no reason to go bringing them to us," Dick Hohn cut in using a sour tone of voice and staring hard at Joe Christi. "They're just a couple of dirty-eared steer tramps."

"I'd walk a little softer, if I was you, Dick," said Turner. He flipped up the corner of the duster, jerked up Whitt's dusty head and revealed his dead purple face.

It took a moment for Harvey Blue to recognize Turley Whitt, but when he finally did, he whistled under his breath and said, "Hoss, Gawdamn it!" He spoke over his shoulder to Dick Hohn as he took a step closer and gave a concentrated look at Whitt's hazed-over eyes. "Turner's right, Dick. You might want to walk a little softer!"

"It was a straight-up fair fight, Mr. Walker," Bennie Betts offered meekly. "I saw the whole thing—fair as hell."

"Over a card game," said Turner.

"I believe that," said Harvey, looking closely now at Joe Christi. "I always heard Whitt was a man who couldn't bare losses." He stepped over closer to Joe's horse and nodded at the battered range pistol. "You shot him with that rusty pile of scrap iron?"

"Yep," Joe said flatly.

"Boy," Harvey chuckled, "I bet he felt foolish." He waited a second as if considering something, then said, "Well, Joe Christi, why are you and your friend still sitting on that hot leather?"

"Good manners, Mr. Walker," said Christi. "We ain't been invited yet."

"Hear that, Dick?" said Harvey Blue. "This is a man who kills a big gun like Turley Whitt, and he has good manners to boot."

"Yeah, I heard it," said Hohn, still showing little regard for the two ragged cowboys.

"Well, step on down, Christi," said Harvey Blue.

"And pay no mind to Dick here. He's going to be a little surly for a while. He always thinks of himself as top hand with a gun."

"I *am* a top hand with a gun," Dick Hohn added firmly, his right hand poised as if ready for someone to dispute his claim.

"Well, boss," said Turner, "did I do right bringing them here to show you Whitt's body?"

"Yeah, you did real good, Turner," Harvey Blue replied. While he answered Turner, he looked around for Tony Weaver and motioned for him. "Come up here, Weaver. You two ought to meet one another."

When Weaver stepped in closer and looked Christi up and down, Harvey Blue said, "Weaver here just went up against Cray Dawson. I suppose you know who Dawson is."

"Yeah, he used to be a drover like us. A good man with a gun. He even rode with Fast Larry Shaw for a while," said Christi, returning Weaver's up-and-down look and saying to him, "If you went up against Crayton Dawson, what are doing *alive*?"

Weaver looked stuck for an answer; but Harvey Blue cut in, saying with a laugh, "Oh, I forgot to mention. He was *one of three* who went up against Dawson! The others couldn't turn tail and run as fast as Weaver here."

Weaver, red-faced with shame, still didn't want to say anything that might upset Harvey. He said in a whipped tone, "I was lucky to get away alive—that's a fact. Are you planning on facing Dawson?"

"No," said Christi. "I don't have any plans to face anybody."

"Then why go to the trouble of being so damn good

and fast with a gun?" Harvey asked. "If I was a big gun, my first stop would be facing down Cray Dawson. Why bother with the steer when a bull's walking the line?"

Christi only shrugged.

Harvey said, "I've been curious why he's sheriffing in Somos Santos. Maybe we'll ride over there and see the two of you shoot each other full of holes."

"If nobody here objects," said Joe Christi, ignoring Harvey's remark while he and Bennie stepped down from their saddles at the same time, "I'd like to get this poor bastard in the ground. He's drawing flies." Christi held the lead rope to the donkey in his left hand.

"Sure, go on and get his ass in the ground," said Harvey. "We're all through with him. We'll talk about you some later on."

"I want to know why Turner is calling you boss?" Paco asked, sounding a bit testy.

"All right, Paco," said Harvey. "Here it is, short and sweet. Some of the men think I'd be a better leader than Odell Clarkson, so I locked him and Lonnie in the bank vault."

Paco looked stunned as he saw Harvey, Dick Hohn and some of the men break into laughter. "No, you didn't!" the Mexican said, sounding horrified. "You cannot leave a man that way! It is not right!"

"Not right?" said Harvey in mock surprise. "My, my. I wish you'd said something sooner. I expect they're ready to stretch those two bummers from a barn rafter along about now."

"I'm going back for them!" said Paco. He turned and started back to his horse.

As Harvey spoke, Christi listened while he untied

Whitt's body and took down the shovel tied with it. As Bennie rolled Whitt's body to the ground, Harvey looked at Dick Hohn and gave him a nod.

"Hey, Paco!" said Hohn. "This is for you."

Christi and Bennie saw what was about to happen. Bennie started to say something but Christi gave him a nudge, saying, "Stay out of it."

Before Paco could turn all the way around and face Dick Hohn, a shot exploded from a small-caliber revolver Hohn pulled from inside his shirt and nailed the Mexican high in the right side of his chest.

Turner almost reached for his gun too, but Harvey shouted, "Back off, Turner!"

Turner stood as if frozen in place while Paco hit the ground, crawled a few inches, then fell limply, face-down, in the dirt.

Hohn looked at the smoking pocket revolver with rapt fascination. "I'll be damned. If I thought this little gun would pack such a wallop, I'd have used it long before now."

"Good shot," said Harvey, walking over to the Mexican and nudging him with his boot toe. "Anybody got anything to say about this, get it said. I don't aim to have any bellyaching in this bunch while I run things." His stare went across the men, then settled coldly on Turner. "Buck, you with me?"

Turner stood staring down at Paco for a moment, then said to Harvey, "Yeah, I'm with you. I just wasn't expecting this with Paco." He shrugged. "Leaves us more money to split up though. That's all right by me."

"That's the spirit," said Harvey. "Riding with me, you'll get used to expecting a lot of the *unexpected*." He grinned at Buck Turner, then turned his glance to Christi and Bennie. “While you two boys are at it, how about pitching some loose dirt over the Mexican for me?”

“Sure,” said Christi, “why not?”

“I like that kind of attitude.” Harvey grinned. Nodding at Turley Whitt’s big Colt shoved down in Christi’s belt, he said, “I reckon that’s ole Turley’s shooting iron, huh?”

“Yes, it is,” said Christi.

“You’ll have to tell me all about the gunfight after you get the burying done,” said Harvey, eyeing the shiny Colt. “If I was you, I’d holster that and toss that range pistol as far away as I could.”

“I’m thinking about it,” Joe Christi replied.

“Yeah, I bet you are.” Harvey grinned. He turned with his bottle in hand and walked away.

Joe Christi looked at Bennie Betts and said with resolve, “Start digging.”

Chapter 9

Twenty minutes later, still digging in the rocky ground, Bennie turned to Christi and said, "Jesus, Joe! We've gotten ourselves into a bad fix here." He kept his voice low and ducked his face slightly to keep Harvey and the rest of the men from seeing him. To the west, thunder rumbled strong and deep. The sky along the horizon had turned gunmetal gray.

"I know it," said Christi, looking at the shallow grave, only half the size it would need to be to accommodate the two bodies. "We've got to keep our eyes open and our mouths shut and look for a chance to get away from this bunch."

"I wish we'd never come along with Turner to begin with," Bennie whispered.

"It's not like we had much choice, Bennie," said Christi.

"You're fast with a gun. You could have refused to ride with them," Bennie whispered, looking all around.

"I might be fast," Christi replied, "but I ain't an idiot. It was hard to refuse with two rifles riding at my back."

He stabbed the shovel into the hard ground and pitched the dirt into a pile.

"I'm sorry, pard," said Bennie. "I know it's not your fault we're here."

"Just do like I say, Bennie, and when the time comes we'll—" Christi stopped in the middle of his sentence and jerked around at the sound of a low cough coming from Paco's bloody lips.

"Lord, Joe! He's alive!" said Bennie, jumping back a step as if he'd seen a rattlesnake.

"Shh. Quiet, Bennie," Christi whispered, "or he won't be for long." He took a guarded glance over at Harvey Blue Walker and the rest of the men. "Walk over and get our canteens from our horses like we need a drink. Maybe we can save this man's life."

"A while ago you didn't want to get involved?" Bennie said.

"This is different, Bennie. Go get some water and hurry back," Christi said, looking down at Paco, seeing him try to move an arm and let out a low moan.

"All right, I'm going," whispered Bennie.

Christi leaned down over the wounded Mexican as if getting ready to roll him into the shallow grave. "Paco, can you hear me?" he asked in a low tone. "Don't try to talk. Just open and close your eyes. Can you do that for me?"

Paco opened his eyes with effort, then let them close slowly. His hand tried to reach up onto Christi's forearm, but Christi had to push his hand down to keep anyone from seeing it. "Lay still, Paco. If Walker sees you moving, he'll finish the job on you. Me and Bennie are going to try to save you. But you've got to lay still no matter what—even if I have to throw some dirt over you. Can you understand me?"

"Sí," Paco whispered faintly before Christi could stop him from speaking.

"I said don't talk, Paco. Just open and close your eyes to answer," Christi instructed him again. "Now lay real still for me."

From a few yards away, Harvey Blue called out to Bennie, who came walking back with the canteens, "How's it going over there?"

"It's slow going, Mr. Walker, but we're getting there," Bennie called back to him. "We just need a little water." He shook the two canteens by their straps in his hand.

"Good work," said Harvey Blue. To the men he said with a chuckle, "If it was up to me to dig a hole with a storm coming, I'd have to leave ole Turley and the Mex for the coyotes and buzzards."

"I don't know why we're waiting around here on these two cowhands anyway," said Dick Hohn. "We've all got money that needs spending." He tossed a nod toward the dark horizon. "I hate getting wet."

"Anytime a gunman like Turley Whitt gets shot to hell, I like hearing the particulars," said Harvey Blue. He stood holding a bottle of whiskey, his voice sounding a bit slurred.

"They could catch up to us along the trail," said Hohn, casting a scornful look in the direction of Bennie and Joe Christi. "I don't know why we want a couple of ragged-ass cowhands riding with us anyways."

Harvey Blue threw back a long swig of rye, let out a whiskey hiss, then said, "Hell, you're right. They can catch up to us. Why hang around here when we've all got more money than we know what to do with?" He turned a drunken glance to Buck Turner. "Buck, you're still our rear guard. Stay here and keep an eye on these two cowboys. Make sure they come along behind us when they finish up here. I like that gunman. He smells like a cow, but he's got good manners." Harvey laughed.

"Sure thing, boss," said Turner. He'd looked over a moment ago and saw Christi bowed over Paco's body. Without appearing too eager he wanted to get over there now and see what was going on. Standing near his horse, Turner stepped over, picked up his reins and led his horse to the grave site.

"Anyways," said Bennie, as if he and Christi had been carrying on a conversation as Turner arrived, "I told Yancy, the next time I ride for a greasy-bag bunch like this, I'm going to—"

"They're riding on," said Turner, cutting in. "We're supposed to catch up to them along the trail."

Bennie Betts managed to keep himself between the rest of the men and Christi while Christi had stooped down and poured a trickle of water onto Paco's parched lips.

"Good." Christi turned slightly, the canteen still in his hand.

Turner stopped short in his surprise. "What are you doing?" he asked, watching Christi.

"This man is alive," Joe Christi said in a guarded tone.

"Jesus!" said Turner. He gave a quick glance over his shoulder toward Harvey and the rest of the men, who had begun stepping up into their saddles and turning their horses to the thin trail.

Seeing Turner about to hurry over beside him, Christi warned him, "Don't come any closer. Stay right there and help Bennie cover what I'm doing."

"Right, sure thing!" said Turner. "Jesus!" he said again, his surprise and elation barely under control. "I'm much obliged, Christi, you helping him out. Him and I have kinda gotten to be pals."

Christi gave him a look. "It didn't sound like it a while ago. You said with him dead there'd be more loot to go around."

Turner looked ashamed. "I only said it to look out for myself. Paco knows how that works, riding with a bunch like this." He leaned slightly and tried to look around Christi at the wounded Mexican.

"I said stand still and cover me," said Christi.

"Right." Turner stiffened quickly as if called to attention. "Do you think he'll make it?"

"I don't know," Christi said bluntly. "I'm not a doctor." He took a glance around the rocky terrain, then nodded off to the east. "There's a cattle shack a couple of hours' ride from here. If we can get him there ahead of the storm, maybe we can keep him alive."

Glancing up at a deep clear Texas sky, then judging the distance from there to the dark widening horizon, Turner said, "He can't ride. Not in this shape. Sitting in a saddle will kill him."

"He'll have to," said Christi.

Bennie glanced around at the riders moving out of sight and said, "What about when Mr. Walker realizes we're not joining up with him?"

"You can stop calling him *Mister* now, Bennie," said Christi.

"All the same," said Bennie, embarrassed, his face reddening a bit, "what's he going to do when none of us comes catching up to him?"

"You know him better than we do, Turner," said Christi, looking to Buck Turner for an answer.

"I ain't sure," said Buck, "but a rear guard is not a job you send your favorite man on. If somebody's dogging your trail, it's the rear guard that catches hell first. At least that's the way I look at it. If I don't come back, Harvey will probably figure I got myself et up by a posse. I hate losing my share of the loot, but he won't lose no sleep over me, especially when it's time to give everybody their share."

"But it sounds like you left Schalene Pass in plenty of time. There shouldn't be a posse trailing you this quick," said Christi.

"Maybe, maybe not," said Turner. "You never know how things are going to play themselves out, robbing banks. It's a hazardous business. You'll find out if you ride with the Harvey Blue Walker gang."

"Harvey Blue can go straight to hell, as far as we're concerned," said Bennie.

Giving Bennie a silencing look, Christi said quietly to Turner, "We didn't want to ride with Harvey Blue *before* and we sure don't want to ride with him now."

"But he was real impressed with you shooting Whitt," said Turner. "I just figured you'd want to throw right in with the gang. You both look like you could stand a stake . . . to get back on your feet?"

"Let's get this straight, Turner," said Christi. "We're *on* our feet without anybody's help. We're drovers. We live the way that suits us. The only reason we came along with you and Paco was because you both had rifles and caught us off guard. We're not outlaws, Bennie and me."

"All right," said Turner, "take it easy. We were just doing our jobs."

"What you were doing was shoving your weight around, two rough, tough outlaws wanting to show their boss how bold they were, bringing in the man who killed Turley Whitt."

Instinctively Turner gave a half glance toward his rifle in his saddle boot.

"Huh-uh, Turner," said Christi, "you'd be dead before you got your hand on it. Besides, I'm not crossing you for a fight. Hell, I'm not even a gunman—just a fellow who got into a card game and had to shoot his way out. I'm just making sure we both understand one another."

Turner let out a breath, relieved. "Sorry for how we acted, Paco and me."

Joe Christi only nodded a halfhearted acceptance of Turner's apology. Looking out along the empty dusty trail, he said, "They're gone. You can come on over here," he said to Turner.

"Much obliged," said Turner, stepping over quickly. He stooped down beside his wounded friend. "Paco, can you hear me?"

"Sí," Paco whispered in a failing voice. *"Agua . . . "*

"Here," said Christi, handing his canteen over to Turner. "Give him some water, but not too much."

Taking the canteen and pressing it to Paco's lips, Turner said to the wounded man, "Paco, you're going to be all right—do you hear me? You're going to pull through this."

The Mexican rasped in a faltering voice, "What about—what about . . . our money?"

"Our money?" said Turner, as if having forgotten for a moment. "Well, I expect you can forget about yours, since Harvey thinks you're dead." He looked off in the direction of the settling trail dust as if considering it for a moment, then said, "Damn, I hate to lose my share too." He searched Joe Christi's eyes for some sort of advice. "But I suppose money ain't everything."

Christi said, "Do what you've got to do. I'll go make some bandages out of a bandanna."

"What do want me to do, Joe?" Bennie asked as Christi passed him on his way to his saddlebags.

"Keep digging, Bennie, and you best hurry it up," said Christi. "We still need to get Whitt into the ground."

"Damn," Bennie complained to himself, raising the shovel and stabbing its blade into the unyielding earth. "This digging is the worst job of all."

But in moments he had stabbed and scraped and cleared the grave deep enough to accommodate Turley Whitt's stiffening body. While he rolled the dead gunman into the ground, Joe Christi and Buck Turner had stripped Paco's shirt from him and pressed bandages against the chest wound until the blood finally began to darken and firm into a blackish jell, slowing the flow of any fresh blood.

They raised the Mexican into a slumped sitting position, and Christi looked at the large bump on his back, where the bullet had broken a rib and lodged there just below Paco's shoulder blade. The skin surrounding the large bump had already grown blue and swollen. Paco drifted in and out of conscience, babbling and coughing under his breath.

"That bullet's going to have to be dug out of him, ain't it?" Turner asked.

"Yes," Christi replied, "I'm afraid so. If we don't get it out, it'll give him blood poisoning sure enough." He gave Turner a serious gaze. "Have you ever cut out a bullet?"

"No," said Turner, the two of them lowering Paco back to the floor. Turner stared fixedly at the bloody bandage while Christi pressed more strips of bandanna into the sticky blood. "Have you?"

"Nothing this bad," said Christi. "I cut a bullet out of a man's thigh—that was bad enough." He shook his head and added, "I hope I don't kill this man trying to save him."

"If you do, I believe Paco here would understand," said Turner, relieved that he wasn't to be the one doing the cutting and probing into Paco's back.

"Yeah," said Christi in a wry tone, "I bet he would." He picked up the rain slicker that he'd untied from behind his saddle and folded it into a small square. He laid the slicker over the blood-soaked bandages and pressed it slightly, saying to Turner, "Help me sit him up again, enough to tie his shirt around him and hold everything in place."

"I can ride," Paco murmured weakly as the two lifted him into a slumped sitting position.

"I sure hope so," said Joe Christi, looping the shirtsleeves around the Mexican's thick chest and tying them together behind his back. "All right, Turner, let's get him up and on a saddle. You ride double behind him." As he spoke the first fine sliver of rain blew in from the west and landed on the back of his bloody hand. "We'll be lucky if we get there ahead of this storm."

In moments they had mounted and moved out across the rocky ground, Paco and Turner riding double, Turner sitting behind the saddle, supporting the wounded man. "I hope I live . . . long enough to kill . . . that bastard," Paco whispered weakly.

"You will, Paco," said Turner. "Just keep telling yourself that, and keep hanging on. Be too damn tough to die."

"*Sí,*" said Paco, "too damn tough to die."

By the time they had reached a weathered shack sitting on the side of a hill overlooking a winding creek, the storm had moved in behind them and begun pelting them with sheets of rain.

"There it is," Joe Christi said over his shoulder to Bennie and Buck Turner. Without another word, he nudged his horse forward up the hillside toward the shelter of a lean-to behind the shack. Turner and Bennie followed, Bennie still leading the donkey on the end of a lead rope.

"Yeah, and just in time," Bennie said, casting looks back into the dark boiling sky looming close behind them. "It looks like this is going to be a real gully washer. Nobody in their right mind would want to be out in the likes of *this*."

Chapter 10

"This sonsabitch is slowing us down!" Lonnie shouted to Odell through the blowing rain. "I'm putting a bullet in him and leaving him in the mud!" Lonnie pulled hard on the reins to Potts' horse, dragging both horse and rider along behind him.

"Please!" Potts cried out. "Don't shoot me. I'm doing the best I can! Perhaps if you give me the reins, I can get the animal to move along."

"Give him the reins!" Odell bellowed, leading Jeffrey's horse along beside him. "Some horses won't lead, especially with a storm blowing!"

Lonnie tossed the reins to Potts, saying, "There, you money-counting bastard. I hope you try to make a run for it! I'll kill you deader than hell."

"I won't try, I swear to you," said Potts, taking the reins and right away feeling the horse beneath him settle immediately.

"He ain't going nowhere," Odell said over his shoulder. "He knows that this teller is dead if he does. Do you understand?" Above them thunder pounded. Lightning twisted and curled. Around them wind roared and screamed.

"I understand completely, sir," Potts cried out above the wind and rain, one hand holding his drenched bowler hat down onto his head. "I would never do anything to jeopardize young Jeffrey's life."

"He ain't going to cut out in the midst of this storm anyways. Ain't that right, Potts?" shouted Odell.

"Right you are, sir," Potts shouted in reply.

Clamping his hat down onto his head and hunching low in his saddle, Odell slowed his horse to halt for a moment and shouted to Lonnie above the storm, "We've got to find a place to step up out of this for a while! Another few minutes this whole stretch of flatlands is going to be rushing water!"

"Which way then?" Lonnie shouted, also clamping his hat down onto his head.

Odell looked all around, squinting in frustration, unable to see twenty feet in any direction through the silver-gray blasts of rain. "Damn it to hell! I don't know! One wrong move we could wind up running smack into that sheriff!"

"He said he wouldn't follow us until these two come back alive!" shouted Lonnie.

"Shit!" said Odell. "If he'd been on our trail any quicker, we'd be following him!"

"What?" Lonnie shouted.

"Nothing," said Odell. "Stick close to that banker and let's get moving. Keep headed upward till we get above these flatlands!"

"All right. I'm right behind you!" shouted Lonnie, backing his horse a step and turning it sidelong, searching for Potts in the hard blow. "Get up here, banker. Let's go! Don't be fooling around!"

But Potts neither answered nor appeared.

Lonnie squinted harder into the silver-gray swirl, saying, "Banker, damn it! Get up here!"

"What's the holdup?" Odell shouted back over his shoulder, hearing Lonnie call out to Potts.

"The banker's gone!" Lonnie raged. "It ain't been five *Gawdamn* minutes he gave his *Gawdamn* word! Already he's gone!"

"You let him get away?" Odell shouted as if in disbelief.

"No, I didn't let *him*!" Odell replied. "You said he wasn't going anywhere!" Rain pelted their faces like darts.

"Gawdamm it! I didn't mean for you to quit watching him!" Odell bellowed through the wind.

"I just stepped my horse up there beside you for a second!" said Lonnie. "He promised! Then he took off before the words got out of his mouth!"

"Go get him, damn it!" Odell screamed. "He can't get far. He's a banker!"

"Which way?" shouted Lonnie.

"I don't know!" Odell shouted. "Just get him!"

Jeffrey hunkered down in his saddle, bare-headed, a hand above his eyes for protection against the rain. As he saw Lonnie nudge his horse and disappear into the swirl of wind and water, he felt Odell tug roughly on his horse's reins. "I guess you know that sonsabitch just got you killed, don't you, boy?" Odell shouted at him.

Jeffrey looked quickly at Odell, in time to see him reach for the Colt at his hip. Wildly, and without thinking, the young banker raised his left foot from the stirrup, shot out a kick that landed solidly beneath Odell's chin and lifted him sideways out of his saddle. Odell's Colt exploded upward in a streak of fire as he went airborne, letting the reins to Jeffrey's horse fly from his hands.

"The hell's going on?" Lonnie shouted, hearing the shot from fifty feet away. He jerked his horse around in time to see an obscure image of horse and rider race away and vanish in the rain.

"Get him!" Odell commanded, wallowing and slipping in the mud, trying to gain footing for himself.

But before Lonnie could gig his horse forward, Potts charged out of the rain screaming, his horse slamming into Lonnie from the side.

Lonnie flew from his saddle and landed splashing flat into the mud. "Odell!" he shouted. But before he could say anything more, Potts was upon him, astraddle his chest, screaming, almost sobbing, a letter opener rising and falling in his pale hand.

Lonnie felt the stabs one after another in his chest, his ribs, the side of his throat. At first he'd tried to grab the banker's rising-falling arm. But Potts, in his fear and desperation, moved too fast for him. Lonnie managed to get a hand on the banker's face, covering it, muffling Potts' screams. Yet the stabbing continued until the silver letter opener stuck tightly in Lonnie's breastbone and could not be retrieved. Lonnie sighed deeply and tried to grasp the slippery letter opener. But within seconds his hand fell to the mud and began opening and closing deftly, without purpose.

"I'm coming, Lonnie. Where are you?" Odell shouted into the gray swirl.

Panting, heaving, Potts had flung himself away from Lonnie Freed. Then, as if in afterthought, upon hearing a gurgling sound come from the outlaw's lips, he reached over, grabbed the revolver from the outlaw's holster, cocked it with both hands and pointed it at Lonnie.

"Don't shoot," Lonnie rapsed in a shallow voice.

"I must," the trembling banker sobbed. Taking one hand off the pistol to hold over his eyes, Potts turned his face away and pulled the trigger.

"Lonnie!" Odell shouted, hearing the gunshot. He searched blindly in the sidelong rain.

"He's dead!" shouted Potts, cocking the big pistol again with both hands. "Go away. Please!" He fired the pistol in the direction of Odell's voice, then struggled to cock it again.

"Lonnie, answer me!" shouted Odell, not taking the banker's word for it yet.

"Please go away! He's dead, I told you!" Potts shouted and sobbed.

The bullet whistled close enough to Odell's head that he heard it slice past his ear. He ducked away and turned at the same time, running, splashing through the mud in a low crouch back toward his horse. "All right, I'm gone! Don't shoot!"

Hearing Odell running away, Potts lay panting, gulping for air, the pistol lying slumped in the mud beside Lonnie's body. Listening closely he heard the running stop, then the sound of horses' hooves splashing away from him. He closed his eyes for a moment and let his lips move in prayer. But in the midst of his prayer, he heard splashing footsteps coming toward him again. He raised the pistol and fired wildly, catching only a glimpse of a shadowy figure leap down out of sight in a spray of mud.

"Go away!" Potts screamed, nearing hysteria, his wet hands slipping franticly as he tried to recock the revolver.

"Don't shoot! Please, Mr. Potts, sir! It's me! Jeffrey!"

"Je—Jeffrey!" Potts sounded relieved, but still badly shaken. "Oh, Jeffrey, Jeffrey, Jeffrey!" He broke into tears as he spoke. "My goodness! I might have shot you! Come here quickly! *Quickly*, do you hear me?"

"Mr. Potts, are you all right, sir?" Jeffrey asked, approaching the banker with caution, still trembling a bit from his ordeal.

"Oh, yes, dear me, yes," said Potts. Lying on his side in the mud, propped up on one elbow, Potts cried, wiping tears from his eyes even in the lashing rain, "This is all so terrible, Jeffrey. To think that I have just killed a man!"

"I know, sir," said Jeffrey, stepping in and sitting down in the mud beside him. "But he would have killed you, sir. Don't forget that."

"Yes, I realize that," said Potts, sniffing, regaining some of his customary composure. The two turned their gaze to Lonnie's body lying less than three feet away.

"These were very bad men, sir," said Jeffrey, coming around some, the trembling leaving his voice as shock settled in. "I have no doubt that we were both about to meet a bad end."

"Yes, I believe you are right, Jeffrey," said Potts, turning loose the revolver and reaching a hand out to the younger man. "All things considered, I believe we have both accounted well for ourselves."

"Yes, I think so," said Jeffrey. They shook hands and hunkered back down against the next slamming gust of wind and rain. When the gust subsided, Jeffrey asked, "What must we do now, sir?"

"I believe we must stay in pursuit of Odell," said Potts above the raging storm.

"But we're free now," said Jeffrey. "Shouldn't we get back and let Sheriff Edwards handle things from here?"

"That would be true if we were ordinary citizens, Jeffrey," Potts said loudly beneath a jarring clap of thunder. "But we are both bankers. The town's money is at stake here, and that man is going to go straight for it. We must do our best to know the whereabouts of the money when the law arrives. Ours is a position of trust—don't ever forget." He wagged a wet muddy finger.

"Yes, right you are, sir," said Jeffrey. "It won't happen again."

Odell Clarkson pushed his horse wildly through the wind and rain, aware only that the land beneath the animal's hooves seemed to be rising above the flatlands. When the animal stumbled and almost went down, Odell drew the animal to a walk and let it take him up the side of a hill where he found partial shelter beneath a cliff overhang. "If I ever get my hands on the sonsabitches . . . " he grumbled to himself.

He wiped his face with his wet gloved hands and stared out through a sideways waterfall of rain spilling down from the cliff's edge above him. "Well, I'll be double-dog damned, Odell," he said to himself, barely making out the vague outline of the drover shack perched half way the hillside across from him. "Looks like you ain't run out your string just yet." He looked back, squinting in the direction of Schalene Pass, then nudged his horse forward out into the raging storm.

Inside the shack, Bennie Betts had found enough scraps of dry wood in a corner wood box to start a fire in a battered tin stove. He'd found a tall candle stub in its dusty tray atop a wooden shelf on the wall, and set it aside for later use. In the candle tray lay four wooden matches. He touched the end of the match heads to make sure they were firm and dry.

Paco lay on the floor on his stomach, his shoulders propped up slightly by saddle blankets piled against a wet saddle. Joe Christi had found a few coffee beans in a paper sack rolled up in the bottom of his saddlebags. He'd crushed them with the butt of his range pistol and boiled a pot of weak coffee. An hour passed before Paco stirred and became conscious enough to look around at the dusty shack and say in a shallow voice, "Is it . . . done yet?"

"No," said Christi in a regretful voice. "I haven't started yet." He stood up and walked to the open door of the tin stove. "We needed you to rest first, to get some strength up."

"Now you'd do best to go *back* to sleep, Paco," said Turner, kneeling beside the wounded Mexican.

"Santa Madre," Paco whispered in his native tongue. "I would do best if I . . . had some whiskey." Talking caused him to cough under his thin breath.

"Sorry, Paco," said Turner. "I can't accommodate you there. I wish I could. We could both use a long swig right now." He reached out and pressed a hand gently down on the back of Paco's shoulder.

"I see what . . . you are doing," Paco whispered.

"Oh?" said Turner.

"*Sí,* you are testing, seeing how to hold me down," Paco replied.

"We've got to get that bullet cut out," said Turner. "Me and this cowboy is going to hold you. Christi is going to do the cutting."

"Can . . . I trust him?" Paco's failing eyes went over to the tin stove, where, from its flickering flames, he saw Joe Christi take his knife out of the open stove door.

"He's been straight up with us so far, Paco," said Turner. "That's all I've got for you."

Using all his effort, Paco turned slightly and called out to Christi in his weakened voice, "Hey, cowboy . . . one shot, eh?"

Christi looked at him as he raised the knife in his hand and examined the glowing blade. "Yeah, one shot," Christi said absently, preoccupied with the knife and the thought of what he had to do. "You saw his body."

"*Sí,* I saw him. One shot." Paco managed a faint grin and lowered his eyelids as if drifting off to sleep. "Cut quick and deep . . . cowboy. Do not hesitate."

"I won't," said Joe Christi, walking slowly toward him across the dust-covered floor. "We're ready," he whispered to Buck Turner and Bennie Betts.

Bennie eased over from beside the tin stove and squatted down on the other side of Paco. He and Turner gave each other a look. Joe Christi eased in beside Bennie on the left in order to better get to the wound. With the knife in his right hand, he examined Paco's swollen purple back, determining where to sink the tip of the blade.

"Are we sure we've got to do this?" Bennie whispered. He picked up the loose end of Paco's gun belt, which was lying beside him. He doubled the belt and slipped it in between Paco's teeth.

"Yes, we're sure," said Christi.

"Jesus," said Bennie. As he spoke, a match flared in his quaking hand; he touched the fire to the candle wick. His face had turned ashen and tight. "Won't you need more light than this?" He held the candle tray out to Joe Christi.

No one answered. Christi wiped his shirtsleeve across his sweaty forehead and said grimly, "Hold him down." Then he took the candle tray in his left hand, held it down close, took a deep breath and cut down into the swollen flesh with the sharp point of the blade.

Chapter 11

"Good God!" Odell said to himself, hearing the terrible growling scream come from inside the drover shack. Wet rifle in hand, he'd tied his horse around the corner of the shack and crept up onto the front porch, where he hunkered down beneath a window ledge for a moment before rising to peep in through a dirty window. In the narrow candle glow, he saw three men hover over a fourth like wolves over their prey.

It took a moment for him to get a recognizable look at Buck Turner's face. When he did, he growled under his breath, "There, I've got yas, you sonsabitches." His thumb went across his rifle hammer and poised there. He paused and stared through the dirty window, wanting to get a look at everybody's face, knowing that the men inside were too busy to notice him.

From out of the storm came the faint sound of a horse nickering farther down the hillside. Inside the shack, Turner turned a gaze toward the window in the direction of the sound. Outside the window, hearing the sound himself, Odell ducked down and rolled away just in time.

"Somebody's coming up the hillside!" said Turner. "I heard their horse."

"I heard it too," said Christi. "But keep ahold of him!"

"The pain's knocked him out," said Bennie, sweating profusely.

"Hold him anyway!" Christi barked harshly, without rising from his gruesome work. He worked intently, one bloody finger deep inside the Mexican's broad back, having found the place where the bullet lay lodged between one shattered rib and the rib above it. He tried to hook his fingernail under the edge of the lodged bullet. "We don't want him waking and jerking around!"

"All right, Joe! Jesus!" said Bennie. "I'm holding him!"

"What about who's coming out there?" Turner asked. "It might be the law."

Christi turned his face sideways for a second, just long enough to once again blot his sweating forehead on his wet shirtsleeve. "You're the one worried about the law, not us," he said. "You do what you have to do. I'm trying to keep this man alive."

"I need to turn loose of him to go see," said Turner.

"I said hold on to him!" Christi rasped, his face down close to Paco's bloody chest in the flickering candle light as his finger picked and probed.

Turner started to say something more on the matter, but before he could, the front door flew open with a hard kick from Odell Clarkson's muddy boot. "Don't bat a Gawdamned eye!" Odell shouted. Turner turned loose of Paco, but Bennie held on firmly just as he'd been told.

"Odell!" said Turner. "What are you doing here?"

"You mean how did I get out of that damned town

alive, don't you?" Odell shouted. Before Turner could answer, Odell looked at Paco's unconscious face lying sideways against the saddle. Christi remained bowed over the wounded Mexican, still working intently. "Turn around here, you sonsabitch, and get your hands up!" shouted Odell.

"I can't," Christi replied bluntly. "If I do, this man will die."

"Not before I put a bullet in his head, he won't," said Odell. His eyes took in Bennie and Christi. "Now turn around, both of yas! I ain't telling you again." In his white-hot rage, the still unattended bullet graze on his head began to bleed down into his eye and drip from his nose.

"Joe, what do I do?" Bennie asked in a shaky voice, needing some guidance.

"Hold on to him, Bennie," said Christi with resolve.

"Have it your way!" said Odell, raising the rifle, taking aim on Christi's back.

"Wait! Don't shoot, Odell!" said Turner. "This man has done you no harm! Neither has Paco! The Mexican took that bullet over you! He heard what happened and tried to go back for you! Dick Hohn shot him! I swear to God!"

"You're a lying bastard, Turner, and now you're going to die!" He swung the rifle barrel away from Christi and Bennie for the moment and toward Buck Turner.

"Got it!" said Christi, seeming to pay no attention to Odell. He rolled the bullet upward from inside Paco's back on the crooked tip of his finger.

"All right, Odell, maybe I've got it coming!" said Turner, spreading his hands high, as if offering Odell a better target. "But Paco took that bullet for you, and that's the God's truth that I'll die with."

Odell looked troubled and confused for a second. He raised a hand to wipe blood from his eye. Doing so gave Christi the time he needed to slip his bloody hand over to Paco's gun belt and raise the Mexican's Colt cocked and pointed at Odell's chest. "Mister, I've got no dog in this fight," he said, "but what this man's saying is true. I saw it. The Mexican was headed for his horse to ride back after you. Harvey Blue Walker had his man shoot him down."

Odell squinted through his bloody eye and asked Buck Turner, "Who the Gawdamned hell are these two?"

"There just a couple of drifting cowboys who's helped me and Paco out, Odell," said Turner, his hands still up and spread, not taking the time to explain to Odell about Christi shooting Turley Whitt. "Like he said, he has no interest here except to say what he saw happen. I admit I'd heard Harvey was going to jackpot." He hung his head a bit and said, "I'm ashamed I didn't come tell you right away. Fact is, I never really believed he'd do it."

Odell considered the cocked gun in Christi's hand, and let the rifle sag a bit. "The Mex wouldn't stand for it, huh?" he said, keeping a close eye on Christi and Bennie.

"He went plumb growling-ass wild over it, Odell," Turner replied quickly. "I've never seen nothing like it. It shamed me proper."

Odell ran the information back and forth in his mind, realizing Christi could drop the hammer as quickly as he himself could. Finally, he said grudgingly to Turner, "I ought to kill you, Buck, you lousy turd."

"And I wouldn't blame you, Odell," Turner replied, managing to ease his hands down a bit. "But we're both in a tight spot here. It'd be best if we could stick together. Besides, if you're out to kill Harvey for what he done to you, I'm on your side all the way."

"Oh, you can bet I'm going to kill Harvey Blue Walker, sure as hell," said Odell, lowering the rifle more, and Christi put down his pistol as well.

"Was that your horse we heard nickering, Odell?" Turner asked. "Because if it wasn't, we've got company coming already."

"I heard it too," said Odell. "It wasn't mine." He lowered the rifle the rest of the way and said, "It sounded like somebody's riding up the hill."

"I suppose there's law on your tail?" Turner asked, already knowing the answer.

"Oh, hell, yes," said Odell. "Me and Lonnie left that vault with both the president and his teller under the gun. I expect we'll be hearing from the sheriff anytime."

"You left Lonnie watching them?" Turner asked.

"No," Odell replied bluntly, appearing reluctant to talk about it.

"Then where is Lonnie?" Turner asked.

"They killed him, it sounded like," said Odell.

"They? They who?" Turner probed.

"The two bankers," said Odell. As if dismissing the matter he asked, "Is Paco going to live?"

"He's got a chance," said Christi, "now that that bullet's out of him. Sometimes a small bullet stuck inside a man is more dangerous than a big bullet that goes clean through him."

"Yeah?" said Odell, giving the ragged dressed cowboy a smug once-over look. "How come you know so much about bullets?"

"The *bankers* killed Lonnie Freed?" Turner asked with an incredulous expression, not letting Odell change the subject.

"Gawdamn it, I don't know!" said Odell, getting agitated. "We stopped in the storm, one of them tried to get away. I heard a shot. I called out to Lonnie, but the banker answered . . . told me Lonnie's dead." Odell looked crestfallen and shook his head. "Hell, I had to turn and cut out with him shooting at me."

"A banker?" said Turner, having difficulty accepting the story.

"Didn't you hear me say *banker* the first time?" Odell responded, his hands tightening on the rifle stock.

"All right. Sorry, Odell," said Turner. "That just sounds hard to believe, is all."

"Believe it, Turner," said Odell. "And believe this too. We best be getting Paco and ourselves into some saddles and the hell out of here. The sheriff in that town is coming after us. I saw it in his eyes."

"If you put this man on a horse too soon, you'll kill him," Christi cut in. "Me and my pard here will stick around and take care of him until he's strong enough to sit a horse."

"Oh, will you?" said Odell. "And what then?"

"Then he's on his own," said Christi. "I'll help a man get over a gunshot if I can, but I won't shoot it out with the law because of him."

Clearly agitated with Christi, Odell, asked, "Who the hell said you're calling any of the shots here, cowboy?"

"Nobody had to say. I'm calling them for me and my pard," said Christi, the pistol still in his bloody hand, his hand lying loosely in his lap.

"Let's make sure you understand one Gawdamned thing before we talk any farther," said Odell, turning the rifle back slightly toward Christi. "No Gawdamn ragged-assed steer pusher is going to have any say on who does what or any other—"

"Odell," said Turner, cutting him off before things got out of hand, "this man killed Turley Whitt in a straight-up gunfight."

"I see." Odell stood stunned and silent for a moment, nodding his head as if trying to decide what to do or say next. Finally, he lowered his rifle and chastised Turner, saying, "Why didn't you tell me that before now, instead of letting me act like some ill-mannered. . . ." He let his words trail to a halt, then turned his attention back to Joe Christi. "How did you and Whitt come to lock horns anyway?"

"Over a poker hand, but that's not important right now," Christi said. "If you've got riders close on your trail, you better both get moving."

"And leave Paco," Odell said, "after him taking a bullet for me?" He looked at Turner for direction.

"Nobody got a look at me or Paco," said Turner. "Remember? We both laid back and guarded the trail behind Harvey and the boys."

"Are you riding with me or not then?" Odell asked pointedly.

"I'm with you, Odell," said Turner. "I still want to get

my part of the money. I figure I've got it coming, so does Paco . . . especially after what they done to him."

"If you're going, you best hurry up and get out of here," Christi cut in, wanting the outlaws out and away from him and Bennie when an angry posse showed up with killing on their minds.

"Take care of Paco for me, Joe Christi," said Turner. "Whether he lives or not, I'll always be obliged to you for helping."

"Get going," said Christi, motioning the two toward the door with the pistol barrel.

Bennie scooted over closer to Christi and Paco and sat watching in silence while Buck Turner gathered his wet saddle and slung it over his shoulder. When the outlaw had picked up his wet rifle and headed out the door behind Odell, Bennie let out a long breath of relief. "Jesus, I'm glad they're gone," he said, still staring at the door as if the two might come barging back in.

"So am I, Bennie," Christi said, reaching around beside Paco and slipping the big revolver back into its wet holster.

"You think we can make a posse understand that we had nothing to do with any of this?" Bennie asked, finally taking his eyes off the door.

"We'll have to," said Christi. "If nothing else, we'll tell them what happened between me and Whitt at Morris' gun shop."

"You think Morris will admit to it?" Bennie asked. "He didn't want anybody to know about the gambling in his back room."

"I know," said Christi, "but if it comes down to something as serious as you and me getting blamed for that bank robbery, he wouldn't let us down."

"I hope you're right, Joe," said Bennie, with an expression of apprehension.

Joe Christi gave him a wry grin and said, "So do I, Bennie. So do I."

Chapter 12

Behind a tall swaying pine a few yards below the drover shack, Arvin Potts flagged his hands trying to hurry Jeffrey back toward him from the direction of the lean-to shelter, where four horses and the donkey stood huddled together against the storm. Jeffrey slid and rolled the last few feet of the way down the hillside until Potts caught him and settled him against the side of a tall swaying pine. The two huddled behind the pine as the shack door opened and closed.

"Thank God, they didn't see you, lad!" Potts whispered. The pair watched wide-eyed and attentively as Odell and Buck Turner walked down off the front porch and splashed toward the lean-to. Through the window, the glow of a candle remained.

In a panting voice, Jeffrey said, "You're right, sir. There are more of them!"

"Could you tell how many more there are?" Potts asked in a whisper, staring at the two obscure figures disappearing into the lean-to.

"I don't know," said Jeffrey, "but more than one or two I'd say. There are four horses and a mule up there."

"I see." Potts thought it over. "But these two are leaving, so there will only be two."

"I'm afraid to guess, sir," said Jeffrey, his breath sounding better as he calmed down. "But do we stay here and watch about the ones inside or follow the two who are leaving?"

"Yes, that is our quandary," said Potts, rubbing his wet chin. Lonnie Freed's gun belt was buckled around his own waist. He tapped his wet fingers on the pistol butt as if doing so had been his custom for years. "I daresay, we could rush the house."

"Really?" Jeffrey said.

"But that might not be prudent," said Potts. The two watched Turner and Odell lead their horses out of the lean-to, mount up and rein the animals onto the narrow slick trail reaching up the hillside. "No," Potts said, "rushing the house would be far too dangerous. I propose that we stay here and keep an eye on these fellows. Sooner or later, this storm will let up, and Sheriff Edwards and his posse will arrive."

"But how do we know the sheriff's posse will come this way?" Jeffrey inquired.

"Oh, they will," said Potts. "I'm certain that after a storm like this they will have to spread out and search for some sort of sign in order to get back on the hunt—don't you suppose?"

Jeffrey saw doubt in his mentor's eyes. "Yes, I believe you're right again, sir," he said.

"Then I suggest we sit tight here and wait for help to arrive," said Potts.

"But it's awfully wet and windy here, sir," said Jeffrey, swaying a bit on a sharp gust of wind. Their horses stood huddled together beneath another tall pine farther down the hillside.

"That it is," said Potts, "but we must make do and meet this challenge with perseverance."

"Yes, sir," said Jeffrey. He sat down against the swaying pine and hunched himself up inside his thin, wet suit jacket. "All we can do is wait."

For the next hour and a half, the two sat together while the storm continued to rage. Inside the shack, Christi and Bennie waited and watched over Paco. Farther down the hillside Sheriff Edwards and his eight-man posse moved steadily closer, having circled above the flatlands in a stretch of low hills above countless debris-filled streams of runoff water.

When they reached a fork in the muddy trail and weren't sure which direction the gang might have taken, Edwards divided his men into two search parties and proceeded. But that had been hours ago; now the sheriff stood up in his stirrups and gave a troubled look in the direction of two rifle shots. "Did that come from Capson's party?" he asked William Tyler, the town barber who rode beside him.

"I wouldn't think so," said the barber, who rode without a hat, wearing only a wool muffler drawn down over his bald head. "We're supposed to use a single pistol shot for a signal, remember?"

"Of course I remember," said Sheriff Edwards, still gazing off in the direction of the rifle shots. "I'm just wondering, is all." He looked back at the other two townsmen, John Fletcher and Mann McNalty. The two rode behind him and Tyler, looking wet and miserable and half asleep in their saddles.

Seeing Sheriff Edwards look back, McNalty tugged his wet coat collar up and said, "Damned if I ain't ready to call it a day, Sheriff."

"Me too," said Fletcher. "I'm aching in parts of me I forgot I ever had."

Before Sheriff Edwards had time to answer them, a single pistol shot rang out on the trail ahead of them. "There!" said Edwards. "Now that's the signal I've been wanting to hear." He gigged his horse forward up the narrow, slick trail.

"But how did they get circled up around us?" asked Tyler, adjusting the muffler onto his shiny wet head.

"I don't know," said Edwards. "I reckon they got ahead of us in the storm some way." He looked off toward where he'd first heard the two rifle shots. "But now I'm awfully curious what the rifle shots were about."

"I'm cold, tired and wet, and I want to go home," said McNalty, stopping his horse while the other two reined their horses in behind the sheriff, who had started up the trail.

"Then go home, McNalty," Edwards called back over his shoulder. "Let everybody in town know that you didn't hunt down their savings for them. That'll make you *real* popular for a long time to come."

"He's right," said Fletcher. "I want to go home too, but for the town's sake, let's give it a little while longer."

"All right, damn it to hell," McNalty grumbled pushing his horse forward behind the others.

Before they had traveled a thousand yards up the mud-slick trail, Sheriff Edwards saw Potts in the upper distance, standing beside the tall pine, waving his arms back and forth slowly above his head. "My goodness!" said Edwards. "It's Arvin Potts!"

"Hurry on then!" said Tyler. "It's about time we got some luck going for us!" He started to gig his horse forward quickly, but the sheriff grabbed the horse by its bridle and held it back.

"Damn it, Tyler!" Edwards barked. "We can lose that luck just as quick if you go tearing up there and get your eyes shot out!"

"Take it easy, Sheriff," said Tyler. "I know what I'm doing."

"The hell you do! Listen to me, all three of you," said Sheriff Edwards. "This could be a trap for all we know. Spread out along this hillside. Soon as we get within a hundred yards of Potts, step down and lead your mount the rest of the way."

"Sheriff, I hardly think that's necessary," Tyler protested in a scoffing tone.

"You do it, Tyler," Edwards raged, his patience giving out on him, "or so help me, I'll crack your skull with a gun barrel."

"All right, all right, Sheriff!" said Tyler. "I'll do as you say!"

Edwards let go of Tyler's reins and nudged his horse forward again. At a hundred yards he looked side to side and saw the other three men spreading out. He stopped and stepped down, keeping an eye on Potts, who calmly walked back into the cover of the pine and slumped down onto the wet ground. A few minutes later Potts still sat slumped as the four men led their horses up closer, guns in hand, and stopped along the hillside, looking up at the drover shack.

"That's close enough, men," Edwards called out as quietly as he could to the other three, motioning for them to sink to the ground for cover. When they did, he walked the rest of the way up to Potts, seeing Jeffrey squatted down against the tree trunk. "Are you two all right, Potts?" he asked.

"We are now, Sheriff," said Potts, his face looking haggard and frightened. He pushed himself up from the ground and plucked at the seat of his wet trousers. "Some of the gang is up there." He pointed at the shack. "Two of them rode off a while ago, but there are more still up there."

"Good work, Potts," said Edwards, motioning to the men along the hillside to keep down. "How did you two manage to get away from Odell and his partner?" He eyed the gun belt around Potts' waist.

"Young Jeffrey found an opportunity and kicked Odell off his horse."

"But Mr. Potts stabbed the other one with a letter opener!" Jeffrey cut in, as if not wanting to take the credit.

"*A letter opener?*" the sheriff said in surprise. "Potts, that's amazing. Those two men are hardened criminals."

"It was terrible, Sheriff," said Potts. "But the main thing is, we haven't lost track of the town's money." He nodded toward the shack. "I doubt if it is up there in the shack, but I'm certain those men can lead us to it."

"Then let's try to take these birds alive if we can,"

said Sheriff Edwards, turning his gaze upward to the weathered shack.

Joe Christi turned his face from the window and looked at Bennie Betts, who sat beside Paco on the floor, a canteen and wet rag in his hands. "They're getting ready to come calling, Bennie. I best try to let them know who we are before any shooting starts."

"What are you going to tell them, Joe?" Bennie asked.

"The truth, Bennie, just like it all happened," Christi said. "If we start off truthful we won't have to worry about getting tangled up in a lie afterward."

"But you're not going to mention shooting Turley Whitt, are you?" Bennie asked.

"Not unless I have to," said Christi, turning his gaze back out the window and seeing the sheriff step behind the same tall pine that sheltered Potts and Jeffrey. "Here we go, Bennie." He raised the creaking window and quickly stepped to the side. "Sheriff! Can you hear me? We ought to talk."

After a short silence, Edwards replied, "Yes, I hear you. Talk about what, the bank money?"

"We don't have any of your bank money," Christi called out. "We're not the men you're looking for."

"Then throw out your guns and step out with your hands raised high," said Sheriff Edwards.

"We're going to do just that, Sheriff," said Christi. "But first I want to make sure I tell you our side of the story on equal footing."

"Who's in there with you?" Edwards asked.

"If you're really asking how many are there in here,"

Christi said, "there's my friend and me, and a wounded man named Paco. He's down and out, got a bullet hole in his chest."

"Who shot him?" asked Edwards.

To himself Christi said, "Damn it!" After a slight pause he said, "One of Harvey Blue Walker's men shot him and left him for dead. We've patched him up some. Walker's men were here, but they left a while ago."

While the two spoke, Tyler the barber had crouched below the cover of the hill line and run over beside Sheriff Edwards. "What the hell are you doing here, Tyler?" Edwards asked. "I motioned for all of yas to sit tight!"

Tyler ignored Edwards' question and said, "You don't believe him, do you?"

"I don't know," said Edwards. "Right now my biggest concern is getting the shack empty and getting the guns out of everybody's hands. Then I'll let you know who I believe and who I don't—if that's all right with you?" His voice had a sarcastic bite.

"It'd be a big mistake to believe anything this man has to say. He's one of the gang. You can bet your life on it!"

"I don't want to bet anybody's life on it," said the sheriff. "That's why I'm listening to him. That's why I'll go along with him, if that's what it takes to get this thing done and get back after our money. Now get down and keep your mouth shut!"

"Sheriff?" Christi called out. "Did you hear me?"

"Yes, I heard you," Edwards replied. "It sounds like you've got yourself tangled up into something you're wanting to get out of."

"That's the truth, Sheriff," said Christi. "Me and my pal here are just working drovers. We're not bank robbers."

"I understand," said Edwards. "You need to tell me the whole story so I can sort it out some. If you're innocent men, you've got nothing to fear from the law."

"Have we got your word on that, Sheriff?" Christi asked.

"You do," said Edwards. "Now pitch out your guns and walk onto the porch with your hands high."

Christi turned a glance over his shoulder and said, "Are you ready to walk out there, Bennie?"

"As ready as I'll ever be," Bennie replied, standing and holding Paco's big Colt and drawing his own range pistol from his holster. He walked toward the open window beside Joe Christi, ready to pitch both pistols onto the porch. "What about him?" he asked, nodding toward Paco lying unconscious on the floor.

"We did all we could to save his life," said Christi. "I reckon that's what I felt one man ought to do for another. What happens now is between him and the law."

"Seems like everything you done is a waste of time, if he ends up swinging from the end of a posse's rope."

"From what little I've heard about Sheriff Edwards, I believe him to be a fair man. He'll keep his posse under control," said Christi.

"I hope you're right about him," said Bennie, holding his pistol, looking reluctant, yet still ready to toss it out the window at his partner's command, "but what if you're wrong?"

"No matter," said Christi. "We've got to face up to this thing if we're ever going to get it straightened out."

His hands went down, drawing his range pistol from his holster and Turley Whitt's big Colt from behind his belt. "All this over a hand of cards," he murmured. He reached down and picked up the repeating rifles that leaned against the wall.

Chapter 13

Sheriff Edwards breathed a little easier watching the four pistols drop out of the front window and land, each making its own thud, on the front porch of the shack. He breathed even easier when Christi reached and lowered the two rifles as far as he could before turning them loose and letting them fall.

"All right, Fletcher, McNalty, get ready," Sheriff Edwards called out to the two men, who still lay thirty yards apart on the hillside. Their attention should have been directed to covering the shack with their rifles, but Edwards suspected that their only interest right then was in getting into some dry clothes and a hot meal in their bellies. He looked down at the excited barber, who reminded him of a dog straining on its leash, and said, "Tyler, you hang back here until they're all out."

"Stay back here? Away from all the action?" Tyler gave the sheriff an incredulous look. "Why?"

"Because you're too damned eager," Edwards replied.

"Well, excuse me for taking all this so seriously, Sheriff!" said Tyler.

Edwards raised a hand to cut him off, saying, "We

don't have time to discuss this. You're just too damn keen on shooting somebody. Now do like you're told. I need you here . . . with Jeffrey," he added. Then he said, "Mr. Potts, I want you on my right side a couple of feet back."

"You do?" Potts looked surprised.

"That's right. I do. Get up. Let's go," said the sheriff.

Potts rose quickly from the ground and hurried to catch the sheriff, who'd started forward up the hill, waving the other two men ahead with his rifle barrel. "Stay back a foot or two, like I said," Edwards instructed the nervous banker.

"Should—should I draw this pistol?" Potts asked, his voice stammering in uncertainty.

"That would be a good idea, Mr. Potts," said Sheriff Edwards. He saw the front door of the shack open slowly and watched the two ragged drovers ease out onto the porch, their hands held high above their heads.

"Stay like that," said Sheriff Edwards, "and we'll all get along just fine." He motioned them down off the porch with his rifle. As Fletcher, McNalty and Potts drew in, forming a half-circle around the front of the shack, Edwards said to the banker, "Mr. Potts, you and the others keep your guns on these two while I look around inside for others."

"Yes, Sheriff," said Potts, his voice sounding stronger than it had a while ago.

Edwards stepped up onto the porch, but stopped for a moment before entering. "Are you sure there's nobody else in there except the wounded man?" he asked Christi.

"You have my word, Sheriff," Christi said firmly.

"All right then," said Edwards. "Mr. Potts, if you hear

that I'm in trouble in there, feel obliged to shoot these two."

"Yes, sir, Sheriff Edwards," said Potts, getting bolder now that some responsibility had been placed upon him.

The sheriff paused for a moment to see if Christi had anything to add. When Christi offered nothing more on the matter, Edwards nodded to himself. "All right, fair enough." He crept inside the door with his rifle cocked and ready.

Potts, Fletcher and McNalty stood tensely waiting for word from Edwards inside the shack. While they waited, William Tyler made his way up the muddy hillside and stopped beside Arvin Potts.

"Goodness gracious, Tyler!" Potts whispered harshly, "What are you doing? The sheriff told you to wait down there with Jeffrey."

"Aw, come on, Arvin," said the barber. "Quit taking yourself so damn serious. This situation is under control. Edwards is getting to be like some old woman if you ask me."

From the open door to the shack, Sheriff Edwards called out angrily, "Nobody *asked* you, Tyler!" He stepped out onto the porch, his knuckles squeezed white around his rifle stock. "And I'm not going to tell you again. If you disobey my orders one more time, I'm running you out of here! As far as I'm concerned, if you can't do like you're told, you're not fit to ride with a posse!"

"Take it easy, Sheriff," said Tyler. "I just thought it made good sense that you might need some more help up here." He looked at the other three men and added, "I mean, some real help, from somebody who knows how to handle a gun and won't wet themselves if they have to."

"You're a barber, Tyler!" Edwards fumed. "Don't start taking on airs." To the other men he said, "Fletcher, you and McNalty get inside. Keep an eye on that wounded man. That ought to be something you two can handle."

The two started forward but Fletcher stopped abruptly and asked, "He ain't armed, is he?"

"For God's sake, Fletcher," said Edwards, "he ain't hardly even alive." Shaking his head in disgust, he waved the two into the shack, then turned to Christi and Bennie, with his gun pointed at their chests, and said, "Now then, cowboys, start talking, and make it good. As you can see, I've got my hands full here."

Bennie remained quiet while Christi told the sheriff everything. But he didn't tell him about shooting Turley Whitt, only that he and Bennie had been on their way across the flatlands east of town when Paco and Turner came upon them and forced them to come with them. He told him about what had happened when Harvey Blue told the Mexican about locking Odell and Lonnie in the bank vault, and how Dick Hohn had shot Paco when Paco tried to ride back to town to save Odell from the law.

"Is that everything?" Edwards asked at the end of the story.

"Yes." Joe Christi looked the sheriff in the eye and said, "That's the long and short of it."

"And it's all horseshit!" said William Tyler. "This man is one of the gang! Any fool can see that."

Sheriff Edwards turned his face slowly toward the

barber and said wryly, "Tyler, would you like for me to hand you this badge so you can take over officially?"

"Sorry, Sheriff," said Tyler, "but we all can see this bastard is lying." He pointed at Christi and Bennie. "I saw them both in town the other day! You could tell by the looks of them they were up to no good!"

"Just shut up, Tyler," said Edwards. "You're too damn wound up to make any sense."

"He could have seen us in town," said Christi. "We come through your town now and then, off the drives. We never stay long."

"I know," said Edwards. "I've seen you myself." He stared into Christi's eyes and asked, "Where do you suppose Harvey Blue Walker and his men are headed?"

"I heard them say Somos Santos," Christi replied. "He seemed real interested in why a man like Cray Dawson is the sheriff there."

"And you told him?" Edwards asked.

"I couldn't tell him anything," said Christi. "I didn't know myself, unless maybe it's because Somos Santos is Dawson's hometown."

"Yeah, maybe," said the sheriff, seeming to weigh things carefully. Finally he said to both Christi and Bennie Betts, "Cowboys, you're coming with us. Until we get this straightened out, you're both my prisoners."

"Are we under arrest?" Christi asked flatly.

"Only if you'd rather it be that way," said Sheriff Edwards. "But either way, you're coming with me."

"But we need to get on," said Christi. "We've got to get back to the big southern spreads and get ourselves some work."

"If I find you're part of Harvey Blue's gang, you

won't be looking for work. You'll be wearing leg irons," Tyler interjected.

Edwards silenced the barber with a cold stare. Returning his gaze to Christi, he continued. "I didn't put you boys here consorting with outlaws. Until we get this settled, you might want to stay helpful. This looks bad on the both of yas."

"We weren't consorting with outlaws, Sheriff," said Christi.

"Then show me one thing that ought to make me think otherwise," said Edwards.

Christi took a deep breath and released it, ready to tell the sheriff about the shooting in Morris' gun shop. But before he could say anything, Fletcher appeared at the door of the shack and called out, "Sheriff! Here comes Leon Capson and some others! Looks like one of them is hurt bad!"

"All right, Fletcher, I see them," said Edwards, gazing down the hillside toward the muddy trail. He raised his rifle and waved the four riders up to the shack, seeing one man riding slumped on his horse's neck. One rider led a horse by its reins. A body lay across the horse's saddle, wrapped in a riding duster.

"Oh my goodness," said Potts, seeing the body and the slumped rider. Young Jeffrey stepped out from behind the pine as the riders approached him, and trudged along beside them, leading his mount.

Turning back to Christi, Edwards said, "Whatever you started to say, spit it out, cowboy. We've got to get moving."

"All right, Sheriff, here it is," said Christi. "Bennie

and me were playing cards in the back room of Carl Morris' gun shop."

The sheriff stared at him as if he needed to hear more. Christi took another deep breath and said, "There was a shot came from the gun shop—that was me shooting Turley Whitt. But it was in self-defense. I swear it."

"Turley Whitt?" said Tyler. "This malarkey is getting thicker by the minute!"

Edwards didn't bother telling Tyler to shut up. Instead, recalling the gunshot he'd heard at that time, he said, "I suppose Morris will agree with your story if I press him on it?"

"Yes, I'm certain he will," said Christi. "It was a fair shooting. The only reason I didn't send for you and tell you about it was because Morris said it could cause him trouble. But he wouldn't let me take the blame for a bank robbery. Carl Morris is better than that."

"Yes, he is," said Edwards.

"I know you're in a hurry, Sheriff," said Christi, "but if somebody would take the time to go back to town and ask Morris, it would clear me and Bennie up real quick."

Sheriff Edwards watched Christi's eyes for a reaction as he said, "No need in that, cowboy." He gave a nod toward the four approaching riders. "Carl Morris is one of the men coming up the hill."

"Good enough," said Christi. He and Bennie gave each other relieved looks and stood quietly with their hands held chest high. Potts and Tyler were nearby with their guns trained on them. All four of them watched Sheriff Edwards walk away and meet the riders, who'd stopped fifteen yards away and stepped down from their horses on a flat spot on the hillside.

Fletcher came down off the porch and joined Tyler, saying, "Uh-oh," as three of the riders stepped over and jerked the fourth slumping rider from his saddle and let him fall in the mud. "By God, they caught one!" he exclaimed loudly.

Hurrying to the riders, Edwards gave one of the men a shove just as a boot cocked back to kick the downed man in his face. "Hold on, Bert!" Edwards shouted at the livery man. Taking control, stepping in between the three angry men and the one lying bleeding in the mud, Edwards demanded, "What the hell is going on here?"

"Don't stop him, Sheriff. Let him kick the son of a bitch's brains out!" shouted Leon Capson. "He's got it coming."

"Not while I'm in charge here!" shouted Edwards, waving his rifle. "Everybody back!"

"But he's one of the sumbitches Walker locked in the vault!" shouted Collins, still maneuvering for a place to bypass the sheriff to try to get in a kick.

Edwards aimed his rifle at Collins' foot. "Don't make me clip a toe off of you, Bert!" he shouted.

Leon Capson stepped in and said, "Easy, Collins." He called over his shoulder to the third man, saying, "Orsen, bring that horse up here and show the sheriff the kind of men we're dealing with."

Orsen Miles jerked the reins to the horse with the body lying over its back and brought it forward.

"Oh no," said Sheriff Edwards, already realizing what had happened. He braced himself as Miles threw back the corner of the duster and showed him Carl Morris' bloody face, his dead eyes wide-open, his mouth agape.

"How'd it happen?" Edwards asked, a look of dread on his face.

"We found him hiding behind a log, with a rifle. He got off two shots and fell face forward onto the ground. But both shots hit ole Carl dead center."

"Jesus," Edwards murmured. He looked down at Lonnie Freed, who babbled under his breath and tried to scrape his way across the muddy ground with his fingertips; a blood trail followed in his wake from the stab wounds in his chest.

"We brought him back to hang him, Sheriff," Capson said bluntly.

"No, you're not a lynch party. This is a legal sheriff's posse!" Edwards said in a stern tone. "He'll get a trial like everybody else gets."

"But a trial for what?" said Bert Collins. "We all saw him shoot Morris. There's no question about what happened. A trial makes no sense at all, not if we aim to keep moving and catch up to the town's money!"

Edwards didn't bother to argue the point. Turning and looking at Christi and Bennie, he said firmly to Collins and Miles, "Get him up on his feet. I want to hear what he says about these two." He nodded toward Christi and Bennie.

Collins and the others looked up the hill at Christi and Bennie, as if seeing them for the first time.

"So your party caught a couple yourselves. Good going, Sheriff!" said Capson. "We can hang all three and save ourselves some time!"

"These men say they're not a part of the gang," said Sheriff Edwards.

"Well, I just bet they do," said Capson, chuckling

darkly under his breath. "They can tell all that to the devil, far as we're concerned."

"I won't tolerate that kind of talk, Capson," said Edwards. He looked at Collins and Miles, who had dragged Lonnie Freed to his feet, and said, "Get him on up there. See if he can identify these others before he dies on us."

Bennie gave Joe Christi a worried look, seeing the two posse men drag Lonnie Freed up and stand him wobbling in front of them.

"Do these men ride with you?" Edwards asked the dying outlaw.

Lonnie Freed shook his head no, and dropped it onto his chest.

Edwards gave him a skeptical look and jerked his head back up by his hair. "Would you tell me if they did?" he asked. Again Lonnie shook his head no, this time more firmly. "That's what I thought," said Edwards, dropping Lonnie's bloody head.

"What about him identifying the Mexican?" Tyler asked the sheriff.

"Take him inside and see," Edwards said to the two posse men holding Lonnie up. As they dragged Lonnie up the steps and into the shack, Edwards said to Christi and Bennie Betts, "I don't have time to take you two back to town right now. Looks like you're headed with me to Somos Santos. Any objections?"

"Do we have any choice?" Joe Christi asked.

"Yeah," said William Tyler, butting in. "Your choice is, we can leave you hanging from a tree with a note nailed to your chest."

Chapter 14

Immediately after the storm, Harvey Blue had broken the men up and sent them off in different directions. All the way to Somos Santos, the riders remained spread apart across the wide rocky land, often as far as three or four miles, making it difficult for anyone searching for their trail to realize that they were a band of men instead of separate travelers riding in twos and threes together.

Alongside a creek in a stand of cottonwoods three miles from Somos Santos, Harvey Blue Walker stood beside his horse, while Dick Hohn distributed five hundred dollars to each member of the gang. As the men filed past Hohn and took their money, Harvey studied the look on some of their faces and said, "Remember, men, this is only temporary. I'm going to see to it you all get the rest of what's coming to you as soon as we get across the border."

Stuffing his money down into his shirt pocket, Freddie Tapp grumbled something under his breath as he walked back toward his horse.

Dick Hohn looked up from counting money out into

Eddie Rings' hand and said to Tapp with a cold stare, "What's that, Freddie? Something bothering you?"

Tapp only shook his head.

"Because if there is," said Dick Hohn, "don't be bashful. You speak right up. Let us all hear what's on your mind."

Buttoning his shirt pocket, Freddie said, "I only said, I don't like nobody handling my money. Once I've stole it, I like putting my hands on *all* of it when it suits me."

"You're a part of this bunch now," said Hohn. "You'll do like you're told."

"I always do like I'm told, Hohn," said Tapp. "But I've got a right to voice my damned opinion anytime it suits me." He glared at Hohn.

"Damned right you do," said Hohn. "And you've got a right to take a bullet in your gullet too, if you keep shooting off your mouth." He gave Rings a slight shove out of the way and took a step toward Tapp.

"Everybody hold it!" shouted Harvey, seeing that Freddie Tapp wasn't backing down. "This is something we all agreed upon, for our own good! If you men want to go into Somos Santos one and two at a time while I check things out, this is how you've got to do it. Consider this money a draw. You can't go in there with your whole role sticking out of your pockets, can you?"

Tapp held his hand poised near his holstered Colt as he answered Harvey, "No, we can't, boss."

"Then relax, Freddie," said Harvey. "Get that crook out of your back. We're all out for the same thing here. Settle down."

"I am settled," said Tapp, his eyes still on Hohn, his

hand still poised, "as settled as I'm going to be around Dick here."

"What's that supposed to mean?" Hohn asked harshly.

"It means if you and me happen to have a disagreement, I ain't taking a bullet from a hideout gun while my back's half turned to you."

"You sonsabitch!" Hohn tensed like a rattler about to strike. But he saw Freddie Tapp matching him move for move, and decided to stop.

"Different when a man's facing you, ain't it?" said Eddie Rings, who had stepped away, but stood watching as if he might throw into the deadly game.

Hohn considered it quickly. A nerve twitched in his set jawline. He knew Harvey Blue considered him his right-hand man. He knew Harvey stood watching with curiosity to see how he handled this.

"Shut up, Rings. This is none of your business," said Hohn. He eased down a bit, and said to Tapp, as if no longer taking him seriously, "Hell, Freddie, I mighta known if somebody was going to bellyache it'd be you. You'd gripe if somebody dipped your boots in gold." He tried to put forth a thin trace of a smile, to test the situation. "Now get on out of here so I can give these men their money."

"Yeah, Freddie, damn it," Earl Duggins joined in. "You got your money. Now get away so's I can get mine!"

"Yeah, Freddie. Get to town and buy yourself a rubber-bellied whore. It looks like you need one pretty bad," Harvey laughed, having gotten himself a good look at how far Dick Hohn could go before his bark became loose. Freddie Tapp was no more than an average gunman, yet he'd stood his ground with Hohn. This was good to know, Harvey told himself.

A ripple of laughter rose and fell among the men. Freddie Tapp made it a point not to turn away from Hohn until he'd backed away a few steps and Hohn had done the same. When Hohn reached into a canvas bag to take out another handful of money to distribute, Tapp let his gunhand fall at ease to his side. He walked farther away and stood sullen beside his horse until Earl Duggins had collected his money and walked up to him counting it.

"Make sure it's all there, Earl?" Tapp said under his breath. "It's getting to where you can't trust nobody these days."

"When it comes to *my* money I never did anyway," Earl grinned, folding his bills and stuffing them down into his trousers. "Say, pard, I hope you didn't take no offense at what I said over there."

"If I did you'da known it before now," said Tapp, still simmering a bit from his confrontation with Hohn.

"I was just trying to keep down any shooting among us," said Earl. "We've got lucky, with all that rain washing out our tracks. Why start shooting and let the world know we're here?"

"You're right," said Tapp. "It just sticks in my craw, the way Hohn has come in here and rooted himself a wider place at the trough than the rest of us—especially the way he killed the Mexican."

"Yeah, I know what you mean," said Duggins. "But you got to hand it to Harvey Blue. The bank job in Schalene Pass was slicker than socks on a rooster. This is the kind of work I can stand a lot of."

Tapp let out a breath. "That's the truth. It felt plumb

eerie, leaving a town with all that gold and money, and nobody shooting at us. It's been damned near a week now and no sign of the law on us." He grinned with satisfaction. "It's enough to spoil a man."

"And I need spoiling," Tapp laughed.

In the midst of their conversation, Eddie Rings walked up, stuffing his money up inside his wide hatbrim and placing his hat back atop his head. "What's so funny?" he asked, offering a bemused smile.

"Nothing," said Tapp. "I'm obliged to you for a while ago."

"Don't mention it," said Rings, tossing the matter aside. "I like Harvey's ideals on bank robbing, but I can't say I'm real pleased with who he choosed for a segundo."

"That's sort of what we was just now talking about," said Duggins, now that he saw Rings felt the same way they did.

"Really?" Eddie Rings looked to Tapp for affirmation.

"Yes, really," said Tapp. He looked past Rings and Duggins and watched Hohn continue passing out money to the rest of the men. "But let's not talk about it here and now. Let's ride into town and dip ourselves into some good whiskey."

"Sounds good to me," said Rings. He turned and called out to Harvey Blue, "Hey, boss, we've got our draw. Can us three ride on in?"

"Yeah, go ahead," said Harvey. "Remember not to do anything to attract attention. If you see me and Dick, don't let on like you know us."

"Yeah," Dick Hohn added, giving the three a look of

superiority, "you're going there for whiskey and women, but don't forget this is also a serious business trip."

"How *could* we forget?" Rings asked Tapp and Duggins in a joking manner, keeping his voice down.

Jimmy Shaggs stood barefoot, sweeping the boardwalk out front of the sheriff's office in Somos Santos. From his right ankle a four-foot length of chain held him attached to a heavy ironsmith's anvil that sat firmly on the rough plank floor. Having reached the end of his chain, Jimmy sighed and cast a look toward Deputy Hooney Carter, who sat in a wooden chair leaning back against the front of the building.

"I don't hear no broom swishing," Deputy Carter said flatly, his hatbrim pulled low on his forehead. A sawed-off shotgun lay across Carter's lap. His hands were loosely on it, yet as he began to speak, his thumb had slipped deftly across the gun hammers and rested there.

"That's because I'm getting ready to move," Shaggs responded, eyeing the deputy and noting the thumb with keen interest.

"You're supposed to tell me just as soon as you're fixing to move," said Carter.

"I was going to tell you, Deputy," said Shaggs. "Jesus, give a man time to announce his intentions."

Without raising his hatbrim or looking toward Shaggs, Carter said, "You best learn to get it timed down. The second I don't hear that broom swishing, I better hear you telling me what you're doing."

"I've never had this kind of treatment anywhere in my life," Shaggs protested, looking down at the metal cuff circling his bare ankle. "A damned anvil on a damned chain? It's damned inhuman!"

"Thank you," Carter said idly. "It's sort of my own personal system." A flat smile came to his lips. "With your help, I think we can make it work."

"Damn it to hell," Shaggs grumbled under his breath. But aloud, he said, "All right, I'm moving the anvil, Deputy."

"There. See how well this works if you give it a chance?" Carter said, wearing the same flat smile beneath his lowered hatbrim. His thumb slid down off the gun hammers.

Swinging his broom up under his arm, Shaggs stooped down, picked up the heavy anvil with a grunt and carried it a few feet farther away. Sitting the anvil down with a thud, he immediately began sweeping dust and flecks of dried mud into the rutted street. "I'm sweeping now, Deputy," he called out to Carter.

"There's a good lad." Twelve feet away Carter grinned to himself.

Grumbling under his breath, Shaggs continued sweeping fervently, as if taking out his anger on the dusty planks. At length he looked up along the street and saw three riders maneuver their horse among buggy and freight wagon traffic toward the Ace High Saloon. "Freddie Tapp," Shaggs whispered to himself, "you rotten old bastard rat. I wonder what you can do for me."

Realizing he had stopped sweeping, he quickly started swinging the broom back and forth again, hoping he hadn't raised Carter's interest.

But it was too late. Carter called out, "Shaggs? Are you still with me here?"

"I'm with you, Deputy! I just stopped long enough to scratch my backside," Shaggs said, sounding irritated and put upon.

"Next itch you get, you tell me before you stop to scratch," Carter said without looking his way.

"If I itch, you'll hear about it," Shaggs said, growing more agitated by the second. For a moment he'd considered telling the deputy about Tapp and the other two riding in. But now he grumbled under his breath and swept with a vengeance, stirring up a knee-high cloud of dust, giving Carter a heated stare. "Otherwise, I wouldn't tell you, Deputy Carter," he said to himself, "if these black-hearted sonsabitches steal everything but the jailhouse hinges."

Shaggs watched the three men while he continued sweeping back and forth. They stepped down from their horses, hitched them in front of the saloon and walked through the bat-wing doors, Tapp going in last and giving a quick look back over his shoulder.

"How long before the sheriff gets back?" Shaggs asked while he swept.

"Don't you concern yourself with Sheriff Dawson's comings and goings," Carter replied.

Now that Freddie Tapp and the two other riders were out of sight inside the saloon, Shaggs asked, "What if I knew something or saw something that the law ought to know about, Deputy? Do you think I'd get some special consideration for letting the sheriff know?"

Something in the tone of Shaggs' voice caught the deputy's attention. He rocked his chair forward from against the wall and raised his hatbrim with a push of his finger. "Anything you've got to say to Sheriff Dawson, you'll have to say to me first. I'll decide if it's worth wasting the sheriff's time or not." He stood up as he spoke and gave Shaggs a closer look. "If you know something we need to know, I'll see to it you get rewarded for your help."

"Yeah, I bet," Shaggs grumbled under his breath. Shaking his shackled foot he said, "Rewarded how? With a lighter anvil?"

Carter smiled. "Now that you mentioned it, I suppose a lighter anvil might be looked at as a good reason to cooperate with the law."

"Yeah, well, forget I brought it up," said Shaggs. "If I've got anything to say about anything, I'll wait until I can tell it to Sheriff Dawson."

"Suit yourself," said Carter. "But Sheriff Dawson has a lot on his mind today. His wife is leaving him today." Carter cradled the shotgun and scratched his neck and said, "Oh, let me correct myself. It's not his wife—just a woman he lives with out at the Shaw place. She was Shaw's woman, not to mention his dead wife's sister." Carter grinned. "Can you beat all that?"

"Damn," Shaggs mused. He stared at Carter for a moment, then asked, "Did Sheriff Dawson tell you all that?"

"He didn't have to," said Carter, liking the idea that he had such information about the sheriff. "I listen when I should listen."

"Yeah," said Shaggs, deciding to tell the deputy and see where things would lead. "Well, listen close right now." He gave a sidelong nod toward the three sweaty horses in front of the big clapboard-sided saloon and said, "I just saw Fredrick Argyle Tapp and a couple of others ride into town. Ever heard of Freddie Tapp?"

"I can't say that I have." Carter grinned.

"Last I heard there's over three hundred dollars on his head," said Shaggs. He watched Carter for a reaction.

"Do tell," said Carter, staring studiously at the batwing doors of the Ace High Saloon.

"Does telling you this get me a lighter anvil?" Shaggs asked with a trace of sarcasm.

"No," said Carter, "but it gets you one boot."

"One boot?" Shaggs asked in disgust.

"Yeah," said Carter, "so you won't have to go around completely barefoot." Without taking his eyes off the saloon, he motioned Shaggs toward the office door with his shotgun. "Come on, let's go. I'm going to stick you in a cell and see if what you're saying is true."

"Oh, it's true," said Shaggs, seeing that Carter wasn't going to do anything for him. "And it won't be hard collecting that three hundred. Everybody I know says once Tapp gets a few drinks in his belly he never puts up much of a fight with the law." He studied Carter's face to see if the deputy had taken any interest in what he'd told him.

"Not bad information," said Carter. "Keep it up, you might get yourself another boot."

"So are you going after him now?" Shaggs asked.

"Huh-uh," said Carter, relaxing a bit. "I'll just hold back a few minutes and let him get that couple of drinks you're talking about."

"Good idea," said Shaggs.

PART 3

Chapter 15

Inside the Ace High, Freddie Tapp, Earl Duggins and Eddie Rings had slapped trail dust from their shirts with their hats and ordered whiskey from Kat Sullivan who tended bar during the day until her husband, Payton Sullivan, owner of the Ace High, arrived in the late afternoon to run a faro table and help his wife attend to the larger evening crowd.

"Are you boys going to chase down the rye with a mug of beer?" Kat asked, standing with the bottle in her hand. Tapp had thrown back three shots of whiskey as quick as she could get them poured. The other two men weren't far behind him. As Kat spoke, her free hand hooked into the handles of three clean beer mugs from a shelf beneath the polished oak bartop.

Eddie Rings gave her a suggestive grin and leaned over the bar, saying, "The only *chasing* I'm interested in is chasing you up the stairs and into one of them rooms." He banged his empty shot glass on the bar and gave a nod toward a row of rooms along a landing atop a set of stairs.

"I don't chase," said Kat Sullivan, playing it off, filling the three mugs and setting them on the bar. "Besides," she added, sliding one of the mugs over to Freddie Tapp, who stood tossing back a shot of whiskey, "those rooms haven't been used for business since my husband and I took this place over six months ago."

"My goodness, then!" said Rings, not giving up. "Ain't it about time we went up there and shook out the sheets, you and me? I ain't chased myself down a big-busted redheaded gal since my cousin Cleo fell and broke her leg."

"Long as you didn't cause it," said Duggins, raising his shot glass in a salute before tossing back a drink.

Kat filled Rings' empty whiskey glass, feeling his eyes on her bosom. "I can't stand it," Rings growled. He reached out and grabbed her wrist before she had time to pull her hand out of his way.

"Look, boys," she said, keeping her head. "I don't know how we got started off on this *chasing* subject. But the fact is, my husband and I own this place. I haven't gone belly to belly for years, and I don't run any whores." She waved the thought away with her hand. "I've been out of that business too long to even talk about it." She tried to wrench her wrist free, but Rings only tightened his grip.

"So what?" said Earl Duggins, leaning over beside Rings, staring at Kat's ample bosom. "That doesn't mean you've forgotten how."

Kat managed a quick glance around the nearly empty saloon, seeing two old miners and a passed-out teamster, none of them noting her situation. She was on her own and would have to handle these men as best she could. "What's wrong with your friend here?" she asked Duggins. "Doesn't he want you drinking any more whiskey?"

"Huhn?" Duggins grunted, looking confused.

"I can't pour it for you if he's holding my hand," Kat explained. She gave Duggins a look that seemed to challenge him to do something about Rings.

"Damn it, Eddie!" said Duggins, giving Rings a rough shove. "Let go of her pouring hand. I've got some serious drinking to do."

Rings turned Kat's hand loose but said, staring at her, "Before this night is through, I'm taking you up them stairs and lifting your ankles in the air."

"Ha, you're just dreaming with your eyes wide-open!" Kat replied, keeping her cool, smiling and bantering with Rings. "Besides, you can't afford me. You'd have to sell your horse and rifle just to see me loosen a strap."

All three men laughed. Rings tossed back a swallow of rye and said, "I don't have to *sell* a thing." His hand jerked a thick roll of folded bills from his shirt pocket and slapped it down atop the bar. "There, that ought to be enough to loosen every strap you've got!" Dollar bills fluttered off the roll like birds set free.

"Lord! What a roll!" said Kat, staring, too impressed to hide her response.

"Put that away, Rings," said Freddie Tapp, who had only stood by drinking in rapt silence while Rings and Duggins had made their play for the woman bartender. He stood holding a shot glass in each hand. Half a mug of beer sat in front of him on the bar. Beer foam clung to his thick mustache.

"Are you talking to me?" Rings asked, giving Tapp an

angry look. He turned slightly toward Freddie Tapp, leaving his roll of money lying on the bartop.

"Yeah, I am," Tapp said flatly, his voice already taking on a boozy thickness.

"Nobody tells me what to do with my money," said Rings.

Kat stood watching with a worried look on her face.

"Easy now, fellows," said Duggins. "We just now got here. Don't let these first drinks go to your heads." He offered a nervous grin. "You know we're supposed to be on our best behavior." He leaned in close to Rings and said in a low tone of voice, "You've never drunk with Tapp before, have you?"

"No, why?" Rings asked Duggins without taking his cold stare off Freddie Tapp.

But before Duggins could answer a voice called out from the bottom of the stairs, "All right, gentlemen, that'll be enough horseplay for today."

The three men turned as one toward Payton Sullivan, a tall, dapper man wearing a light gray swallow-tail coat and a well-tucked necktie garnished by a single silver diamond in its middle.

"Payton!" Kat said quickly. "Everything is under control here! Let me handle this!"

But Payton didn't seem to hear his wife. He walked toward the bar at an easy gait, his hands at his sides, his hair still glistening from where he'd wet it in the washpan before combing it.

"Who the hell are you?" Rings asked, sizing the bar owner up and down, feeling the whiskey at work, starting to boil inside his skull.

"Me?" said Payton Sullivan, an intrepid smile coming

to his lips. "Why, I'm the man who is going to sit you down and take all that money away from you, while you thank me for doing it."

"Is that a fact?" said Rings, still sizing up the man, but letting his poised gun hand relax a bit. He offered a trace of a smile himself.

"Not only a fact, gentlemen," said Payton with confidence and authority, "that's the gospel."

Kat let out a sigh of relief, seeing her husband settle the three. As Duggins and Rings settled and reached for their shot glasses, she picked up the bottle and once again began to pour.

"I'll be a dog's ass if it's a fact," said Rings, snatching up the thick roll of bills from the bar and fanning it. "What's your game, mister?"

"In this case, straight draw poker, as hard as we can deal it," said Sullivan. He gestured a clean, manicured hand toward a poker table and said, "Sit at your own peril, sir."

"I like this sumbitch," said Rings, chuckling, starting toward the card table.

But before he'd taken a full step, another voice called out harshly, "Everybody freeze!"

In the rear door of the building, Deputy Hooney Carter stood with his sawed-off shotgun cocked and pointed.

"What the hell?" said Duggins.

"Fredrick Argyle Tapp," Carter called out, moving forward toward the bar, "step aside with your hands raised! You are under arrest!"

"Oh shit," said Duggins under his breath, a frightened look coming to his face.

Freddie Tapp turned slowly, facing Carter and his cocked shotgun. His face took on a crazed expression. A string of spit appeared from his lip. A low growl came up from his chest.

"Are you Tapp?" Carter asked, knowing the shotgun had caught the three off guard. "If you are, just step aside easy-like," Carter offered. "We'll make this as easy as we can—"

Carter cut himself short, seeing Tapp's hand snatch the pistol up from his hip, already exploding wildly on its way out of the holster.

Seeing the fury begin, Kat Sullivan dropped down behind the bar at the same instant Carter hurled himself to the side, his shotgun exploding into Tapp's hail of pistol fire.

Duggins and Rings both drew and fired, but their action was only an attempt at covering themselves as they got out of the way. Duggins made a dive across the tops of tables and chairs, his double-action Colt firing as fast as he could pull the trigger. Rings had ducked beneath a whir of slicing buckshot and rolled away on the dirty floor, firing in Carter's direction.

On the floor behind the bar, Kat heard her husband cry out in pain as a stray bullet hit him high in the chest. She snatched the shotgun from the shelf under the bar as she screamed out, "Payton! I'm coming!"

Firing as he went, Tapp stepped over and snatched up a heavy poker table by its leg. Holding it in front of him as a shield, he shouted like a wounded panther and advanced on Carter, who lay sprawled on the floor. Carter scooted backward, aiming the shotgun as bullets raised splinters from the floor and whistled past his face. "Stop, you sonsabitch!" Carter cried out, half an order, half a plea.

Smoke and blue flame erupted around the corner of the oncoming poker table. Carter pulled the shotgun's trigger and saw the upper right edge of the table disappear in a swirl of chewed-up wood. Behind the bar, Kat Sullivan had popped up in defense of her husband, who stood staggering in place, as if dumb-founded, his hand pressing the wound in his chest.

"I'll save you, Payton!" she shrieked. But she stood up only in time to see another stray bullet hit her husband and spin him on the heels of his shiny English quarter boots like some impassioned stage dancer, blood flying from a new wound in his chest and spraying from the exit wound in his back. Looking past her husband, Kat saw gunfire coming from Eddie Rings, who lay firing from beneath a pile of chairs.

But just as Kat swung the shotgun toward Rings and fired, poor Payton in his staggering waltz swayed into the path of the buckshot, the blast lifting him so quickly that one boot flipped off his foot. "Oh, no! Payton!" Kat screamed.

"Halt! Gawdamn it, *halt*!" Carter screamed, hurriedly scooting away as the bullets continued to fly at him from behind the encroaching table. He dropped the empty shotgun and drew his pistol, firing, seeing three fresh bullet holes appear in the tabletop. "Why won't you *stop*?" he bellowed.

From his cell in the sheriff's office, Jimmy Shaggs leaned to the side and pressed his face between the bars for an angle of vision across the office and out the front window. In the failing evening light, he grinned as he flinched at the sight of gunshots flaring through the bat-wing doors of the Ace High Saloon. "Give them hell, Deputy," he said to the empty office, chuckling cruelly to himself. When the shots had begun, Shaggs watched the miners and the drunken teamster come flying through the bat-wing doors and disappear behind cover.

Now, as the firing seemed to wind down, Shaggs saw one man come crashing through the large saloon window and scramble to his feet. He raced to his horse at the hitch rail, flung himself into the saddle and sped out of town in a rise of dust.

"Chickenshit!" Shaggs laughed aloud, watching the rider fade into the evening gloom. A moment later, another man hurried out of the saloon on his belly, crawling and thrashing wildly like a terrified snake. He shot forward off the edge of the boardwalk as more gunfire exploded inside the saloon, and managed to come up into a crouch and hurry to his horse.

Jimmy Shaggs turned his attention away from the fleeing man and went back to the flashes of fire beyond the bat-wing doors. He whistled to himself as a shotgun blast ripped one of the doors from its hinges and left the other one banging back and forth as if struck by some powerful unseen force. "Damn, those boys mean business."

Along the boardwalk townsmen had taken cover behind crates, water troughs and freight wagons, some of them drawing pistols, others arriving with rifle and shotguns of their own. One man slung open the door to the sheriff's office and stood panting, looking all around until his eyes found Shaggs standing with his hands grasping the bars.

"Sorry." Shaggs shrugged and grinned. "Sounds like everybody's over at the Ace High."

"Son of a bitch!" the man growled, slamming the door behind himself.

Inside the saloon, the battle raged. With the bullet-riddled table still in front of him, Freddie Tapp had made a rush on the bar when Kat dropped her shotgun and two fresh loads onto the polished oak bartop and scrambled over the bar toward her downed husband. Seeing Tapp grab up the shotgun and quickly begin to load it, Carter called out, "Drop the gun! Damn it! You're not under arrest! Hear me? You're not—"

"Come and get me!" Tapp bellowed.

"Good Lord!" Carter had stopped short and hurried away for cover behind the stove, seeing Tapp click the freshly loaded shotgun shut. "Hear me, Tapp?" he shouted, his fingers trembling and shoving fresh rounds into the chamber of his smoking Colt. "I ain't arresting you! Jesus! I'm sorry I brought it up. Gawdamn it!"

Buckshot exploded against the front of the heavy iron stove, sending off a shower of metal sparks and causing the pellets to strike the walls and ceiling in every direction. "It's commenced, you son of a bitch," Tapp raged like a man possessed. "Get on out here and let's *die*!"

Carter hurriedly clicked his reloaded Colt shut and fired, this time at Tapp's legs, the only part of him visible beneath the shielding tabletop. "Stay where you are!" Carter shouted as he fired.

A bullet struck Tapp above his right ankle and caused him to stumble to his knees, still holding up the table in front of him. He let go of another blast of buckshot. This time some of the steel pellets knocked a lit lamp from the wall and sent oil and flames spewing across the floor.

"Jesus!" screamed Carter. "We're on fire!" Seeing that Carter had emptied both shotgun barrels, and hearing no pistol shots coming from behind the table, the deputy ran quickly across the floor, raising his pistol and pulling the trigger, only to hear the hammer click on an empty cylinder.

Knowing he'd gone too far to back out now, Carter charged into the tabletop with his shoulder, knocking it and Tapp a few feet backward. He shoved the tabletop aside and threw himself upon Tapp, who lay with his pistol open, having been in the process of reloading. "You crazy sonsabitch!" Carter shrieked, striking the big man repeatedly with his pistol barrel. "Give up!"

"Go to hell," Tapp screamed in response, jerking a knife from his boot and swinging and stabbing the big blade at the deputy.

Chapter 16

Hearing the battle rage from a half mile away, Sheriff Dawson put his horse into a run until he came sliding to a halt in the middle of the street. Seeing flames begin to lick out and upward from the broken window and the bat-wing doors of the Ace High Saloon, he jumped down from his saddle, drawing his rifle from its boot, and gave Stony a slap on the rump, sending the animal out of the way.

"Sheriff!" a townsman called out from behind a stack of nail kegs in front of the mercantile store. "They're burning the place to the ground!"

"How many are in there?" Dawson called out over his shoulder, already running in a crouch toward the burning building.

One of the miners who'd been in the saloon when the fight started yelled above the sound of breaking glasses coming from inside the Ace High, "There's only one left, Sheriff! Hooney Carter is in there fighting like the devil with him!"

"Deputy, you better hope you're in the right," Dawson said under his breath.

As he ran up onto the boardwalk into the thick black smoke, Kat Sullivan came running out into his arms, sobbing uncontrollably. "Sheriff, I killed Payton! I didn't mean to, but I killed him!"

"You take it easy, Kat," said Dawson, looking around for someone to take her from him. Seeing no one, Dawson hurried her away from the smoke and sent her sobbing toward the townsfolk who'd begun to move in closer, some of them forming a bucket brigade to extinguish the fire. Dawson hurried inside, fanning smoke and staying low in a crouch, his Colt up and ready.

"Carter? Can you hear me?" he called out, hearing a struggle going on somewhere ahead of him in the black smoke. "Where are you?"

"I'm over here, Sheriff," Carter called out, his voice sounding strained and gasping for breath. "Come help me drag this crazy sumbitch out of here!" He coughed in the thickening smoke.

Dawson fanned his way across the floor, toward the smoke-obscured image of Carter and Tapp grappling with each other. Carter held tight to Tapp's leg while Tapp kicked at him and tried to crawl away. A knife handle stuck up from Carter's shoulder, where Tapp had sunk it to its hilt.

"You're not taking me nowhere!" Tapp bellowed in the thick smoke.

Seeing the crazed look on the outlaw's face, Dawson stepped in without hesitation, drew back his rifle and slammed the butt of it sidelong against Tapp's jaw. Tapp's head swung sideways and came to rest on the plank floor as though he'd fallen asleep.

"Son of a bitch is a lunatic!" Carter said. Coughing

and gagging, he grasped Dawson's leg and clawed his way to his feet.

"Help me get these men out of here," Dawson shouted to two townsmen who had ventured inside the burning saloon. Feeling his breath become stifled more and more by the heat and smoke, the sheriff motioned the townsmen toward the body of Payton Sullivan lying crumpled in a pool of blood. The townsmen ran to the body as Dawson and Carter grabbed Tapp by his boots and dragged him outside through the bat-wing doors. They didn't stop dragging him until they reached the middle of the dirt street.

Checking the look on Dawson's face, Carter said in a choking voice, "I know what you're thinking, Sheriff. But I swear none of this could be helped." He pointed at Freddie Tapp and said, "This man, *Fredrick Tapp,* is a wanted criminal."

"You better hope he is, Deputy," said Dawson. "Where did you see his poster?" He stooped down over Tapp and snapped a set of handcuffs on his wrists.

Carter looked stunned for a moment. But recovering he said, "I didn't actually see a poster on him, but he's wanted."

"Then where did you get your information?" Dawson asked pointedly.

"I—That is, it came from a reliable source," said Carter, stalling as long as he could before telling Dawson where he'd heard it.

"What reliable source?" Dawson asked even more pointedly.

"Aw, hell," Carter said with regret, realizing what he'd done. He stared for a moment at townsmen hurrying back and forth past them, carrying buckets of water and throwing them on the raging flames. "Sheriff, I heard about it from that snake Jimmy Shaggs."

Dawson slumped and shook his head. "All right, Deputy, get yourself over to Doc Isenhower's and sit tight until I can locate him and have him get that knife out of your hide," he said. Looking down at Tapp, he heard the other man groan and saw him struggle back into consciousness. "I'll get this man locked up and get back out here and help put out the fire."

"Obliged, Sheriff," said Carter, turning and limping away, holding a hand up to his throbbing shoulder near the protruding knife handle. As Carter spoke, Dawson bent down and helped Tapp struggle up to his feet. Tapp wobbled in place.

"All right, Fredrick Tapp," said Dawson, giving the man a nudge in the direction of the jail, "let's go." As the two walked away from the middle of a suddenly busy street, Dawson looked at the dust kicked up by Tapp's comrades, who had spurred their horses into a flat-out run. "Who are your friends, Tapp?" Dawson asked the bleary-eyed outlaw.

"I'm not saying, Sheriff," Tapp replied, "but I expect you'll be meeting them soon enough."

Duggins and Rings didn't slow their horses or look back toward Somos Santos until they rounded a turn in the trail and came very near running over Harvey Blue and Dick Hohn.

"Whoa!" Harvey called out, his horse rearing as Duggins and Rings slid their animals to an abrupt halt.

Dick Hohn had drawn his gun and almost fired before recognizing the two men. Looking past them at the thick black smoke in the sky, he asked Rings, "What the hell is going on back there?"

"Harvey, we've got to get out of here pronto!" said Duggins.

"Why? What are you talking about?" Harvey asked, seeing the tearful look on Duggins' face.

"It's that sheriff!" said Rings, struggling to settle his horse. "He came looking for Tapp before we hardly got settled in at the bar!"

"I don't think that was the sheriff," Duggins offered, still trying to catch his breath. "I believe it was the deputy."

"Sheriff, deputy—what's the difference?" said Rings. "Whoever it was, I never seen nothing like it. He came into that saloon all by himself and stood right up to Tapp with no regard to us two standing there with him."

"What's all the smoke coming from?" asked Hohn, nodding toward the sky above the town.

Duggins looked down as if ashamed as he said, "The saloon was on fire when we left."

"The what?" said Harvey, shocked. "Good God, man! You burned the saloon?"

"We didn't burn it," said Rings. "But there was shotguns going off in every direction! We're lucky we got out of there alive!"

"And you left Tapp behind?" Hohn asked in a critical tone.

"We had no choice, Harvey," said Rings, answering to Harvey Blue instead of Hohn. "Tapp turned into a wild man. Started shooting, screaming, foaming at the mouth like some wild dog!"

"Damn it!" said Harvey. "That's the way Freddie gets after a couple of shots of rye."

"Then this sheriff must've known it," said Rings. "It sure looked to me like he pushed Tapp awfully hard."

"It was not a sheriff," Duggins corrected him. "It was a deputy."

"Damn it, whichever it was, he sent us packing, and far as we know, he's killed poor Freddie by now," said Rings.

"Damn," said Harvey almost to himself, studying the high drift of black smoke across the sky. "Why does a man like Dawson take such good care of this little bump in the trail?"

While Harvey contemplated the matter, Hohn turned to Rings and Duggins, saying in a cynical tone, "I suppose you two didn't waste any time leaving ole Freddie to fend for himself?"

"We did what we had to do," Rings replied harshly. "I don't answer to you for saving my own life."

"Stop it, both of yas," said Harvey, snapping out of his deep thoughts. "We've got to keep serious heads on our shoulders about this Dawson and his town."

"You don't mean you're still thinking of doing some robbing there, do you?" Rings asked with a look of disbelief on his face.

Without answering Rings, Harvey said, "You two ride on back and meet the others on the trail. Me and Dick are riding into town to see what we can learn about this place."

From inside the stagecoach, Carmelita saw the smoke rising above Somos Santos as the trail winded around the town from the west. Leaning out through the window in the door, one white-gloved hand cupped to her mouth, she shouted up to the driver, "Stop this stage at once!"

The driver also looked at the boiling smoke and called down to her, "Ma'am, I can't turn back. It's company policy."

"I did not say *turn back,*" Carmelita shouted above the sound of the rolling wheels and the horses' hooves. "I said *stop*!"

"I can do *that* rightly enough," said the driver, already sitting back against the long reins and drawing the brake handle at the same time.

No sooner had the stage rumbled to a halt than Carmelita jumped out of it, hiking the hem of her gingham dress up out of the dirt. From inside the passenger compartment, a traveling seed peddler stuck out his head and asked, "What on earth has happened over there?"

"I do not know," said Carmelita, "but I intend to find out."

"Ma'am, I already told you I can't turn back," the driver said again, leaning down to her. "It's too far off the big trail. That's the reason we stop at the relay station on the flats and never go right into town."

"Throw down my bag," Carmelita said flatly.

"What?"

"You heard me. Throw down my bag," she repeated with determination. "I am going to walk to Somos Santos from here."

"Ma'am, you can't do that!" said the driver. "It's up and down rocks and gullies. There's rattlesnakes out there can stand straight up and spit in your eye. Besides, it's probably that worn-out livery barn. Everybody's been expecting it to either burn down or fall over for the past ten years."

"We heard gunshots," said Carmelita, holding up her hand and motioning for the driver to toss down her bag. "My *husband* is sheriff there," she added, seeing the eyes of the seed peddler and two other passengers on her. "I am going." Having referred to Cray Dawson as her *husband* surprised even her. She'd never done that before.

"Have it your way, ma'am," said the driver, standing up from his hard seat and stepping atop the stage. He unstrapped the stack of luggage that held the well-worn leather travel bag Dawson had given Carmelita for her journey back to Mexico. "I wish you wouldn't do this, though," the driver added, pitching the bag expertly to the dirt near her feet. "The company doesn't like to encourage passengers hopping on and off anytime they please."

"I am certain they will understand," Carmelita said, stooping slightly, picking up the heavy bag and using both hands to hold it against her. She stepped back and gestured for the stage to leave.

"Women." The driver sighed, shook his head and slapped the reins to the horses' backs.

Before the stage had gone a hundred yards, Carmelita had walked off of the trail and begun making her way across the rocky ground. Knowing that Somos Santos lay over four miles east of the main stage trail, she raised the leather bag, balanced it atop her head and paced herself, walking unhurriedly yet steadily toward the black smear on the otherwise clear and cloudless sky.

A four-mile walk represented no problem for her, even in the heat of the day; but the weight of the bag and the rough up-and-down terrain soon forced her to stop for a breather in a thin slice of shade along a gully wall overgrown along its edge with a stretch of coarse buffalo grass. A thin stream of water from the recent storm still ran down the center of the gully. Carmelita touched her palms to the surface of the shallow stream, then pressed her palms to her face.

Lying back in the sparse shade and closing her eyes for a few minutes, Carmelita did not hear the two men who had followed her shoeprints in the powdery dust and led their horses up quietly behind her.

"You saw her, didn't you?" Odell Clarkson said in a whisper to Buck Turner even though they were thirty yards from Carmelita's gully. "I hope to hell this ain't some trick the heat's playing on me." He rubbed his glare-strained eyes.

"If it is, it's tricked us both," said Turner. "Are we going to do what I think we're going to do?"

"Why, hell, yes," said Odell. "I know we're on serious business here. But a man would be a fool to see something like that and not pounce on it. How would a fellow ever live it down if word got out?"

"That's true," said Turner. "I just wanted to make sure we're both of the same mind here. I have a hard and fast rule regarding women I find alone and unprotected. I take them right then and there with no ifs, ands or buts about it. It saves me from wishing I *would've* for the rest of my life."

"I think it's only reasonable to feel that way," said Odell. "I consider this one act of vengeance against Harvey Blue. Wherever he's at right now, I know he's not getting ready to do what we are." He grinned and stared toward the gully.

Chapter 17

Odell stayed back with the horses while Buck Turner slipped forward on foot. When he got closer, Turner flattened himself on his belly and crawled the last few yards rather than have the sun give him away by casting his shadow out across the gully.

Carmelita snapped her eyes open at the rustling sound in the grass above her. She jerked herself up from against the hard rocky side of the gully and turned quickly, seeing the smiling face of the man crouched on the egde of the gully only inches above her. "Don't bolt on me, ma'am," said Turner, his words not meant to settle her, but rather to warn her. "There's no place to run or hide. So stand still and don't make us shoot you."

As Buck stood up and stepped down through the buffalo grass over the gully's edge, Odell Clarkson came walking up, slowly leading the horses. "Oh! Lord God!" Odell chuckled. "My eyes weren't lying!" He looked Carmelita up and down, his eyes glistening like those of a hungry wolf, and said, "Just when you think the whole miserable Gawdamned world has jackpotted you for life, something like this just falls down out of the sky."

"It's enough to make a man believe in heaven," Turner said over his shoulder, his eyes fixed on Carmelita. To her he said, "You speak *inglis*, you pretty thing? *Hablo inglis,* eh?"

"*Sí* . . . I mean, yes," said Carmelita. "I do speak English."

"Well, now that's just dandy," Turner said, his smile widening, his eyes still fixed on the woman. "It means you won't have no problem at all understanding what I tell you to do."

"You are making a big mistake," said Carmelita, reaching for any weapon she could find. "I am waiting for my husband. He is picking me up from the stagecoach." She nodded at the leather travel bag sitting in the dirt.

"Yeah," said Turner, "in a pig's eye. We saw where you got off the stage. Nobody is fool enough to walk two miles out across this furnace if there's somebody coming to meet them. You were walking to town." He unsnapped his gun belt and let it fall to the ground.

"Whoa, hold on, Buck," said Odell. He dropped the horses' reins and slid down the edge of the gully in a stir of rocks and dust. "Don't forget who runs things here." He walked in closer to Carmelita. "I go first."

Turner stooped down and quietly picked up his gun belt without protest. "Well, so long as I get some when you're finished."

"You are making a big mistake," Carmelita repeated, her voice starting to tremble in spite of her effort to keep it strong and fearless. "My husband is a sheriff—"

"Big mistake? So what?" Odell snapped, cutting her off. "Life is full of mistakes. Some is just sweeter than others." He grasped the front of her dress and she knew his next move would be to rip it off her.

She grabbed his hand before he made his move. "Wait, *por favor*!" she said, reverting to her native tongue. "I will take it off. Do not ruin it."

"Oh?" Odell chuckled and gave Turner a look and a grin, still gripping her dress. "But will you make us like the way you do it? Will you undo it and sort of let it fall, real easy-like?" He grinned.

Carmelita said with quiet resolve, "*Sí,* I will do whatever you tell me to." She reached behind her and unsnapped the dress at her neck, then undid the buttons and let her dress fall down around her ankles.

"Oh, my God," Odell breathed, seeing her standing before them in only her undergarments. "Step over here in the shade."

"Hold on," said Buck Turner, a curious look coming to his face. "Did you say your husband is a sheriff?"

Carmelita had reached up atop her head and found the long pin that held her hat in place. She planned to draw the pin at just the right moment and plunge it into Odell's throat. But now she lowered her hands and used them to cover her breasts.

"*Sí,* he is a sheriff," she said quietly, the fear and dread evident in her trembling voice. Her knees quivered in the harsh glare of sunlight.

"Damn it, Turner," said Odell, "this is not the time to go asking questions that make no—"

"Sheriff *where*?" Turner asked, raising a hand to cut

Odell off. Finally Odell seemed to get the message. The two exchanged looks.

"In Somos Santos," Carmelita replied.

Odell and Turner stood in stunned silence for a moment. Then Odell asked, challenging her, "Yeah? Then what's his name?"

"Crayton Dawson," Carmelita said quietly and without hesitation, figuring she had nothing to lose.

Turner let out a chuckle. "I'll be damned."

Odell stepped over and quickly rummaged through Carmelita's leather travel bag. He found nothing to connect her to Cray Dawson until he closed the bag and saw the engraved brass name beneath the handles. "C. Dawson," he said to Turner in a bemused tone. "Buck, she's telling the truth."

"I'll be damned," Turner said again.

"Pull your dress up, little lady," Odell said to Carmelita. "What are you doing out here anyway?"

"I was on the stagecoach. I heard shooting and saw the smoke," she said, nodding toward the black smoke. Quickly pulling her dress up, she buttoned it behind herself. "If you let me go, I promise I will not tell him about this."

"I don't think so," said Odell. "A man can always tell when another man has looked upon his woman—don't you think so, Buck?"

"Without a doubt," said Turner. "I've never seen it fail. One look at her and he'll know."

"No, he won't. I swear it to you!" said Carmelita. "All you have to do is ride away. No one will ever know."

After a moment of contemplation, Odell grinned and

said to Turner, "I've always wondered how it would feel to have a big gunman backing me up. I bet if we play our cards just right, we can get Cray Dawson to help us kill Harvey Blue and the rest of those snakes."

When Dawson finished helping the townsmen put out the fire at the Ace High, he walked back to his office, his shirt soaked in sweat, his face streaked with soot. Deputy Carter met him inside the door, supporting his right arm in a sling. "Well, what did they say about me, Sheriff?" Carter asked anxiously. "Are they asking for my badge over this?"

Dawson wiped his blackened face on a bandanna and just stared at the deputy for a moment. "Carter," he said finally, "nobody mentioned you. Everybody was busy putting out the fire." He looked past Carter at Jimmy Shaggs and Freddie Tapp, standing in the same cell. Shaggs looked frightened. "What're they doing in the same cell?" Dawson asked.

"I put them together when I got back from getting the knife out of my shoulder. I thought it would be easier to look after them both this way." Carter shrugged and tried to change the subject. "So you think this might all blow over? Everybody will forget all about it?"

"Blow over?" said Dawson, as he walked to the wall. "I don't think so, Deputy. The Ace High meant a lot to the folks in this town." He took down a brass key ring that hung on a wall peg and walked over to the cell. "They're not likely to forget all about it." He opened the cell door and motioned for Shaggs to step out. Freddie Tapp stood grasping the bars with both hands, not yet realizing why Dawson had made such a move. He still appeared a bit stunned from the beating he'd taken earlier.

"Much obliged, Sheriff," said Shaggs, giving Carter a harsh stare. Lowering his voice he said, "This crazy bastard was hoping Tapp would kill me in my sleep for jackpotting him."

"Who jackpotted me?" Tapp asked, looking confused.

Nobody answered Tapp.

Hearing Shaggs, Deputy Carter said, "You didn't just jackpot Tapp—you jackpotted me too. You set me up to get me killed, you little weasel!" As he spoke, he became more infuriated, until he finally made a lunge across the floor toward Shaggs, grabbing for him awkwardly with his left hand.

"That's enough, Carter," shouted Dawson, stepping in between the two, then shoving Shaggs into the empty cell and quickly closing the door. "You've had enough trouble for one day."

Carter stood back seething in anger. "Yeah, and it's all this sneaking little bastard's fault!" he hissed.

"Ha!" said Shaggs, taunting Carter a bit now that he felt safe under Dawson's protection. "It's your own damn fault, you greedy turd! Tell the sheriff here how you was going to collect the bounty on Freddie Tapp all by yourself, and not share it with nobody!"

"He lied to me, Sheriff," said Carter. "Told me Tapp would be an easy catch once he had a few drinks in him. Turns out Tapp is a lunatic when he's drinking. You saw how hard he was to take down."

"A lunatic?" Tapp bristled a bit, starting to realize

what Shaggs had done to him. "A bounty on me? From where? I ain't wanted nowhere that I know of."

"You are now, you pig-brained bastard," Shaggs snickered under his breath. "I put the deputy right on you!"

Carter pointed at Shaggs and said, "See, Sheriff? He set this up and jackpotted me sure as hell!"

Tapp looked at Shaggs through the bars separating their cells. "You told this man there's a price on my head? After us riding together for the English spread?" A second passed as Tapp boiled inside, figuring it out. Then he exploded and dived into the bars, his arms going through them, reaching for Jimmy Shaggs. "I'll kill you, you son of a bitch!" he screamed. Shaggs hurried to the far side of his cell, but then began to jump up and down, laughing and taunting Freddie Tapp.

"Both of you settle down!" Dawson shouted.

Tapp jerked himself away from the bars, cursing under his breath. He walked over and flopped down on his cot against the back wall. Shaggs ran his fingers back through his hair and said, "That just makes up for the way you treated me when we *rode* for the English spread. I've waited a long damn time for the chance to piss in your ear!"

Turning to Carter, Dawson said, "See, Deputy? You should never have taken his word on this. There's an old grudge at work here. Plus, you knew how bad Shaggs has had it in for you ever since we arrested him. All you had to do was go through that stack of wanted posters in my desk drawer."

"Tapp rides with Harvey Blue Walker and his gang, Sheriff," said Jimmy Shaggs, injecting himself into the conversation. "He told me so while you were busy putting out the fire your deputy started."

"Why, you—" Tapp clenched his fists and pounded himself on the knees. "If I ever get my hand around your neck—" He stopped short and sat staring, his eyes sharp and filled with dagger blades.

But Shaggs ignored Tapp and gave Carter a flat, cruel grin. "I'm thinking you'd be better off if I was your deputy, Sheriff Dawson, instead of this—"

"Shut up, Shaggs!" said Dawson. He looked back at Tapp and asked, "Where is Harvey Walker?"

"I don't know what you're talking about, Sheriff," said Tapp. "What am I going to be charged with?"

"Shooting up the saloon, contributing to the burning of the saloon, resisting arrest—"

"But I wasn't wanted for anything, Sheriff!" Tapp protested.

"Then you should have given this deputy the chance to find that out," said Dawson.

"Damn it, how long will I have to be in here?" Tapp asked.

"Until the circuit judge rides through here," said Dawson. "It could be as long as a month or more. I've never seen a wanted poster come through here on you or Harvey Blue Walker, but I know he's a thief and a killer. But so far whatever he's done in Texas hasn't caught up with him."

"In that case, why do you want to know about him?" Tapp asked. "Just to harass some poor ole boy?"

"He got you there, Sheriff," Shaggs chuckled.

Dawson gave Shaggs a sharp look of warning, then said to Tapp, "I've never laid eyes on Harvey Blue

Walker, but I've heard plenty, all of it bad. I consider it my job to try to know his comings and goings."

"Then you better ask somebody who gives a Gaw-damn what you want, Sheriff," Tapp said abruptly, " 'cause I ain't telling you a thing."

Outside, across the street from the sheriff's office, Harvey and Dick Hohn stepped down from their saddles at a charred hitch rail in front of a burned heap of smoldering rubble. Looking all around at blackened frame timbers sticking up from the Ace High's remains, Harvey said, "Whooieee! Looks like a nice long drink of rye might be out of the question here."

He stood only a few feet away from a gathering of sweaty, soot-smeared townsmen, all of them holding water buckets in their hands. Faces turned toward him, wearing flat stares. "Mister," said a tired, raspy voice, "losing this saloon is like losing a member of the family here. So keep any funny remarks to yourself, if you know what's good for you."

Dick Hohn bristled and started to jerk his pistol from his holster. But Harvey stopped him with a quick glance, then replied to the townsmen as a group, "Sirs, each and every one of you have my most sincere apologies. What I said was crude. I hope you'll all forgive me."

"Well," said one townsman, noting the guns and rough demeanor of the two strangers, "I suppose we're all a bit touchy today. Your apology is accepted, sir. And I hope you'll excuse my testiness. This all happened when three ne're-do-wells rode in, got drunk and shot it out with our sheriff's deputy."

"Oh?" said Harvey, appearing shocked. "I hope your deputy taught them a thing or two."

"He should've waited for our sheriff to get here," said the man. "They killed the saloon owner. Two of them got away. The one the deputy did manage to take into custody stabbed him and beat the hell out of him before our sheriff came riding in and took over."

"That must be some sheriff you have," said Harvey.

"Yes, he is indeed." Raising a hand to his hatbrim, the man said, "I'm Farrel Galbrath, owner of the Galbrath Family Dinner House." He gestured up the rutted street toward an old adobe building, where a large wooden sign bore a handpainted plate piled high with potatoes and chunks of meat. "If my establishment can be of service, please feel welcome."

"Much obliged," said Harvey, also touching his hatbrim. "I'm Horace Smith. This is my partner, Bill Thomas. We're cattle buyers from up Abilene way." He also gestured toward the big wooden sign and said, "I'd feel better if that was a big hand holding a bottle of whiskey, but under the circumstances . . ."

"Oh, I'm certain it will be all right if I serve whiskey, beer or whatever else a body needs," said Galbrath, "just to accommodate until we've got ourselves a saloon rebuilt." He looked for support from the other townsmen. "Don't you agree?"

The other townsmen all nodded and murmured in agreement.

"Do you suppose your good sheriff would go along with something like that?" Harvey asked, wanting to find out what he could about Cray Dawson.

"Yes, I believe we do," said Galbrath. "Our sheriff is

none other than Crayton Dawson. Perhaps you've heard of him?"

"Dawson, Dawson," said Harvey pretending to have to think hard for a moment. "Yes, it seems I do recall that name."

"If you're a Texan, I wager you *have* heard of him," said Galbrath, broadening his chest in pride. "He's the man who stood side by side with Lawrence Shaw and brought a merciless gang of killers to justice."

Harvey snapped his fingers. "Ah, of course! Cray Dawson—now it comes to me. A fine *heroic* man, from what I've heard."

"Yep," said Galbrath. "He's from here, you know."

"Sure enough?" Harvey asked as if in awe. "A local fellow who came back to his roots."

"Yes, in a nutshell," said Galbrath. He hooked his blackened thumbs in his sooty vest pockets. "Dawson loves this town. That's something you can count on."

"Well, then," said Harvey, "you can't imagine what a load you've just taken off my mind. We came here wondering if this bank—and this town—is a safe place to deposit our working capital."

"Oh good heavens, yes!" said Galbrath. "We have *big* depositors, men who are known not only across Texas but across this entire country—in Europe even!"

"Galbrath, you talk too much," said a voice among the townsmen.

"Well, pardon me," Galbrath said sarcastically, "if I just happen to be one who believes in promoting Somos Santos."

"Gentlemen, my friend and I will have to come back later for food and drink. We have men outside town waiting to hear what we think of your bank. If you'll excuse us, we'll just go get them and return pronto." Harvey grinned, then stepped back over to his horse and up into the saddle. Dick Hohn followed suit.

Chapter 18

On their way out of Somos Santos, Harvey and Dick Hohn heard the sound of horses' hooves rounding a turn in the trail and managed to get off into the brush and scrub oak before the riders saw them. "Damn! It's a posse!" whispered Harvey. Then both his and Hohn's eyes widened at the sight of Paco lying forward on his horse's neck, the horse being led by William Tyler.

"Jesus, looks like that Mexican must've come back from the dead!" said Hohn.

"Huh-uh, he wasn't dead," said Walker, pointing at Bennie Betts and Joe Christi riding along handcuffed, flanked by two posse men who carried rifles in their hands. "I've told you that little hideaway gun ain't worth a snap when it comes to killing. Those two boys saw he was alive and decided to turn good Samaritan on us."

"He's alive now, but he won't be once I get another chance at him," said Hohn.

"This ain't a business built on *second* chances, Hohn," Walker said in a warning tone. They watched the posse ride by and head into Somos Santos.

"What's this going to do to our robbing the bank?" Hohn asked.

"It slows us down a bit," said Harvey. "We can't do anything while they're there. We'll lie low and wait until they leave here. Then we'll go right on with our work."

Hohn looked apprehensive. "I don't know, Harvey. Maybe we ought to forget this one and go onto the next. Things are getting crowded around here."

Harvey looked at Dick long and hard. "You heard that restaurant owner. This town is holding some serious money in its bank. Nobody knows it but us right now. But if we fool around and don't act on it, word will get out. We'll miss a hell of a job."

Hohn watched the riders grow distant in their own rise of dust. "Yeah, you're right. There is no reason in the world for a big gun like Dawson wearing a badge here, unless there's big money willing to pay a price to keep him here."

"Now you're talking." Walker grinned. "I was starting to worry about you there for minute." He heeled his horse forward back up onto the trail, with Hohn right beside him.

On the trail into Somos Santos, Joe Christi looked back over his shoulder, as if summoned by intuition. But he didn't see the two riders, only a drift of trail dust beneath the wide Texas sky, and above the dust an endless terrain of cliff, brush and boulder.

"The hell are you looking for, *outlaw*?" William Tyler said harshly, riding behind Christi, leading Paco's horse by its reins. As he spoke, Tyler gave a rough jerk on Paco's horse's reins, causing the wounded man to bounce painfully. It was an act of torture that Tyler had inflicted on Paco frequently during the ride to Somos Santos.

"Nothing," Christi said in a tight response, knowing that the last thing he said would cause Paco more pain.

"Worried about the Mex living, eh?" said Tyler, not content to let a chance at torturing Paco pass him by. He jerked the reins again. Paco moaned.

Christi gritted his teeth.

"He's killing him, Joe," Bennie Betts whispered beside Christi. "And there ain't a damn thing we can do about it."

"I know," said Christi. "Paco will just have to hang on. We're almost there."

"No talking up there, outlaw!" Tyler shouted behind them, giving another stiff yank on the reins.

Paco let out a sharp yelp and almost fell from his saddle. Hearing it, Christi dropped his horse back, ready to reach up and kick Tyler from his saddle and take a chance on Tyler shooting him. But before he could act, Sheriff Edwards, who rode ahead of him, quickly circled his horse and rode in closer to Tyler, saying, "Give me the reins!" He reached out and snatched the reins from Tyler before Tyler had time to even respond.

"Hey, Sheriff!" Tyler said, appearing surprised at Edwards' action. "What are you doing? I'm leading the sonsabitch, ain't I?"

"You can't be trusted to do a *damned thing*, Tyler!" the sheriff barked. "You know that this man's word might be the only thing standing between these two and a prison cell!"

"That's right. I do know it," said Tyler. "But I also

know that these two are part of the gang no matter what anybody tells you! Far as I'm concerned, we'd save everybody time and energy if we hanged them both from the nearest tree!" He glared at Christi and Bennie.

"As soon as we get into town, you're finished riding with me, Tyler," said the sheriff. He gigged his horse forward, leading Paco's horse behind him.

"All right, fine," Tyler called out, "and that's one less vote you can count on come election time!"

"The day I have to count on support from an unreliable bastard like you is the day I'll sail this badge off a cliff," Edwards grumbled, going in front of the riders as the main street of Somos Santos came into view.

Behind the sheriff, Potts and Jeffrey rode side by side, Potts leading Lonnie Freed's horse. No sooner had the confrontation between Edwards and Tyler settled down than Jeffrey looked at Lonnie Freed and gasped. "Mr. Potts!" he said, trying to keep Sheriff Edwards and the others from hearing.

"Yes, Jeffrey, what is it?" Potts asked, turning to the excited young man.

Pointing back at Lonnie Freed, Jeffrey said, "I—I believe he's dead, sir!"

Potts stopped abruptly, causing the riders behind him to bunch up and also come to a halt. In front, Edwards turned in his saddle, circled and stopped. "What's going on, Potts?" Edwards asked gruffly, still stinging from his run-in with Tyler.

"This man is dead, Sheriff," Potts said.

The riders stared at Lonnie Freed, who sat slumped in his saddle, wearing a grim gray expression, his eyes barely open and staring blankly ahead. "Freed?" said Edwards, reaching out and tugging on the handcuffed outlaw's coat sleeve. "Are you still with us?"

Freed toppled sideways without response.

"Damn it!" Edwards tried to stop the falling outlaw, but his effort came too late. Freed fell to the ground face-first with a sickening thud.

"Serves the sonsabitch right," said Tyler. "Leave him where he lays."

"Why don't you stop being an asshole, Tyler?" said Capson, one of the men with rifles flanking Christi and Bennie Betts. He slipped his rifle into its boot and stepped own from his saddle.

"An asshole?" said Tyler, indignant. "What right do you have calling me an asshole? I'm only saying what the rest of you won't say! I'm glad this man is dead." He looked Christi and Bennie up and down. "Now, if we'd only hang these two, we could get on with this manhunt without interruption."

Sheriff Edwards sat in silence, starring down at Freed's body. Stepping down from his saddle to help Capson, Bert Collins the livery owner, said to Tyler, "You really are an asshole, Tyler. There's such a thing as respect for the dead."

"I had no respect for that stinking bank robber when he was alive. I sure as hell have no respect for him now that he's dead." He gave Collins a frown. "Maybe it's my honesty that the rest of you can't stand. I don't mind saying that this man deserved to die. I would not have hesitated a second to kill him myself."

"You're all cold piss and hot air, Tyler," said Collins, as he and Capson raised Lonnie Freed's body and draped it over the saddle.

"Oh, am I?" said Tyler. "I haven't seen much out of you this whole trip." He looked at Potts and said, "Arvin, you're the only one here who has shown any fur on your navel. You stabbed this man full of holes. What say you? Shouldn't we get rid of them?"

Potts looked away as he spoke, as if avoiding having to see Freed's body. "I am the president of the bank, sir," he said. "I think it only fitting that you call me, Mr. Potts, all things considered."

A couple of the other men snickered quietly.

"Well, la-de-da," said Tyler. He gigged his horse forward ahead of the others and, cursing them under his breath, rode on into Somos Santos.

Orsen Miles pushed his horse forward beside Edwards and said, "Suppose I better go tell him to get back here with the rest of us, Sheriff? This looks bad on all of us, him breaking ranks. There's no telling what he'll say about us to that sheriff."

"To hell with him," said Edwards. "Anybody listens to Tyler for five minutes they'll see what kind of an aggravating turd he is."

Ahead of them Tyler lopped his horse recklessly up the middle of the street and slid it to a halt in front of the sheriff's office. Dawson, standing on the boardwalk and observing the smoldering remnants of the Ace High Saloon, turned his attention to the rider. Then he saw Edwards and the rest of the posse come riding in at a much slower pace.

"You must be the sheriff," said Tyler, eyeing the badge on Dawson's chest.

"I am," said Dawson. "What can I do for you?"

Tyler gestured toward Edwards and the others. "I'm

part of a sheriff's posse. We're in pursuit of the Walker gang. Did they have anything to do with that?" He jerked a nod toward the burned saloon.

"One of the men in custody rides with Walker," said Dawson. "But he's not saying much."

"You have one *jailed*?" said Tyler, unable to conceal his excitement. "Damn good work!" He leaped from his saddle and bounded onto the boardwalk, hurrying right past Sheriff Dawson until Dawson's flat hand stopped him cold.

"Are you the posse leader?" Dawson asked.

"No. I'm William Tyler, town barber in Schalene Pass. I've been riding—" Tyler didn't get to finish before Dawson cut him off.

"Then settle down, Mr. Tyler. We'll wait until the leader gets here."

"Sure, all right," said Tyler, backing up a step. "I don't mean to be pushy, but we don't have lots of time to waste." He looked Dawson up and down and said, "You must be the gunman turned lawman we've all heard about. Crayton Dawson, is it?"

"I'm Sheriff Dawson." Dawson gazed away from Tyler toward the rest of the posse.

"We happen to be holding some of Walker's gunmen prisoner ourselves," Tyler said, taking on an air of importance. "One of them is shot all to hell. We'll be needing the use of your jail while we're here. Any objections?"

"We'll see," said Dawson. He saw the glint of the badge on Edwards' chest.

"It's a simple question, Sheriff," said Tyler. "Will you accommodate us or not?"

Noting the impatience in Tyler's demeanor, Dawson said flatly, "I think I'll wait and talk to your sheriff. It'll keep me from repeating myself."

Dawson and Tyler stood in silence while Edwards and the posse rode up and stopped at the hitch rail. Seeing the badge on Dawson's chest, Edwards touched his hatbrim and said, "I take it you're Sheriff Dawson?"

"I am," Dawson replied, also touching his hatbrim. Having seen the riders arrive, Deputy Carter had slipped quietly out the office door and stood against the wall holding a shotgun. Nodding toward him, Dawson said, "This is my deputy, Hooney Carter."

Acknowledging Carter with a nod, Edwards said, "I don't know how much Mr. Tyler here has told you, but I'm Sheriff Malcom Edwards from Schalene Pass. We're tracking the Walker gang for robbing our bank." He nodded sidelong at Christi and Bennie, then at Paco on the horse he led and the body of Lonnie Freed draped over a horse led by Potts. "This is what we've managed to run down so far."

"This is Sheriff Crayton Dawson, Sheriff Edwards," Tyler said, cutting in. "He's got one of Walker's men in jail here. Walker's men burned down the saloon!"

Tossing a look toward the rubble of the bar, Edwards shook his head. "Is that a fact, Sheriff Dawson?" he asked.

"Yep," said Dawson, "in a manner of speaking. There was a gunfight, and the saloon caught the brunt of it."

"Sorry to hear it," said Edwards. "Do you mind if I take a look at that man, hear what he might be able to tell me? They've taken the savings and operating capital of just about everybody in my town. Schalene will dry up and blow away if I don't get that money back."

"You're free to ask him whatever you want, Sheriff Edwards," said Dawson, "but I'll tell you ahead of time he's not much of a talker."

"Give me five minutes alone with him," said Tyler. "I'll have him talking."

Without acknowledging Tyler, Dawson said to Edwards, "I don't tolerate anybody getting rough with my prisoners, Sheriff."

"Don't worry," said Edwards, giving Dawson a look that told him not to pay any attention to Tyler. "I've never mistreated a prisoner in my life unless he got out of hand on me."

Dawson left the boardwalk as Edwards and his men stepped down from their saddles. After looking at Lonnie Freed's dead face in passing, Dawson turned his gaze up to Joe Christi and Bennie Betts. He noted their hard-worn hats and range clothes, and their brush scarred horses and tack. Seeing something familiar about the two, he asked Edwards, "You caught these fellows riding with Walker?"

"No," said Edwards, "we found them holed up in a shack, tending to this one." He pointed to Paco, who appeared to be more dead than alive. "They claim they were just rendering assistance to a wounded man."

"That's the truth, Sheriff," said Bennie, cutting in. "Me and Joe here are just working cowhands. We done some gambling in Schalene Pass, then got caught up in all this on our way home."

"Shut your lying mouth!" Tyler shouted, stepping heatedly toward Bennie with his rifle stock drawn back.

Once again Tyler stopped cold when Dawson pressed a hand flat on his chest. This time Dawson gave him a shove. "That's twice you've tried to make a move past me, mister," said Dawson.

"Hold it, everybody!" said Edwards, stepping in and giving Tyler another shove. He turned to Dawson, saying, "I hope you'll overlook Tyler here, Sheriff. He's gotten plumb out of hand. I told him I'm sending him back to Schalene as soon as we get these prisoners situated."

"I understand," said Dawson. He turned back to Bennie and Christi. "Have I seen you two around this part of the country before?"

Bennie Betts answered, "You sure have, Sheriff. Me and Joe here worked for Gains Bouchard's Double D spread, the same as you did, only at different times of course."

"Joe Christi," said Dawson as he began to recognize the two from a couple of times when their trails had crossed on cattle drives to Abilene and Ellsworth. As Christi nodded, Dawson looked back at Bennie.

"And I'm Betts—Bennie Betts," he said. "We worked for Bouchard off and on. You and us know the same ole boys at the Double D. They'll all vouch for us . . . except for Gains himself, God rest his soul." He swept his hat from his head in respect.

"Knowing the same people ain't getting you two owlhoots off the hook," said Tyler. He fell silent under Dawson's cold gaze.

Then Dawson turned to Joe and Bennie and said, "I'm afraid he's right about that part. If you've been riding with Harvey Blue Walker, the best thing you can do is come clean and help this sheriff find him."

"If we rode with Walker or anybody else," said Joe Christi, "I expect I'd admit it by now and take what's coming to me. But the fact is, we don't ride with Walker."

Edwards said, "In that case, the man the sheriff is holding in jail here shouldn't have any trouble telling us that and clearing your name, should he?"

"I expect not," said Christi, swinging his leg over the saddle and sliding down with his hands cuffed in front of him. Looking at Dawson, he said, "I've always heard you're a square shooter. Let's go see that man and get it done."

"All right by me," said Dawson. Turning to Carter, he said, "Deputy, go get the doctor and get him over here. This man looks like he needs some medical attention."

Carter nodded grudgingly. "I'm on my way, Sheriff," he said.

Chapter 19

From the first cell, Sheriff Edwards stepped out and took a break from trying to get Freddie Tapp to tell him whether or not Bennie and Joe Christi rode with the Walker gang. Tapp had remained belligerent and uncooperative. "March them both out and hang them," he offered, "soon as the doctor gets that one fit enough to stand on his own feet." He nodded through the bars toward young Dr. Wilson Isenhower, who sat cleaning and dressing Paco's wound in the next cell. "That's what you lawdogs do best, ain't it? String a fellow up?"

Nobody answered.

Seeing Edwards leave Tapp's cell, Dawson stepped away from the doctor and Paco in the next cell, saying, "How about some coffee, Doc?"

"Later, thanks," Dr. Isenhower said without looking up from his patient. On the other side of the doctor and Paco, Joe Christi and Bennie Betts sat on a cot in the third cell, near the bars, still rubbing their wrists where the metal handcuffs had irritated them. Sheriff Edwards had unlocked their handcuffs and locked them in the same cell with Jimmy Shaggs. Concentrating on his patient, the young doctor said through the iron bars to Bennie and Joe Christi, "You boys did a respectable job getting the bullet out of this man, all things considered."

"Heck, it weren't me, Doc," Bennie said. "Joe here did all the cutting work on him."

"Be that as it may," said the doctor, above his glasses, "good job, sir." His eyes went back to his work, swabbing around Paco's exit wound with a cloth dampened with alcohol.

Joe Christi only nodded and sat quietly, watching the doctor at work, but keeping his eyes guardedly searching the jail and the lawmen for any glimpse of a way to escape. From the start, it appeared to him that Bennie's and his chances of clearing themselves grew worse at every turn. Now, with the iron-barred door closed between him and the rest of the world, cold reality had set in.

"Cray Dawson strikes me as a fair and honest man," said Bennie under his breath, "so does Sheriff Edwards. They'll get us cleared, don't you think?"

Joe Christi only nodded in reply. He agreed with Bennie about both of the sheriffs, but he wasn't about to trust them with his life if he had any say in the matter. So far it appeared to him that their situation had only grown worse at every turn. Now that his wrists were free of the cuffs, he wanted to keep them that way. He couldn't sit still and helpless in a jail cell and watch Bennie's and his freedom slip farther away.

They had drawn the cot over to the bars for a better view of the doctor attending to Paco. Jimmy Shaggs stood beside the cot, grasping the bars with both hands. Christi had recognized the thin, pale miscreant as soon as they had entered the cell. Now that Dawson had left the doctor with Paco in the next cell alone, Christi said under his breath, "Shaggs, are you one of the ones I heard tried to gun down Cray Dawson?"

Seeing this as a chance to build himself up in someone's eyes, Shaggs said, "I was one of the backup men for Teddy Bryce."

"So I heard," said Joe Christi. "But I heard it didn't do much good. Cray Dawson killed Bryce real quick. I heard he killed you too."

Jimmy Shaggs gave him a curious look and asked, "Where the hell did you hear all that?"

"From the other backup man," said Joe Christi.

"Yeah? Give me a name," Shaggs challenged him, to see if he was telling the truth.

"Tony Weaver," said Joe, watching Shagg's beady eyes, knowing Shaggs had to believe him.

"Jesus," said Shaggs, "where'd you run into Tony Weaver?"

"He's riding with Harvey Walker. He told us the whole story."

"That sumbitch," said Shaggs, "did he mention how he ran out on me, put me in this fix I'm in?" He nodded at the anvil sitting on the floor of his cell and reached out a bare foot, touching a dirty toe to it. "Carter's got me weighted down. I can't even go to the jakes without this blasted thing chained to my ankle. Sheriff Dawson told him to take it off, but the dumb bastard has lost the key to it. Now we've got to wait for the blacksmith to come cut it off." He shook his head. "The deputy's got it in for me."

"What brought that on?" Joe asked, the two still whispering while the doctor ignored them and continued dressing Paco's wound.

"Just the usual jailhouse stuff." Shaggs shrugged his thin shoulders. "Complaining about the food, the way I'm being treated. I teased him some, trying to wear him down so I could catch him off guard."

"Nothing worked?" Bennie asked, getting into the whispered conversation.

"Naw, he's one of them real serious, *crazy* types, always wanted to get his hands on a *real criminal* like me so's he can prove how tough he is. I hate him *real* bad." Shaggs grinned slyly. "I thought for sure I'd get him killed, siccing him on Tapp. But you know what they say: 'God don't always answer prayers.' "

"That ain't how they say it, is it?" Bennie asked, looking confused. "I believe it's 'God answers prayers sometimes by saying yes and sometimes by saying no.' "

"Oh?" Shaggs' eyes gleamed with mischief. "All I've heard Him say is '*maybe*.' "

"I've never heard that," said Bennie, giving Christi a look.

"He's kidding, Bennie," said Joe. "Shaggs, you know me and Bennie have never rode with Walker, or any other gang. We just drove herds for whatever greasy-bag outfit comes along."

"I know it," said Shaggs. "I was wondering what that was all about when they brought you two in here. All I ever heard of you doing is practice gun handling and playing poker. Has that turned out to be a bad combination?"

"Yes, you might say," Christi offered upon quick reflection. "The thing is, we ran into Walker's men. One of them had shot the Mexican and we patched him up."

Bennie cut in, adding, "Next thing you know, here we are, accused of being outlaws. Everything we think might clear us just keeps burying us deeper."

"All this because you helped out ole Paco?" Shaggs said, musing over the situation.

"Yep, that's the size of it," said Christi.

"Well, tough rinds." Shaggs chuckled, offering no sympathy for the two. "That's what you get for doing something good for somebody. I say I'll let a sumbitch die and rot before I'll stick my neck out like that. Sounds like you boys are just getting what's coming to you."

"Stop acting like an ass, Shaggs," Christi said, taking on a firm tone with him. "Is there some way you can help us out?"

"You mean speak to the law on your behalf?" Shaggs' grin widened. "Damn, Christi, you must want to get the both of yas hanged!"

"No, Shaggs," said Christi. "It's too far gone for somebody speaking for us. We've got to get out of here and get on the run. Nothing else is going to do us any good."

Shaggs stooped down beside the bars, as if picking his toenails, and said closer to Joe Christi, "So what you want is for me to help you and Bennie break out of here. Send the two of you on your way, maybe wave goodbye to you while you're leaving?"

Christi stared at him. "You're welcome to go with us, of course."

"Oh." Shaggs looked surprised. "Well now that's mighty white of you!" he said.

"You know what I mean, Shaggs," said Christi. "You're included in what we do."

Shaggs smiled and settled down. "Much obliged," he said. "But the fact is, I don't want to leave here just yet. I enjoy seeing all these folks I haven't seen in a while. It's like a good ole get-together. We can swap stories and get caught up."

"But you'll help Bennie and me?" Christi asked hopefully.

"Sure, I can do that for you," Shaggs said with a cocky air. "But the question is, what will you do for me?"

"What do you need?" asked Christi.

"I need for you to kill Tony Weaver for me as soon as you see him."

Christi's expression turned grim. "I'm afraid I can't kill for you, Shaggs. Not Weaver, not anybody else."

Shaggs looked puzzled. "Why the hell not? He's a good-for-nothing run-out-on-you-pard bastard that's got no business living anyway."

Christi shook his head. "I can't help it, Shaggs. If killing Weaver is the only way I'm getting out of this mess, I'll just have to buck up and ride it out."

"Doggone it, Joe," Bennie cut in, sliding down the bars beside Christi. "You killed Turley Whitt. Why can't you kill Weaver if that's what it takes to get us out of here?"

"That was different, Bennie," Christi said. "Whitt tried to kill me. That was self-defense. This is like being a paid assassin."

"You killed Turley Whitt?" said Shaggs, as if suddenly in awe.

"Self-defense," Christi repeated.

"Yeah, but still!" said Shaggs. "You killed him? No tricks, no backup man, nothing?"

"That's right—he did," said Bennie.

"And you can't kill Weaver for me?" Shaggs asked Christi, ignoring Bennie Betts.

"You heard what I said, Shaggs," said Christi. "So let's forget it." He straightened up on the cot and stared forward, seeing the two sheriffs pouring themselves coffee from a blackened tin pot on the wood stove.

"All right," said Shaggs, still whispering. "I must be out of my mind, but I'll do it. I'll help you two bust out of this place."

Christi looked back at him. "I'm obliged," he said. "Just let me know what you need us to do."

"All you've got to do is snatch the deputy's gun when I set him up for you, Christi," said Shaggs. "But if you want this to work, you better not question anything I do until that time comes. Can you go along with that?"

"You mean we've got to trust *you*, Jimmy?" Bennie asked, as if such a thing would be impossible.

"Yeah, something like that," Shaggs said.

"We'll trust you, Shaggs," Christi cut in. "Just help us get out of here."

"All right then," said Shaggs. He picked up his anvil and held it to his chest. After stepping away from Christi, he said loudly, in a chuckling voice, "Help you get out of here? You mean break jail?" His eyes went to Sheriff Dawson. "Hear this, Sheriff! One of Walker's boys here wants me to help him and his idiot friend break jail?"

"You dirty bastard!" Bennie shouted, jumping up

from the cot. Christi caught Bennie around the waist and held him back.

Shaggs stood across the cell, shouting through the iron-bar door, "See this, Dawson? I want to report a jail-break! They're trying to get me involved in busting out of jail! Do I get anything for turning them in? He just told me everything! What do I get for jackpotting these two?"

Dawson stepped sidelong, opened the front door and called, "Get in here, Deputy. Shaggs is making new enemies for himself."

Carter hurried inside, cursing under his breath.

Shaggs laughed louder at Bennie, watching him try to wrestle free of Joe Christi. Holding the heavy anvil tighter, Shaggs said in a scornful tone, "You stupid bastards want *me* to help *you*? Are you crazy? Look at me! Where the hell am I going? I'm chained like a Gaw-damned circus bear! Who the hell do you think you are, tormenting me this way?"

"Settle down over there, Shaggs," Dawson warned him.

But Shaggs' voice went louder as he called out, "Deputy! Hurry up. Take me to the jakes! These fools have got my belly all worked up."

Dawson stepped over and through the open iron door to where Dr. Isenhower attended the wounded Mexican. "How's it going in there, Doctor?" Dawson asked, watching Carter hurry over to the other cell and fumble with the keys until he unlocked the door.

"I'm glad you didn't lose these keys too," Shaggs said to Carter with sarcasm.

"Shut up and come on, Shaggs," said Carter, standing

aside and letting Shaggs walk past him to the rear door leading outside to the privy.

Paco lay unconscious on the cot, his blurry eyes only opening now and then. "He's infected," said the doctor, finally getting to answer Dawson. Taking off his glasses and dropping them into his wrinkled shirt pocket, he added, "But I've seen worse. A little rest and some proper treatment, he should pull through."

"Good," said Dawson. Looking at Christi and Bennie, he said, "If you men are innocent and ever expect to get out of this thing, I'd advise you to not start palling around with Jimmy Shaggs. He's slippery, and he'll leave you hanging any chance he gets if it's a matter of saving his own skin."

"He was lying to you about me and Joe planning to break jail, Sheriff," said Bennie.

Christi cut in flatly, "No, he wasn't, Sheriff. I talked to him about the possibility of it." He stared Dawson squarely in the eye and said, "I get the feeling Bennie and I could really come up wrong here if we're not careful. I don't want to spend my life in jail for something I didn't do."

"I understand," said Dawson, "but breaking jail is not the way to clear yourselves."

"Then you tell us what is," said Christi.

Dawson appeared to be stuck for an answer.

Chapter 20

In the short space between the back of the jail and the plank door of the outhouse, Deputy Carter stopped Jimmy Shaggs and said, "As a deputy, my main job is being in charge of prisoners. It looks bad on me, what happened with Tapp, and you set it all up." He pointed his finger for emphasis. "If you cause me any more trouble, I swear to God, I'll take you to a creek and drop you, anvil and all, right in the middle of it."

"Stop trying to act tough, Carter," Shaggs said with confidence. "Dawson is giving you some free rein with the prisoners hoping you'll make up for being an idiot. But I've seen what you are—you're nothing. If something bad happens to me you'd most likely hang for murder."

"Oh yeah?" said Carter. "I can put a bullet in you anytime. All I have to say is that you tried to escape."

"Bullshit!" said Shaggs. He jiggled the anvil against his chest. "Who in their right mind would believe I tried to make a run for it? You stupid turd! Putting this anvil on me is the best thing that could've happened to me. I hope that blacksmith never shows up to get this off me.

I've got you right where I want as long as I'm wearing this." He grinned. "I wonder how old you were before your ma and pa saw you were an idiot."

Carter gritted his teeth, and clenched his fists; but he didn't raise a hand toward Shaggs. Instead he rasped in anger, "Get in there and take care of your business! The quicker I get you back in the cell, the better I'll like it."

"Then you best open the door for me, *Deputy*," said Shaggs, mockingly. "Your anvil idea has me at a disadvantage."

"Gawdamn it!" Carter fumed, swinging the door open and stepping back away from the circling flies inside the outhouse.

"Don't run off, Deputy," said Shaggs. "I might need you to tear out some old *Harper's Weekly* pages for me."

"Son of a bitch," Carter growled, slamming the door behind Shaggs. He stepped a few feet away from the smelly outhouse and stood watching the door with his hand on his pistol.

"What's the matter, Deputy? Law work ain't turning out as pretty as you thought it would be?" Shaggs snickered, peeping out between two wall planks. After a silent pause, he said, "You know, it's really a damn shame you and I can't get along. I'm pretty sure those two will make a break for it before long. Catching them in the act would be a feather in your cap—mine too for tipping you off."

"Don't waste your breath, Shaggs," said Carter. "I'm through listening to anything you've got to say."

"I know that, Deputy," said Shaggs, "All I'm saying is that it's a shame we got off on the wrong foot. We coulda helped one another—that's a fact."

"Shut up, and *hurry up*, Shaggs," said Carter. "The only dealings I want to have with you would be if I could put a bullet in your ear and not get caught doing it."

"All the same, I feel a little bad about how we've gotten along," said Shaggs through the closed plank door. "If I hear anything more out of these two, you can bet I'll tell you first thing. Maybe that'll make things better. What do you say?"

"Go to hell, Shaggs," said Carter. He stepped closer and shook the outhouse door. "And hurry it up in there. I'm stuck with guarding you fools while everybody goes to dinner."

"I'm coming," said Shaggs, who hadn't even used the facility. All he had done is set the anvil on the rough privy box and stood observing the deputy through the wall cracks. He unbuttoned his trousers, pulled his shirttails up a little and stood righting them as he said, "Open the door for me, Deputy."

Grumbling, Carter opened the door and saw Shaggs finishing dressing, tucking in his shirttails and buttoning his fly before turning around and hefting the anvil to his chest. "I'll tell you what, Deputy," he said. "Even though you're mad at me, if I hear anything, I'll warn you."

"Yeah, yeah," said Carter, "let's go." He wanted to give Shaggs a shove, but he dared not while the thin man struggled along with the heavy weight in his arms.

"Next time I ask to come out here, it won't be to use the jakes. It'll be to tell you what their plans are."

"I'm sure they'll be real careful telling you anything,

Shaggs, after you shooting off your mouth about it," Carter grumbled.

"Just be ready, Deputy," Shaggs said over his shoulder, plodding along barefoot, looking up at the late-afternoon sky, judging how long it would be before nightfall. Smiling to himself, he walked through the rear door and back to his cell with Carter right behind him, rifle in hand. Once the outlaw stepped back inside the cell, Carter locked the iron door and turned to Dawson, who stood behind his desk talking to Sheriff Edwards and the doctor.

"Ready for that cup of coffee now, Doctor?" Dawson asked.

Rolling down his wrinkled shirtsleeves, the young doctor replied, "I'm afraid I can't take you up on it, Sheriff. I've taken longer here than I thought I would. I have the Shelburtons' baby on its way anytime. I must go check on Lydia Shelburton."

"Too bad, Doc," said Dawson. "Sheriff Edwards and I wanted to take you to over to Galbrath's restaurant for dinner."

"I've never had one lawman buy me dinner, let alone two," said the doctor. "Another time, I hope. I really must get going."

"Another time, and at your pleasure, Doc," said Dawson, watching the serious young doctor throw on his frayed suit coat.

"You're probably not missing much, Doctor," said Edwards. "I expect that by now my posse men have made a big whole in that's restaurant's food supply."

Perfect, Shaggs said to himself. Inside his cell, he'd listened intently even though he sat on the side of his cot and stared down at the heavy anvil on the floor between his feet.

"Carter, look after the prisoners," said Dawson, a moment after Dr. Isenhower had left. Lifting his hat from atop his desk and putting it on, Dawson added, "We'll bring your dinner back to you."

"Yeah, obliged," Carter said grudgingly.

Outside the jail, Edwards said to Dawson, as they closed the door and stepped down to the street, "If you don't mind me asking, how did there come to be ill feelings between your deputy and your prisoner?"

"Carter's a hardheaded young man out to prove himself, Sheriff," said Dawson. "Jimmy Shaggs is a petty thief trying to do the same thing. I expect they each remind one another too much of themselves to ever get along. I'm certain you've seen that more than once, with all your years behind that badge?"

Edwards chuckled. "I expect I have . . . although I can't say I ever had it figured down so close to the bone the way you seem to." He looked Dawson up and down. "Does that come along with being a big gun?"

Dawson smiled thinly as they walked on toward the restaurant. "I never thought of myself as a gunman, Sheriff. I had something that needed doing so bad it was eating me up. Riding with Lawrence Shaw beside me might be all that kept me alive. Anyway, I got it done, I came home here to Somos Santos, and that's pretty much that. Everything else is all scraps and hides."

"You're being modest," said Edwards. "I heard more, much more."

"You know how things you hear can get blown up, Sheriff," said Dawson.

"Yeah," Edwards said. "But I've heard enough I can tell the difference."

Dawson nodded. To change the subject, he asked, "How soon are you and your men headed back onto Walker's trail?"

"First thing come morning," said Edwards. "I know you can't come with us, but I'm obliged for anything you hear about that money. Losing it is going to break my town, I'm afraid."

"Anything I hear, Sheriff, you'll get it before it cools off," Dawson said. They walked on to the Galbrath Family Dinner House and heard the coarse voices of drinkers, which would have sounded more appropriate coming from behind the bat-wing doors of a saloon.

Jimmy Shaggs sat avoiding the harsh stare coming through the bars from Bennie Betts. When Carter had brought Shaggs back inside, instead of putting him back in the cell with Christi and Bennie, Sheriff Dawson had insisted that Shaggs be placed in the cell with Paco for his own protection. That was exactly what Shaggs had wanted. As for Bennie Betts' cold stare, it didn't bother Shaggs one bit. Bennie had no idea what was going on, Shaggs reminded himself.

Bennie and Christi weren't smart enough to keep up with him, Shaggs thought, smiling to himself. The two had shown themselves to be weak, having to ask his help in making a jailbreak. His smile widened as he thought about the looks on their faces when they'd had to seek his help, about the shock in their eyes when he'd blurted out their intentions to Sheriff Dawson.

Looking out the front window, he saw that darkness

had fallen over the town like a shroud. It had been no more than ten minutes since the two sheriffs had left. He glanced over to where Carter sat half dozing at the sheriff's desk. *Good enough.* Shaggs stood up, yawned, stretched and stooped down to his anvil.

Carter's eyes snapped open when Shaggs said, "Hey, Deputy, wake up! I've got to go again!"

"You can wait, Shaggs," said Carter.

"Can I? Are you sure?" Shaggs asked pointedly.

His tone of voice caused the young deputy to look over at him curiously.

Standing beside his anvil, Shaggs stared at Carter but cut a sidelong glance toward Christi and Bennie in the next cell, implying that he'd heard something more from the two. "I really think you ought to take me out back right now. There could be a mess if you don't."

Carter got the message. "All right, damn it," he said, pushing up from his chair and walking to the key hanging from its wall peg. He picked up his rifle from against the wall.

At the cell door, Carter gave Christi and Bennie Betts a look. He saw nothing telling in their flat expressions as he unlocked the door and stepped inside, his eyes going up and down Shaggs, seeing the anvil sitting against his ankle, the four-foot-long chain lying half circled on the cell floor. On the other cot in the cell, Paco lay unconscious, a patch of red already seeping through the new bandange the doctor had put on his wound.

"Pick up your anvil, Shaggs. Let's go," said Carter, his right hand on his gun butt, his left hand loosely holding his rifle. He stepped around to clear Shaggs' way to the open barred door.

"Sure thing, Deputy," said Shaggs, stooping down to pick up the anvil. But instead of holding it to his chest and struggling to the door with it, he flung himself toward Carter, saying, "Deputy! Catch this!"

The sight of the heavy anvil coming at him left Carter no choice. He threw out his arms, dropping his rifle and catching the heavy slab of iron. The weight of it sent him staggering backward until his back jammed against the bars separating the cells. At the same time, Shaggs swept down and snatched up the rifle off the floor.

Christi and Bennie looked stunned. But in Christi's case it was only for a second; he snapped out of it, seeing what was happening in time to make his own move. As the deputy slammed against the bars with both arms full, Joe reached through the bars and snatched Carter's Colt from his tied-down holster.

"Ah damn it!" Carter said as realization set in. The big anvil dropped from his hands and jarred the floor.

"Ooops!" said Jimmy Shaggs, stepping in closer with a wide grin. He swung the rifle butt sideways with such force and quickness, Carter didn't see it coming. But he felt it. His head snapped sideways as the blow caught him full on his jaw and flung him across the cell.

"Jesus!" said Freddie Tapp from the cell on the other side of Shaggs. He hurried to the barred wall separating them and started speaking fast. "Shaggs, I never meant what I said about killing you. You was always a-okay in my way of thinking! I always said you never got as well as you deserved! I just wish I could call back any hurtful things I might have said!"

Pointing Carter's rifle at Tapp, Shaggs cut him off, saying, "Shut up, Freddie! You're going!"

"All right!" Tapp looked relieved. "You won't be sorry! We'll rob and plunder from here to the Canadian border."

"Not if you're going with us," said Christi, taking the key Shaggs handed him through the bars. "If I ever get all you outlaws shook out of my life, you're never getting near me again." He hurried over with Carter's gun in one hand, the cell key in the other. "Come on, Bennie! Let's get out of here!"

"I won't rob nothing until after we split up then," said Tapp, trying to be as accommodating as he could. "I give you my word on that."

Christi stared at him. "If you get us into trouble, Tapp, you'll wish to God you were never born."

"I understand," said Tapp, stretching out his hand and catching the cell key that Christi pitched to him. Hurriedly opening his cell door, Tapp pitched the key to Shaggs' outstretched hand.

"Are you sure you won't go with us, Jimmy?" Bennie asked. He nodded at the knocked-out deputy lying on the floor. "This fellow is going to be awfully mad when he wakes up."

"I've got it all figured out," said Shaggs, giving Bennie a confident grin of satisfaction.

"I'm sorry I doubted you," said Bennie. But Shaggs only gave a toss of his hand.

Out of the cell, Christi hurriedly went through the sheriff's desk, took out the pistol he'd taken from Turley Whitt, shoved it into his waist and kept rummaging. He picked up a gun belt wrapped around a one-piece slim-jim holster. He unrolled it, glanced at the bullets lining it to make sure they were the right caliber, then slung the belt over his shoulder. He saw a small hideout gun, grabbed it, checked it, saw that it had been put away loaded and shoved it down in his trousers.

Stepping up beside him, Shaggs handed Christi the cell key and the key to the anvil chain he'd been hiding in his clothes since the day he'd stolen it from Deputy Carter. "Do me a favor," he said. "On your way out, stick these keys in the outhouse, on the beam above the door."

"Sure thing," said Christi, taking the keys. "Are you sure you want to let go of these?"

"I'm absolutely sure," Shaggs replied.

"All right," Christi said with resolve. Turning, he said to Bennie, "Grab yourself some shooting gear and plenty of ammunition. Once we get shed of this place, they're never bringing me back here alive."

While Christi, Bennie and Freddie Tapp grabbed guns and ammunition, Jimmy Shaggs smiled and dragged the knocked-out deputy from his cell by his boots and left him lying in the cell Tapp had just vacated. After locking the cell door, he said across the room to Tapp, "As far as anybody knows, you're the one who did all this. Is that okay with you?"

"What the hell do I care?" Tapp shrugged, snatching a rifle from a rifle rack along the wall.

Christi, on his way to the rear door, stopped long enough to say, "Shaggs, I'm much obliged—"

"Yeah, yeah, I know," said Shaggs. "Now get going. I figure you've got about a half hour head start before they'll be on your trail." He watched Bennie and Tapp hurry out the door.

"We're gone," said Christi, right behind them.

Shaggs sighed at the empty office. He walked into his cell, left the door wide-open and scooted the anvil to his cot along the wall next to Paco's. He sat down on the cot and cuffed the anvil chain to his ankle. Then he lay down on his cot and shut his eyes.

Chapter 21

Deputy Carter awakened in the quiet of the sheriff's office, his jaw throbbing, his head aching, and only a blurred sense of what had happened to him moments earlier. But as the fog began to lift from his brain, he pulled himself to his feet and looked all around the swaying office. Seeing the opened drawers of the desk, the open cell doors and the rifles missing from the rifle rack, he moaned aloud, "Shaggs, you son of a bitch." But he said the words with no idea that Shaggs lay in the cell next to him.

"You can't blame this on me, Deputy," Shaggs said, the sound of his voice startling Carter.

Carter looked over at him and blinked his eyes as if in disbelief. "You—you hit me," he said, but it sounded as if he had some doubts. "What are you still doing here?"

Shaggs chuckled and swung up on the side of his cot, the chain on his ankle jingling as he did so. "It's all like a bad dream, ain't it, Deputy?"

Carter held on to the bars for support and shook his head, trying to clear it, as Shaggs said, "First of all, I didn't hit you. If I did, you wouldn't be standing up there this soon. I would have beaten your head in." He reached down and shook the chain on his ankle. "Second of all, I'm here because where the hell could I go with this thing chained to me?"

"You had it off," said Carter. "I saw it! I don't know what you're trying to pull, but it ain't going to work."

"Just watch," Shaggs said in a lowered tone.

Before Carter could say any more on the matter, the front door opened and Dawson and Edwards walked in. "Holy cats!" said Edwards. The two lawmen ran across the office and out the open back door, drawing their pistols on their way. Behind them Carter yelled out, "It was Shaggs, Sheriff! He did it! He set it up!"

Five yards away from the back door, Dawson stopped and stared toward the livery barn. "We're wasting time on foot. They've stolen horses and lit out. Gather your posse while their trail is still warm."

They hurried back inside the jail. Edwards called out to Carter, "How long have they been gone?"

But Carter looked dumbfounded. "I don't know. Shaggs knocked me out."

The two lawmen looked at Shaggs in the next cell. The thin outlaw shrugged in bewilderment. "He's out of his mind, Sheriff," he said. "Look at me! Do I look like I could do anything, the shape I'm in?"

Dawson kept a suspicious eye on Shaggs and said to Edwards, "Get your men and go, Sheriff. I have to settle things here before I leave. I'll meet you along the trail."

"We'll keep watch for you," said Edwards, holstering his pistol on his way to the front door.

As soon as Edwards left, Dawson looked all around for the key to the cells. Not seeing it anywhere, he walked over, stooped down behind the stove and pulled a spare key from beneath it.

"I swear, Sheriff," said Carter, talking fast as Dawson unlocked the cell door, "Shaggs did this! He had the shackle off his ankle. He threw the anvil at me, knocked me out with my rifle, locked me up and turned the others loose!"

Dawson gave him a skeptical look, then glanced over at Shaggs, who only shrugged again and jiggled the chain in his ankle. "We'll get to the bottom of this, Deputy," Dawson said. "Is your jaw broken?"

"I don't think so," said Carter, trying to work the stiff swollen side of his face. "It's sore as hell."

"Go get Brady," said Dawson, "and bring him back here as quick as you can."

"Wayne Brady, the telegraph clerk?" said Carter, sounding surprised. "What for?"

"I want him to stay here and keep an eye on you and Shaggs while I get on the trail after those three outlaws," said Dawson.

"On me?" Carter said. "But, Sheriff, I—"

"Go get Brady," said Dawson, "and hurry it up. We've let Edwards' prisoners break our jail. We've at least got to help him track them down."

Dawson unlocked Shaggs' cell and stepped inside before Carter was out the front door headed for the telegraph clerk's room above his small brick office a block away.

"I swear, Sheriff," said Shaggs, standing up from his cot and spreading out his arms, "I have no idea what Carter's talking about. Tapp suckered him into his cell, snatched his rifle and knocked him colder than a duck's dinner. I told them to stop. They wouldn't listen to me. I couldn't go because of this anvil. For a minute there I was in fear for my life."

"Are you through, Shaggs?" Dawson said flatly, stopping in front of him.

"Yeah, I suppose," said Shaggs, giving the sheriff a curious look. "You're not going to pistol-whip me, are you?"

"Don't give me ideas," said Dawson. "Turn around and put your hands on the wall. I better not find that cell key on you."

Shaggs turned around and did as he was told. "Don't worry, you won't, Sheriff." He grinned at the wall.

"Nobody takes a key with them when they break jail, Shaggs," said Dawson as he ran his hands up and down Shaggs' thin bony sides.

"Since I've never been a jailbreaker, I wouldn't know," said Shaggs.

On the next cot, Paco coughed and raised his head a few inches, saying in a dry, raspy voice, "*Agua, por favor* . . . water."

Finishing with Shaggs, Dawson stepped over and bent down to the Mexican. "I'll get you some water. How are you feeling?"

"Rough," said Paco, rising sideways, stiffly, on one elbow. The pain in his shoulder caused him to wince and moan slightly. He looked all around at the bars and said weakly, "Whose jail am I in?"

"Somos Santos," Dawson said, walking away and out of the cell without taking his eyes off Shaggs, who had slumped down on his cot. The sheriff returned with a dipper of water from a water bucket, stooped down and helped hold it as Paco took a drink. "You're a prisoner of Sheriff Edwards from Schalene. You're here until you're well enough to travel back with him."

"*Sí,* I remember some things now." He looked around through dark, cloudy eyes. "Where is the drover who cut the bullet out of me?"

"You mean Joe Christi," said Dawson.

"*Sí,* Joe Christi," said the Mexican. "He saved my life. Me, a stranger—can you believe that?" With his free hand, Paco made a vague sign of the cross on his chest.

Dawson studied Paco's eyes for any sign of deception and saw none when he asked, "Do Christi and Bennie Betts ride with you and Walker's gang?"

"No, they do not," said Paco. "You have seen how ragged they are, no? How little they have? Would they live that way if they had money from a fat, juicy bank?" He lay down on his back again and closed his eyes for a moment, running out of strength. "Those two are not in trouble because of helping me, are they?" he asked. His eyes opened again as if grim possibilities had just dawned on him.

"There's a posse on their backs right now for breaking jail," Dawson said down to him. "Who knows how that might turn out?"

"*Sante Madre,*" Paco said almost to himself, rising back on his elbow. He shook his head and struggled up on the side of the cot. "You must let the posse know that those two are not robbers."

"I will," said Dawson, giving Shaggs a dark stare as he said, "I just hope I can get to them in time."

* * *

Christi and Bennie had taken Tapp's advice and brought along extra horses from the livery barn. They rode their first horses nonstop out through the darkness across the dangerous rocky terrain until the animals began to froth and blow, struggling too hard for the small distance of ground they managed to put behind their tired hooves. At a junction on the dark trail, where to their left lay a stretch of hills and beyond it a straight trail toward the border, Tapp reined his tired horse to a halt and slid down from his saddle.

"Boys, you're both doing good for this being the first posse you ever had down your shirt." He loosened the saddle and stripped it, blanket and all, from the tired horse's back with one hand. In his other hand he held the reins to his fresh mount. Tossing the saddle atop the fresh horse, he said, as he made the cinch and snugged it with a snap of his wrist, "I estimate we've put over a couple of hours between us and them. This crossroads is a good place to split up if we're still going to."

Changing their saddles to their own fresh mounts, Christi said, "I believe we should, Freddie, unless you want to ride for the border with us. Any luck at all, Bennie and me will fade into the bracken and ride straight for the Grande on the back trails. There's nothing'll see us going that way except but rattlers and jackrabbits."

"Go on then," said Tapp. "I almost envy you two, getting out of here that direction."

"Ride with us then, if it suits you," said Christi. "I didn't mean what I said back in that jail. You didn't bring our trouble on us. I did."

Tapp stopped for a moment and gazed west into the starlit sky, as if considering the offer for a moment. But then he shook his head and said, "Aw, hell, I've got to play this out the way it fits. All I ever wanted to be was an outlaw. If a man gets to do what he wants in life, he can't complain about how it ends." He gave the tired horse a shove on its rump and sent it walking off the trail.

"That's as good a way as any to look at it," said Christi. He and Bennie tightened the cinches on their fresh horses and grabbed their saddle horns. They had started to swing up when the sounds of rifles cocking and a loud voice caused them to freeze.

"Don't nobody move a Gawdamned muscle!" the voice bellowed from the darkened shadows alongside a sunken boulder just off the trail. "We'll take them Gawdamned horses now," the voice demanded. "So step away!"

"The hell you will," said Tapp, turning slowly, knowing that whoever held those rifles didn't want to fire them and hit the very horses they wanted to steal. "Walk your rifles away from here and stick them straight up your asses! You ain't taking these horses!"

"Freddie?" the voice said in surprise, softening a bit but still cautious.

"Odell?" Freddie said, sounding equally surprised. Before the voice could even answer, Freddie Tapp asked, as recognition set in, "What the living hell are you doing out here?"

"Me?" Odell asked. "What the Gawdamned hell are you doing out here?" He sounded completely astonished that he had found himself standing in the dark, in the middle of nowhere, about to steal one of his own men's horses right out from under him. Joe Christi and Bennie remained frozen in place, listening. But Christi held his right hand poised, ready to go for the big Colt at the first opportunity.

"Jesus," said Tapp, feeling a bit relieved but still not stepping away from his horse until he knew about Odell's situation. "Me and these two drovers broke out of jail in Somos Santos earlier. We're headed—" He stopped and chuckled in disbelief. "Hell, we thought we had this land all to ourselves."

"Drovers?" said another voice, this one sounding familiar to Christi and Bennie. "You don't mean Joe Christi and Bennie something-or-other; do you?"

"It's Betts," Bennie said.

"Yeah, it's us," Christi said. "Buck Turner?"

"Yep, it's me," said Turner, sounding as dumbfounded by the hand of fate as Odell did.

"Jesus," said Bennie in awe.

A stunned silence followed; then Odell broke it, saying, "Tapp, I ought to kill you!"

"Hold on, Odell," Tapp said. "I never had anything to do with you getting jackpotted. You can ask Buck. Ain't that right, Buck?"

"I have no idea who knew *what* about it," said Turner. "All I know is, we best all put it away for everybody's sake, especially when these parts are crawling with posses."

"That's my take on it too," said Tapp. "But I don't see Odell lowering his rifle any."

Odell uncocked his rifle and let it droop in his hand. Turner did the same, saying to Christi, "What become of Paco? Is he dead?"

"He was still alive when we left him in the jail in

Somos Santos," said Christi. "A posse came by the shack after you left. They took us all with them, hunting Harvey Walker."

"Ain't we all hunting that rotten son of a bitch," said Odell. Having walked closer, he eyed Freddie Tapp. "What is Harvey up to, Freddie? And don't lie to me."

"He wants to rob the bank in Somos Santos," said Tapp. "I expect he's about ready to let her rip most anytime now."

"I've got a little surprise behind that rock. It'll make robbing that bank a snap," said Odell, grinning slyly. "I think it'll get Cray Dawson to kill ole Harvey for me to boot." He nodded toward the large, half-sunken boulder, saying, "Buck, go bring that surprise out here."

"This is where Bennie and I ought to leave," said Christi, watching Turner disappear behind the rock for a moment, "before we hear something we shouldn't."

Freddie Tapp and Odell looked him and Bennie up and down. "You ain't all three riding together now?" Odell asked Tapp.

"No," said Christi, answering before Tapp could. "We broke jail together, but that's it as far as I'm concerned. I just want to get out of here and let some dust settle. Go somewhere and let everybody forget I was ever born."

"What do you say, Freddie?" Odell asked. "Should we let them leave?"

"They've both been on the square with me," said Freddie. "I say let them go."

"Good enough for me," said Odell. Wagging his rifle toward the trail, he said to Christi, "Go on then. Cut out of here. Just keep your mouths shut."

"We will. You can count on it," said Christi. But before he and Bennie could turn and step up into their saddles, Turner stepped back into sight from behind the boulder holding Carmelita by her wrist. "Damn it," Christi said under his breath. "I can't leave her here."

"Well now!" said Tapp greedily, looking at Carmelita in the pale moonlight. "Things are already looking up. When you said a surprise, you weren't blowing air!" He rubbed his hands together. "I hope we're all three good enough friends to share equally."

"She's Cray Dawson's wife, Tapp," said Odell, reaching out, taking Carmelita by her arm and pulling her away from Turner. "Does that bring any possibilities to mind?"

"Yep," said Tapp, "but only one that I care to act upon right now."

"Huh-uh, Tapp," said Odell. "She's strictly to be used for making Dawson do what we want him to." As he spoke, he pulled Carmelita tight against his chest and began stroking her long, dark hair. "We want to rob the bank without Dawson interfering, we send a couple of her fingers to Dawson in a cigar box. We want Dawson to kill Walker for us. If he refuses, we send him one of her ears. When it's all over and done, maybe then we do ourselves a little celebrating with her. But first we take care of business."

Christi and Bennie stood watching, seeing the woman tremble in fear as Odell breathed into her ear and held his hand firm and low on her belly. "There goes Mexico," Bennie whispered. "We can't leave her here, can we, Joe?"

"I can't, but you can, Bennie," said Christi. Under his breath he added, "Get on that horse and ride. Look for me over around Mama Rosa's outside of Mexico City, soon as I can get things straightened out here."

"No," said Bennie, stubbornly. "If you ain't going, neither am I. If I leave you behind now, I've got a feeling you're never going to make it to Mexico."

"All the more reason for you to ride away right this minute, Bennie, while you still can," Christi whispered. "There's no need for both of us not getting away. That makes no sense at all."

"Maybe it don't make sense," said Bennie, stepping back away from his horse and holding the reins loosely in his hand, "but that's how it is. Either we both go, or we both stay."

"Thought you two were so set on getting out of here," said Odell. "What are you drovers whispering about over there?"

"About maybe sticking here and riding with you three after all," said Christi. "That is if you'll have us."

Tapp chuckled with satisfaction. "Oh yeah, Christi, we'll have you all right. I've seen enough to know you're about cool and steady as a man gets. All you've got to do is say the word—"

"Slow down, Tapp," Odell warned, cutting him off with his harsh tone of voice. "You can kiss his ass in private. This is about business."

"Then let's talk business, Odell," said Christi, getting his attention. "You want Walker dead. I want to kill him for you. Let's partner up and get it going."

"Oh?" said Odell. "Is this all it took, seeing this little gal in the moonlight? Think you're in for a part of her?"

"No," said Christi, "but I just thought things over. What am I running for? I'm the man who killed Turley

Whitt face-to-face. I'm not worried about Cray Dawson or Harvey Walker or anybody else. To hell with running off to Mexico. It's time I made some money shooting a gun." He patted the big Colt he'd taken off Whitt.

Tapp chuckled and nodded his head, saying to Odell, "I knew it was just a matter of time before this man was going to turn outlaw. I could see it in his eyes."

"Yeah, you were right," Christi said, his hand resting on the butt of the big Colt. "It was just a matter of time."

Chapter 22

In the night, as the posse made its way across the stretch of flatlands surrounding Somos Santos, Dawson realized that the men would be like tin ducks at a shooting match if they happened upon the escapees along the rocky paths through the hills. Listening to the unmistakable sounds of the men and horses, Dawson had said to Edwards, "We're too loud. They'll hear us coming a mile away. They'll find a good spot and bushwhack us if we're not careful."

"You know these hills better than any of us," said Edwards. They studied the dark outline of the hills lying ahead of them in speculation. "What do you suggest we do, Sheriff?"

"We've made good time, but now I need to scout on ahead," said Dawson. "I can move around a lot quieter on my own. If they hear the posse coming they're going to cut out fast or get themselves into position along the cliffs. Either way I'll be close enough to hear them. It'll keep us from losing them if they run, or getting our eyes shot out if they stick and fight."

In the dark, Edwards pulled a watch from his vest and

stared closely at it, barely making out the hands in the moonlight. "How far ahead are you going to ride? I don't want one of these nervous townsmen shooting you."

"Ten minutes will put me far enough ahead of you to get me into the hills and hear you coming," said Dawson.

Winding his watch, Edwards said, "The men and horses are about ready for a rest anyway. It's long after midnight. I'll clock you ten minutes before we move out."

"Adios," said Dawson. Without another word, he rode away as Edwards turned in his saddle and brought his men to a halt.

Dawson rode fast at first; but he gradually slowed the horse's pace as he neared the hill line. Entering the rocky upward trail, he traveled slower yet, until, after a while, he stepped down from his saddle and led the horse silently up along the cliff's edges.

Dawson's judgment had been correct.

Knowing the posse from Somos Santos would be coming after the escapees anytime, Odell had led the group up into the rocky cliffs above the main trail and searched out a perfect place for an ambush. But having heard the men and horses moving among the rocks, Dawson had slipped forward as silent as a ghost, and although he could not see them, he moved right along with them through the darkness.

Odell Clarkson, Buck Turner and the three escapees quietly lay in wait until, at first light, they heard the soft clicks of horses' hooves walking slowly along beneath them. Carmelita lay under cover of some rocks, her hands and feet tied, a bandanna around her mouth to keep her quiet. As the riders came more clearly into view in the silver-gray of morning, Tapp recognized them and said in a hushed tone to Odell, "It's Edwards and his posse all right. Let's finish them off right here and be done with it."

"Do you see Dawson down there?" Odell asked, squinting for a better look.

"No," said Tapp. "Maybe he didn't come."

"Well, that's the man I want to speak to," Odell continued, as if he hadn't even heard Tapp.

"Speak, hell. Let's kill Edwards and his boys while we've got a chance," said Tapp, his voice rising a bit.

"We're doing this *my* way, Tapp," said Odell. "That woman didn't fall into our hands for nothing. We're going to make good use of her and her lawman husband."

"Okay, Odell," said Tapp, remembering that Odell could be hotheaded when the mood struck him. "I'm right behind you, whatever you want to do."

"Well, thank you *very damn* much," Odell said with sarcasm. "Now if you don't mind, I'll just get their attention." He steadied his rifle down over the edge of a rock and took close aim.

Thirty yards behind Odell, in the morning light, Cray Dawson saw the outlaw getting ready to fire at Edwards and his men. Unable to get a clear shot at Odell without taking a chance on hitting Joe Christi, who was crouched close beside the outlaw, Dawson aimed at the rock a foot from Odell and fired. The shot served as a warning to the posse below and sent them scattering for cover. For Odell, the shot caused him to turn quickly in Dawson's direction and get off a round before Dawson ducked down behind a rock himself.

"Who the hell is that?" Odell asked, startled by Dawson. His forearm stung from tiny particles of chipped rock that had pelted him.

Having turned in time for a good look at Dawson, Tapp widened his eyes. "Damn it! It's Cray Dawson!" he said to Odell. "How the hell did he get around behind us? He'll pick our eyes out from there!"

"Oh no, he won't!" Odell said with confidence. "Turner! You know what to do!"

At the sound of Dawson's shot, Bennie, Christi and Turner all rolled away under rock cover and lay still, trying to peep around the edge of the rocks for a better view. From the trail below, the posse started firing wildly, hitting nothing, but sending bullets ricocheting in every direction.

"Here goes," Turner said to Christi, pushing himself up on all fours. "You boys cover me."

"Wait!" said Christi, but it was no use. Turner sprang into the open long enough to make a run and dive behind the rock where Carmelita lay shaking with fear. Rifle shots from Dawson had kicked up clump after clump of dirt, following Turner until he disappeared from sight.

"Hold your Gawdamned fire, Sheriff!" Odell demanded of Dawson. "I wager you'd never forgive yourself if something bad happens to this little woman!" He waved Turner up from behind the rock. Turner was holding Carmelita against his chest, his pistol pointed at her head.

Dawson froze at the sight of Carmelita; his rifle fell silent.

Odell grinned and relaxed a bit, unaffected by the wild rifle shots coming up from the trail below. "I thought that would get your interest, Sheriff," he called out. "I'm Odell Clarkson, and I'm here to ruin your whole day if you don't play the cards I'm dealing you."

"Turn her loose, Clarkson!" Dawson called out.

"Now don't start talking stupid, Sheriff," Odell said, sounding testy, "or we'll kill her and say to hell with it." He paused for a moment and when the rifle fire below subsided, he said, "Otherwise, I've got a deal for you, Sheriff. If you'll holler down and tell these town birds to stop wasting bullets, I'll tell you how you can save your woman's life."

Without hesitation Dawson shouted loud enough to be heard on the trail below, "Sheriff Edwards, it's me, Dawson! Hold your fire!"

After a tense pause, Edwards called back, "Dawson! What's going on up there? Have they surrendered?"

Odell snickered, "Crazy, ain't he?"

"Just hold your fire. We're talking," Dawson shouted.

Beside Edwards, who was hidden by rocks strewn alongside the trail, William Tyler said to the rest of the posse men, "Hear that? They're talking! We're hiding down here like rats, and they're having themselves a nice conversation." Raising his rifle to his shoulder, he started to take aim, saying, "Well, not for long though, not if I can help!"

Edwards grabbed the rifle barrel and slammed it downward just as it went off. "Damn you, Tyler! Do that again, I'll shoot you myself!" He looked up along the cliffs and shouted, "That was an accident! No more shots now, I promise!"

Up on the cliff, Odell chuckled. "See how nice they can get when they have to work their way down closer, Dawson," said Odell, gauging his voice for Dawson to hear him, but not the men on the trail below. "Let's keep this just between us." He cocked his head to one side. "You ain't scared, are you?"

"No, I'm not." Dawson stepped out from behind the rock, realizing his move made him a clear target, but knowing as well that he couldn't do a thing about it, not without risking Carmelita's life. "All right, Clarkson, here I am." He spread his arms wide and ventured forward, his rifle in his gloved hand, but without his thumb over the hammer. "What is it you want me to do?"

Odell stood up from behind his rock, dusted the seat of his trousers and walked forward until the two stood less than fifteen feet apart. Thumbing back over his shoulder to where Carmelita stood pressed against Turner's chest, Odell said, "Every few seconds I want you to look back there, just so you don't forget and do something rash."

"I won't, Clarkson," said Dawson. "Tell me what it's going to take to get her turned loose."

"You get right to the point, Dawson. I like that," said Odell, smiling. But then his smile vanished quickly and he said, "I want the money from the bank in Somos Santos, for starters."

"The money?" Dawson said, trying not to sound too surprised. "What else do you want from Somos Santos?"

Odell grinned. "I want their *sheriff*"—he pointed at Dawson—"to kill a rotten rat bastard for me."

"Who?" Dawson asked, staring past Odell as he spoke, trying to get a look at Carmelita.

"My *ex*-pal Harvey Blue Walker," Odell said flatly.

"Walker's not in Somos Santos," said Dawson. "As far as I know, he's *never* been there."

"But he's coming," said Odell. "I'm tipping you off right now. He's on his way to rob the bank there."

"When?" Dawson asked.

"Tomorrow," said Odell. "Tapp told me that he and the other two were in town the day Walker came scouting out the bank."

"Walker, in my town?" Dawson asked. "The day Tapp got arrested?"

"He was," said Odell, "and he means to come back and rob that bank. Only, when he does, I want all the bank money to come to me, and I want *you* to kill Walker for me before he can ride away." He grinned and tapped a gloved finger to his forehead. "Maybe right before the bullet hits him in the head, I'll step up beside you and let him know that I was behind the whole thing."

Dawson looked at Odell closely, wondering if he was out of his mind. "How do you think I can do all that, Clarkson? The people of Somos Santos aren't blind. They'll see what's going on."

"They better not," said Odell. "If you bring any townsmen into this, the deal is off and this woman dies. Understand?"

"I understand," said Dawson.

"Good," said Odell. "See to it Walker's gang gets the blame, I get the money and you kill that cheating son of a bitch dead in the street."

Dawson shook his head, amazed at such a plan.

"Clarkson, you must have an awful lot of confidence in me, if you think I can do all that."

"You're a big gunman. I've got confidence you can, Dawson," said Odell. "And you better be *confident* that I'll kill your woman real slow and painful like if you don't."

Dawson looked troubled as he cast another glance at Carmelita, seeing her eyes plead with him above the bandanna concealing her lips.

"Hell, buck up, Sheriff," Odell said with a dark chuckle. "Me and these boys will be right there with you, lurking in the alleys when Walker's men hit town. I wouldn't miss seeing his face for nothing in the world, once he understands what I've done to him."

"When do you turn her loose?" Dawson asked, nodding toward Carmelita.

"Soon as I brush Walker's brains off my vest and heft that bank money on my shoulder," Odell said, "you and the woman walk away hand in hand."

"I don't even have to tell you what happens to you if anything happens to her, do I?" said Dawson.

"Don't start getting your bark on, Sheriff," said Odell. "The best thing you can do is be real friendly with me."

"What do I tell the sheriff down there?" Dawson asked.

"Tell him whatever suits you," said Odell. "Just don't tell him what we're up to."

Dawson thought about it for a second, realizing how shaky Odell's plan sounded. But reminding himself that he had no choice, he sighed and said, "You and your men head out across the hills here. It gets rocky and rough before you circle down and head for Somos Santos from the north. Those posse men couldn't track you across the rock—even if they could stand the trip.

"That-a-boy, Sheriff," Odell said, grinning again. "See how quick you came up with that? We're going to get along just fine, you and me."

"Once I've done what you told me to do, when and where do you turn her loose?" Dawson asked.

"All things in time, Dawson," Odell said, giving his sly grin as he stepped farther away from Dawson. "Do as you're told, you'll get her back so quick you'll hardly know she was gone."

Dawson stood powerless, watching the men pull away from the rocky edge, Turner keeping an arm around Carmelita and his pistol at her head. He waited in silence as they mounted their horses and slipped away quietly, taking their time, knowing they had him where they wanted him. He saw Joe Christi give him a guarded look, but he was unable to discern anything from it.

Once the riders were out of sight, Dawson walked to his horse, picked up the reins and led it the edge of the cliff. "Sheriff," he called out, "keep everybody in check. I'm coming down."

"What about the prisoners?" William Tyler called out before Edwards got a chance to respond. But Dawson didn't answer. He needed to buy all the time he could for Odell and his men to get away. He'd have to deal with the rest of Odell's scheme as it played itself out.

Dawson took his time, rifle in hand, leading his horse down the rocky path to the main trail, where Edwards and his men lay hidden behind rock and some deadfall cedar. He judged it had been a half hour or longer since Odell and the others had ridden away. That was all the time he could give them. At the bottom of the winding path Dawson stopped his horse as Sheriff Edwards and his men rose from behind cover.

William Tyler leaped over a rock, cursing under his breath, and ran forward, passing Edwards and saying loudly to Dawson, "You've got some serious explaining to do, Sheriff!"

Seeing the pistol in Tyler's hand, Dawson cocked his rifle one-handed and, without raising the barrel over a couple of inches, let go a round. The shot kicked up dirt near the barber's feet, causing him to stop abruptly.

"Holster that gun before it gets you killed," said Dawson. His thumb cocked the rifle again.

Tyler shoved his gun down into its holster with a shaking hand; but he cried out to Edwards, "Are you going to let him get away with this, Sheriff? He's shooting at us!"

"Not *us*, Tyler," said Edwards, halting the others behind him with a raised hand. "Just you. You're the one who ran toward him waving a pistol, you fool!" He jerked his thumb back over his shoulder and added, "Now get back here before something more than your pride gets hurt."

Edwards gave him a cold stare as Tyler moved back with his hands chest high and stopped beside him. "Better ask him what kind of deal he's struck with the devil," Tyler asked. If you think he didn't, you're the fool, not me."

Ignoring Tyler, Edwards looked back at Dawson and asked without hesitation, "What went on up there, Sheriff Dawson? Not trying to be an ass like Tyler, but I have to admit, it's dang peculiar, you letting them ride off that way."

Dawson motioned Edwards closer, then said in private to him, "The three we're after have met up with Odell Clarkson and Buck Turner. They're holding the woman I live with hostage. I have to break off of their trail and get back to Somos Santos. Walker and his gang are coming there to rob the bank."

Edwards studied his face for a moment, considering his best move. "Walker's the one holding our bank money anyway. If he's coming to Somos Santos, I won't have to trail these men to get to him. We'll ride back with you."

"No," said Dawson, "keep on their trail. For all I know Walker will have robbed the bank and be gone by the time I get back to town. If you stay on these men's trail, they'll lead you to Walker one way or the other—either before he robs the bank in Somos Santos or along the trail afterward. But you'll get Walker by following Odell—that's the main thing."

"What about you, Sheriff?" Edwards asked. "You'll need help. We're both lawmen. I'm staying with you."

"I'm obliged, Sheriff, but no," Dawson said shaking his head. He stepped up into his saddle as he spoke and turned his horse toward the main trail. "You get on their trail and stay on it. I'll handle the law in Somos Santos."

Chapter 23

After seven miles of hard riding, Buck Turner, carrying Carmelita on his lap, slowed his horse to a walk, saying to Odell, who slowed down beside him, "I've got to pass her around some. She's wearing my horse out." Christi and Bennie and Freddie Tapp sat quietly, their horses also winded and lathering up.

Looking Christi's horse over, Odell nodded at him, saying to Turner, "Hand her to Joe. His horse looks the freshest of the bunch." He turned a scrutinizing gaze to Christi, asking, "Is it all right with you, Joe? Can you stand carrying a soft, warm kitten on your lap for a few miles?"

Christi, not wanting to appear either reluctant or eager, shrugged and said, "I don't mind."

"Ha!" Odell laughed aloud. "I bet you don't! If you did, we'd all be a little bit worried about you."

Turner handed Carmelita over to Christi as if she weighed less than air. Turner grinned. "You two try to keep your hands off one another—you hear?"

"I hear," said Christi, ignoring Turner's lewd implication.

Freddie Tapp had taken a swig of tepid water from a canteen while Turner and Christi made their exchange. Swishing the mouthful of water and spitting a stream, he wiped his hand across his lips and said, "I get her next. I ain't had my hands on a woman's flesh since"—he searched his memory for a moment—"well, it's been too damn long."

"It'll be longer yet," said Odell. "Nobody lays hands on her until we see that her husband, the sheriff, has done what I want him to."

"Hell," said Tapp, "then it'll be too late. She'll be gone!"

Turner and Odell gave each other a knowing glance and chuckled. "Freddie," said Odell, "do I look like the kind of man who can be around a hot cherry pie and not take myself a slice of it?"

Freddie grinned but didn't answer. Odell and Turner had already reined their horses around and put their spurs to the animals. Freddie pulled his horse back a step and said to Christi and Bennie, "You two go on. I'll ride drag for awhile."

On his lap, Christi had felt Carmelita tremble upon hearing Odell's remarks. Gigging his horse ahead of Bennie and Tapp, he felt her long, dark hair on his face as he whispered close to her ear, "Don't worry, ma'am. I'm not one of them. I'll keep you safe."

But Christi's words did not calm her fear. She had no reason to trust him any more than she trusted the others. Yet, since she was in the hands of such men as Odell Clarkson and Buck Turner and Freddie Tapp, she knew she had to examine whatever offer of help came her way. Cautiously she whispered beneath the sound of the horses' hooves, "If you are not one of them, what are you doing here?"

"That's a long story, ma'am," Christi said, speaking into her hair. "My friend and I escaped from your husband's jail with Tapp. We were about to split up when we ran into these two."

"You escaped from jail in Somos Santos. So, your hands are not clean either."

"Putting it that way, ma'am," Christi said, "no, I suppose my hands are not very clean at all. But I won't let these men hurt you, not if I can help it. I hope you believe that."

She didn't answer him; and she dared not allow herself to think that she could trust him. Yet a part of her felt safer in his arms than she had felt in a long time. There was a familiarity in his breath against her ear, a kindredness in his touch— She told herself to stop it, not liking what she felt from this man, at least not under these circumstances.

They rode on until late afternoon. When they stepped down from their saddles, it was only long enough to water their horses and rest them for a few minutes in the sparse shade of a cottonwood tree. While Carmelita sat on a rock alongside a stream, Christi and Bennie looked all around the flat, barren stretch of land surrounding them.

"There's no cover for miles," Christi said after a moment of speculation.

"And there won't be until we get over on the north trail headed back down to Somos Santos," Bennie said.

"That's when we've got to make our move," Christi

said quietly. "We've got to get her away from Odell and not stop until we're out of shooting range."

"It'll be dark by the time we get there," Bennie said.

"So much the better," said Christi. Not risking the others seeing him and Bennie talking together too long, Christi walked down to the water's edge. Seeing that Carmelita had finished cooling herself by dipping water with her hands and washing her arms and face, he said, a bit roughly for Odell's sake, "All right, leave some for the next pilgrims. Get up. Let's go."

Carmelita looked up at him and hesitated. It took her a moment to realize that this change in his voice and demeanor had simply been a ruse to fool the others. Before she could comply, Christi took her by the arm and raised her to her feet, not forcefully, but firmly. Odell smiled, watching Christi lead the woman over to where Bennie stood adjusting his saddle.

"When do I get to carry her some, Odell?" Tapp asked.

"When I see that you can keep from ripping her clothes off, Freddie," Odell chuckled. Nodding at Christi, he said, "Now Joe there looks like he knows how to handle a woman."

"Bull," said Turner, also watching and chuckling. "No man knows how to handle a woman, only how best to let a woman handle him."

"Damn it, all I want is to carry her for a while," said Tapp. "I won't hurt her."

"Maybe later, Freddie," said Odell. He nodded toward Christi, who had just lifted Carmelita up to Bennie, who sat in his saddle. "It looks like our dim-witted friend here is going to carry her for now." He turned his gaze to

Tapp and smiled. "Relax, Freddie. Our two new men are doing a good job looking after her. Let the new men wear their horses down. You'll get all of that woman you want before we're finished." He eyed Carmelita and the two drovers and smiled to himself.

They mounted and rode on, with the afternoon shadows stretching long across the wild grass and creosote brush until the sun slipped down behind the western edge of the earth.

Bennie's estimation had been correct. Darkness had set in by the time they rode onto the north trail that would take them back to Somos Santos. In the clear gray light of a full moon, they sat on the cooling ground long enough to eat dried beef and drink warm water from their canteens. After a few minutes' rest, Odell stood up and dusted his trousers, his rifle hanging loosely in his hand.

"Somewhere along this trail, outside of Somos Santos, Harvey Walker and his gang are just waiting till tomorrow morning," Odell said. "Then they'll ride into Dawson's town and take down the bank the same way we took down the one in Schalene, without firing a shot." He smiled in the moonlight. "From here on, we're going to move real quiet-like." He looked at Christi and Bennie. "You two keep watching about her. As soon as we leave here, tie that bandanna back around her face."

"All right," said Joe Christi. He and the others stood up. He pulled Carmelita up by her forearm, saying, "Come on, ma'am. Time to go."

Odell watched suspiciously as Christi led her to his horse, her hands tied in front of her.

"I'm starting not to like how things are looking between them three," said Turner.

"Don't worry about it, Buck," said Odell. "I've got it covered."

Getting out of the jail in Somos Santos might have been one of the easiest things he'd ever done, Jimmy Shaggs reminded himself, gigging the stolen horse out along the trail in the light of a full moon. All he'd had to do was get Deputy Hooney Carter to take him out to the jakes right before dark, which was something he had decided Carter enjoyed doing since it gave him one more chance to see Shaggs struggle with the heavy anvil.

Once inside the smelly outhouse, Shaggs had taken the cell key and the key to his shackle down from the spot where the escapees had left it. He'd slipped the keys into his trousers, gone back inside the jail and awaited his chance. "And that, fellows, was that," Shaggs said aloud to himself, as if concluding the telling of the story to some future listener. He beamed with self-satisfaction and reined the horse down to a walk.

"Carter turned out to be a dumb sonsabitch," he said to the same imaginary someone who'd listened to his story. He pictured himself throwing back the second or perhaps even third shot of whiskey that same someone had bought him.

Shaggs was so engrossed in the mental reenactment of his jailbreak that he failed to hear the sound of horses' hooves topping a low rise in the trail, coming at him. But on the other side of the low rise, Sheriff Dawson had been more attentive to the night and to the sounds and the dark outlines and images that moved within it.

"Easy, Stony," Dawson whispered to his horse, hearing Shaggs' horse slow down from a trot to a walk on the trail ahead of him. Silently, Dawson reined his horse off the trail and sat in the darkened shadow of a tall cactus until the horse and rider moved up slowly into sight.

In the light of the full moon Dawson watched the deathly thin outlaw move past him along the trail, for a moment no more than ten feet from where the sheriff sat hidden in the velvet black shadow. With no hesitation, other than taking a close second look to ascertain for himself that was indeed Jimmy Shaggs, Dawson nudged his horse in alongside Shaggs, grabbed his reins with one hand and with his other leveled his Colt in the unsuspecting outlaw's face. "Where do you think you're going, Shaggs?" Dawson said harshly.

Startled, Shaggs let out a short scream and tried to bolt forward on his stolen horse. But Dawson held the animal firmly and circled in place with it. "Jesus! God almighty!" Shaggs cried out, but not putting up a fight. His efforts concentrated instinctively on not falling from his saddle. "Sheriff! What the hell? Where did you come from?"

"Raise your hands, Shaggs," Dawson demanded.

Shaggs' hands shot upward in surrender. "How'd you know? How'd you find me?" Shaggs whined, his voice sounding shaken.

"I smelled you." Dawson reached over with Shaggs' reins still in hand and lifted a Starr revolver from the outlaw's waist. He studied the Starr for a second and realized it belonged to Deputy Carter.

"You did, really?" Shaggs sounded puzzled.

Dawson didn't answer. Instead he said, "What are you

doing with Deputy Carter's gun." His gaze hardened on Shaggs.

"His gun," Shaggs said, stalling, but coming up with no explanation this quickly.

"What have you done to my deputy?" Dawson asked menacingly before Shaggs even had time to answer his first question.

"Nothing, Sheriff. I swear to God!" Shaggs cried, still stunned by Dawson appearing from out of nowhere. "Carter's all right. Everybody's all right!"

"Then what are you doing out of jail?" Dawson asked without relenting. He kept his big Colt leveled in Shaggs' face.

"Carter let me go, Sheriff!" the thin outlaw said, talking fast. "See, he decided that since you left him in charge and I had already served—"

Dawson cocked his Colt quickly, the sound and sight of his action stopping Shaggs instantly.

"Sheriff, that's not true!" Shaggs said quickly, as if telling on himself. "In fact that was a damn lie, and I hate myself for telling it! But Carter is all right! You have my word on that."

"Start over, Shaggs," said Dawson.

"Okay, this is what really happened," said Shaggs, sounding repentant, realizing his story would have to be altered a bit from how he'd been telling it in his mind.

"When Deputy Carter took me to the jakes," he said, "I found the keys to both the cell and my ankle chain. They're in my pocket right now. They were just laying there, Sheriff! Why Tapp and the others left them there, who knows?" He shrugged with his hands still raised. "I picked them up and"—he sighed—"God knows I meant to turn them in. But it was just too tempting, Sheriff. I never claimed to be a strong man when it comes to things like this. I expect that's been the reason for most of my failures in life."

Dawson cut him off. "Just save it, Shaggs." He reached a hand behind his back, brought out a pair of handcuffs and said, "I'll find out the truth when we get to town." Cuffing Shaggs' hands, Dawson wasted no time turning the horses and riding to Somos Santos, leading Shaggs by his horse's reins.

The two arrived in the middle of the night and rode up to the rear door of the jail. Dawson took no chances on any of Walker's men being on hand, keeping an eye on the town. He pounded on the door until Carter opened it with a surprised look on his face. "Sheriff Dawson!" he stammered. "What are you doing back so soon?" Carter hooked his suspenders over his shoulders and ran a hand back through his disheveled hair.

Dawson eyed a half-naked woman scurrying out of sight into a small back room. Pulling Shaggs along behind him, Dawson stepped past Carter. "Get her dressed and out of here."

"Yes, sir, Sheriff," said Carter. "She just happened by, and we got to talking about—" Suddenly, he caught sight of Jimmy Shaggs and stopped cold, his face turning ashen. "Shaggs? Is that you? But you're . . ." His words trailed away.

Shaggs grinned silently.

"Yes, it's him," Dawson said flatly. "Get her out of here." He reached out and barely brightened a dim lamp burning on a small wooden table. In the slightly better light, Dawson saw the pile of blankets spread on the rough plank floor. Carter stood slack-jawed, speechless, as if he were in what he could only hope would turn out to be a bad dream.

Carter stammered, tossing his dumbstruck expression at the dark cells along the main wall. "But he—I mean—How did . . . ?"

"You tell me, Deputy," said Dawson, shoving Carter's Starr pistol to him, butt first. "You're lucky he didn't steal your boots, Deputy." Dawson looked down at Shaggs' feet for the first time. Then he turned away in disgust. "Get them off, Shaggs."

Carter groaned and held both hands to his face. "I don't know what to say, Sheriff." His hands trembled as he reached for his shirt, which was lying crumpled on the floor. He picked it up and unpinned his badge from the drooping pocket.

"There's nothing to say, Deputy," Dawson replied, "but pin the badge back on if you want to stand up with me and face the Walker gang."

Carter's expression changed instantly. "Damn right I do, Sheriff!" he said. "I won't let you down. I swear it. I'll make up for all my mistakes. You won't have to worry about me when the fight comes. You'll see."

Catching a glimpse of the woman and a whiff of lilac perfume as she slipped out the back door, Dawson said, "I already know that, Deputy. That's why I hired you. There's not a man around here I'd trust more than you when it comes to a gunfight." He gestured a hand toward the inner office. "Now, if you'll knock off all this craziness, it's time we got to work." He paused for a moment, then said quietly, "They've got Carmelita."

"Walker?" Carter asked, picking up the lantern, his voice and expression already taking on a stronger bearing.

"Odell Clarkson," Dawson said, giving Shaggs a slight shove toward the cells along the inner office wall. Taking the keys he'd retrieved from Shaggs' pocket, he handed them to Carter and watched him unlock a cell door.

"What's he want to set her free?" Carter asked.

"We'll talk about it over coffee, Deputy," said Dawson, not wanting to discuss the situation in front of Shaggs. He looked over into Paco's cell. "How is he doing?"

"He's coming along," said Carter. "He was strong enough to go out back to the jakes last evening."

"Good," said Dawson. "It looks like I'm going to be needing his help."

Hearing the lawmen discuss him, Paco rose stiffly from his cot and looked bleary-eyed into the lantern light.

"Walker is coming to Somos Santos to rob the bank, Paco," Dawson said. "I've never laid eyes on the man. Will you identify him for me?"

"Identify Walker for you? Jackpot the man who had me shot?" Paco sat up on the side of his cot and pushed himself slowly to his feet. "Sheriff, if you give me a gun and lean me against a hitch rail, I will kill Walker and Dick Hohn for you as soon as they show their faces."

Chapter 24

Harvey Blue Walker and his men arose before dawn. The men cleaned, checked and prepared their weapons in the light of the campfire, listening to Walker, who stood looking down into the flames, sipping from a tin cup of coffee. "The setup is going to be the same here as it was back in Schalene Pass," he said. "I want a nice smooth job, no shooting and whooping it up in the street if we can keep from it." He looked over at Dick Hohn, giving him a nod to speak.

Glancing around the fire at Curtis Miggs, Tony Weaver, Marshal Campbell, Eddie Rings and Earl Duggins, Hohn said authoritatively, "We're a couple of men short, so Miggs is riding in alone a half hour ahead of us to watch the streets. Harvey and I will go into the bank while the rest of you stay fanned out around town. When we come out of the bank, we'll ride out quietly. I advise all of you to do the same."

"Sounds smooth enough to me," said Tony Weaver, the newest member of the gang.

Hohn grinned, saying, "Yep. Except for their bank being empty, they'll never know we was there."

A ripple of laughter moved across the men, then settled.

"What about afterward?" Tony Weaver asked Walker, who passed the question off to Hohn with the gesture of a hand.

Dick Hohn replied, "Afterward, we meet five miles on the other side of town. We'll take our cut and separate in different directions."

"What about our cuts from the other bank?" Marshal Campbell asked.

"We cut that up too," said Hohn, giving Campbell a flat stare. "After Somos Santos we'll see to it that everybody gets what's coming to them."

"Wait a minute," said Earl Duggins. "What about Freddie Tapp? He's alive. Ain't we going to break him out of jail before we leave?"

Hohn started to answer, but Walker cut in, saying firmly, "No. Freddie Tapp knew the risks of this business. He's on his own. So will any of you if you mess this job up."

"Oh." Duggins fell silent, but with a look on his face that caused Walker to comment further on the matter.

"After this job is over and we've all taken our part and split up, if any of you who want to go back and break Freddie out of jail, it's up to you." He offered a faint grin and added, "But all that money in your saddlebags is going to make the ride back to Somos Santos seem awfully long."

"I say to hell with Tapp," said Hohn, his hand resting on his pistol butt. "Anybody don't like hearing me say it, now's a good time to step forward and make your feelings known." He looked from one face to the next, then settled his gaze on Duggins. "Earl?" he asked pointedly.

Duggins fidgeted, recalling how Paco had ended up at the end of a similar conversation. "To hell with Tapp," Duggins echoed with a shrug. "I was just curious."

"Don't be," Walker said. "We're going to do a good piece of business for ourselves today. That's all you've got to think about." Having finished his coffee, he swished the grinds around in the bottom of his tin cup and slung them into the fire.

Less than a hundred yards away, Odell and Tapp sat atop their horses watching Buck Turner ride back to them from where he'd been spying on Walker's glowing campfire amid the shelter of rocks. "It's them sure enough," Turner said, sliding his horse to a halt. "They're getting set to ride out to Somos Santos this morning."

"Good," said Odell, already turning his horse to the trail. "We'll ride hard and get there ahead of them."

"What about me carrying the woman a while?" Tapp asked before Odell led the group away.

"Forget it, Freddie!" said Odell. "Bennie and Joe are in charge of her for now." He gigged his horse up into a run, the others falling in behind him.

"Gawdamn it," said Tapp, jerking his horse around and following at the rear.

On Christi's lap again after riding double with Bennie, Carmelita said quietly, "Your friend Bennie told me you are one of the fastest gunman he has ever seen. Is this so?"

"Bennie likes to tell everybody that," said Joe.

"But is it so?" Carmelita asked.

Seeing that she needed to hear something reassuring from him, Christi said, "Ma'am, the fact is, yes, I am fast with a gun. How fast, I suppose I can't say. I killed Turley Whitt. Some say he was one of the fastest guns alive."

"I see," she said, feeling his arms around her. She turned herself a bit sideways on his lap and studied his face closely in the predawn moonlight. She noted for the first time that he carried himself with the same bearing of quiet confidence she had first seen in Fast Larry Shaw and later in Cray Dawson. This was not the time to think about it, yet she allowed herself to wonder briefly why fate seemed to draw her from the arms of one gunman to another.

They rode hard until Odell led them off the trail, amid cover of rock and scrub cedar, to a clear stream less than a mile from the Somos Santos town limits. "This is working out just fine," Odell said, stepping down from his saddle, his rifle in hand, and gazing off toward the first rays of sunlight rising along the eastern horizon. "Water and rest your horses here. Fill your canteens. This might be the last chance we get for a while."

Bennie helped Carmelita down from Christi's lap. Christi stepped down behind her. He unhooked his canteen strap from his saddle horn and led his horse to the water's edge, Carmelita right beside him. As the horse drank, Christi filled the canteen and looked all around to make sure the others were not watching. Whispering to Carmelita, he pressed the small hideout gun he'd taken from the sheriff's office into her hand. "Hide this on you!"

Carmelita's hand quickly went inside her clothes with

the gun and came out empty. She smoothed down her clothes and whispered, "I do not know if I can shoot someone."

"I think you can and will, if you have to," said Christi. "Bennie and I are going to make a move on them any minute. I need for you to take cover when this business starts and to stay put until it's over. If it goes bad for us, you'll have to decide whether or not to use the pistol."

"Sí," Carmelita said, "I understand." Again she ran her hand down her dress, feeling the small pistol lying cold against her flesh.

Twenty feet behind them, they heard Odell say to Freddie Tapp, "I'm leaving you here to watch the woman. Can you do that and keep your hands to yourself?"

"Hell, yes!" said Tapp.

"Stay covered," Odell warned him. "Walker and his men will be coming right by here. Keep an eye toward the trail. If they head over this way to the water, move higher up into the rocks and lay low there."

"No problem, Odell," said Tapp.

"The rest of you mount up and let's move out," said Odell, looking back and forth between Turner, Christi and Bennie Betts.

With his rifle cradled in his arms, Odell stood still while Christi and Bennie started past him, leading their horses. "Oh, I almost forgot," he said, raising his rifle and poking the tip of the barrel against the back of Christi's head. "Joe, you and your idiot friend are waiting here too."

Christi froze in place. "What's this about?" he asked, his hands poised to make a move, but his mind telling him that he didn't stand a chance. Ahead of him, he saw Buck Turner step in and point his rifle into Bennie's stomach.

"We'll hold on to your guns for safekeeping," said Odell. He smiled. Lifting Christi's newly acquired Colt from its holster, he felt the smoothness and balance of it and said, "Damn! Turley Whitt had good taste in shooting gear."

"Why are you doing this, Odell?" Christi asked, standing stiffly, the rifle to his head. "We're on your side."

"I've been double-crossed before, Joe," said Odell. "I didn't like the taste of it. You two came along after this plan was already set. So stay here with Freddie and behave yourselves. You'll get your guns back, and you'll still be part of my gang."

"Joe, what are we going to do?" Bennie asked, his gun already taken from his holster and shoved down into Turner's belt.

Christi let out a breath and replied, "Do like he says, Bennie." Letting his hands down, Christi turned and faced Odell. "You didn't have to do it this way. We'd have waited here like you told us. You didn't have to take our guns."

"Maybe not," said Odell, "but we'll all have ourselves a good laugh about it while we're counting out that bank money."

Christi, Bennie and Carmelita watched Odell and Buck Turner mount up and ride away. Moments after they were back onto the main trail and out of sight, Tapp motioned toward a flat spot on the rocky ground and said, "Everybody sit down and make yourselves comfortable." He eyed Carmelita and added, "You just get over here beside me so's I can keep a good eye on you."

"You better think about whatever you're doing, Freddie," said Christi. "If you touch this woman, I'll kill you. I swear it."

"I said, sit down, Christi," said Tapp, jiggling his rifle. "The man with the gun is the man in charge. Your threats don't work on me." He looked Carmelita up and down hungrily. "There's some things a man like me will risk dying for."

"Joe! Look!" Bennie cut in, pointing over toward the trail. "Here they come!"

The four of them crouched in the cover of waist-high rocks and watched the Walker gang ride unhurriedly along the trail. When the riders had passed the point of turning off the trail toward the water, Tapp breathed a sigh of relief and said, "So far, so good. At that pace, Odell and Turner will beat them there by an hour." He grinned, propped himself back against a rock and turned his attention back to Carmelita. "All we've got to do now is relax and kill some time until Odell gets back."

"Listen to me, Freddie," said Christi, moving around between Tapp and Carmelita. "You and I are going to be riding together for a long time. We shouldn't be arguing over this woman. Odell said to watch her. That's all you're supposed to be doing." He stopped at a point that kept Carmelita out of Tapp's view. Carmelita stood less than three feet behind him.

"Step out of the way, Joe," said Tapp. "You're a powerful big gun, but I'm not the kind of man you want to rile."

Christi continued as if he hadn't heard Tapp. "Besides, what's going to happen when it comes time to set her free? Do you think Dawson is going to do what Odell tells him to do, if it looks like this woman has been harmed in any way?" Reaching his hand behind his back, Christi motioned for Carmelita to hand him the small gun he'd given her.

"I can't," Carmelita whispered, wondering if Christi could even hear her as weak and shaky as her voice sounded.

Christi had barely heard her, and he motioned with his hand more persistently. Still she hesitated.

Tapp managed to grin, although his expression turned tight as his temper began to get the best of him. "I've got news for you, Joe. This woman ain't going to be turned loose, no matter what Dawson does. Odell has already told me I can do what I want to with her. All I'm wanting to do is start the party a little early."

Christi heard Carmelita gasp behind him. Just as soon as Tapp finished speaking, he felt the small gun being pressed into his waiting hand. "You can't mean that, Freddie," said Christi, lowering the gun to his side, keeping it palmed against his thigh as he stepped forward. "What's this woman ever done to you?"

"If you're trying to make me feel guilty, Joe, you can forget it," said Tapp. "I will take my pleasure with that woman. To hell with everything and everybody."

Christi took three more quick steps forward, his arm coming up with the gun. Tapp saw the pistol no more than two inches from his right eye. With another second he could have swatted the small gun away; but he was all out of seconds.

The bright streak of fire from the revolver exploded

into Tapp's eye, causing a blast of blood and brain matter to splatter on Christi's face. Carmelita gasped at the sight and turned her face away as Tapp turned limp and flopped backward onto the rocks.

"Jesus!" said Bennie. He hurried over to Tapp, stepped down and grabbed his rifle. Smoke curled up from Tapp's empty eye socket. A puddle of blood spread beneath Tapp's lifeless head.

Christi stepped back, wiping his sleeve across his blood-smeared face. "At least now we've got a horse for each of us," he said. "Let's get out of here."

"Wait, please," said Carmelita. She stepped in front of him and touched a woman's kerchief to his cheek. "You—you killed him," she said. "You killed him to save me."

Christi looked at her for a moment, taking her forearms in his hands, saying, "We've got to get going, ma'am. We've got to get you to Dawson and let him know that you're all right. Once you're safe, me and Joe has to skin out of here and let things settle down some."

"Where will you go?" Carmelita asked, still badly shaken by what she'd seen.

Christi ignored her and walked over to the horses.

Seeing that Christi wasn't going to answer her, Bennie sidled in close to Carmelita's side and said, between the two of them, "We know folks at the Guizzeman Morales spread not far from Mexico City."

"Bennie! You talk too much," said Christi.

"What's the harm, Joe?" said Bennie. "We'll be in Mexico anyway. The law won't come after us in Mexico."

"You do not have to worry, Joe," Carmelita said. "You

can trust me. I would not betray a man who has killed for me."

Christi didn't respond as he led the horses over and handed Carmelita the reins to Freddie Tapp's bay. "Hurry up, both of you," he said. "This thing's not over yet."

Chapter 25

Hearing a knock on the rear door, Dawson answered it with his Colt drawn and his thumb over the trigger. Looking into Odell's eyes he asked, "Where's Carmelita?"

Behind Odell, Buck Turner started to make a grab for his gun, but his hand froze above his holster. Startled for a second by the gun barrel in his face, Odell quickly composed himself.

"She's nearby, Sheriff. I'm glad to see you've got your bark on this morning. Harvey Walker and his gang are right on our heels."

Lowering his Colt a bit, Dawson said, "Will they hit here the same way they did in Schalene Pass?"

"That's what I'm counting on," said Odell. "He'll send in a couple of men to check things out and wait along the boardwalk for him. A few minutes later, when he rides in, they'll give him the signal that everything is all right. He'll rob this bank without firing a shot. Then the lookout men will cover his back on his way out of town." Odell grinned. "Pretty slick, eh?"

Instead of answering, Dawson said, "What about Carmelita? When do I get her back?"

Odell's grin disappeared. "Freddie Tapp is holding her at a spot where he can see anybody coming from over a mile off," Odell lied. "When I get there with the money, your woman mounts a horse and rides away. What could be smoother?"

Dawson lowered his Colt into his holster, picked up a wool suit coat from beside the door and went outside. Deputy Carter stepped behind him, carrying his sawed-off shotgun. He was wearing a dark frown for the two outlaws. "This is my deputy," Dawson said to Odell. "Him and your man will get in an alley across the street from us."

"Hold it, not so fast," said Odell, not liking the idea of Dawson giving orders. "Maybe that's not the way I've got this planned."

"If you've got a better idea," Dawson snapped back at him, "you better tell us fast. If Walker's scouts see you and your pal they'll know something's up. If they see too much law on the street, that'll stop them too. My deputy needs to be where he can cover the street. I figured you'd want your man keeping an eye on him, same as you'd want to be nearby keeping an eye on me."

Odell backed off, saying, "That's the way we're going to do it. But don't forget who's in charge here, Sheriff." He thumped himself on the chest. "I'm a step behind you, and I'm the one Freddie Tapp better see riding in with the money. Otherwise, the woman is dead."

"Save your breath, Clarkson," said Dawson. "I'm sticking to my end of this deal." He looked at Carter and said, "Go on, Deputy. Get yourself in position."

Carter walked off, ignoring Buck Turner, who, after

getting a nod from Odell, followed him down the shadowy alleyway and out toward the street.

"Harvey Walker and his men are known for shooting up a town. When did he start robbing banks this way?" Dawson asked, walking with Odell to a position that would put them across the street from Carter and Buck Turner.

"Since he stole the idea from me," Odell lied, unable to keep the bitterness out of his voice.

At the front edge of an alley, Dawson and Odell stopped and looked across the street. Carter and Turner were in an adjacent alley facing them. "Now we wait," said Dawson, observing the early wagon and horse traffic coming into town. He laid the rolled-up suit coat at his feet.

They didn't have to wait long before Odell ducked back a step and said to Dawson, "Here comes Curtis Miggs! He's one of Walker's men!"

Dawson cut a glance to the single rider who had just reined his horse to a hitch rail in front of a tack shop twenty yards from the bank. Across the street, Dawson saw Carter give him a quick wave, letting him know that Turner had pointed the man out to him. "Harvey will show up in about ten minutes," said Odell. "You can set your watch to it."

"I will," Dawson said. He raised his watch from his vest pocket, opened the case, noted the time, then put the watch away.

They watched Miggs look all about the town, as he hitched his horse loosely in case he needed a fast getaway. When Miggs stepped up onto the boardwalk and began to browse into shop windows, the manager of the

Somos Santos bank, Gilliam Stuben, came walking from a restaurant a block away, a leather briefcase in hand. He arrived at the door to the bank, unlocked it, slipped inside and locked it behind himself.

Moments later Stuben raised the blind on the front door, unlocked it and turned the sign from closed to open with the flick of a wrist. Dawson checked his watch again. "It's been eight minutes."

"Yep, and they're starting to straggle in now," said Odell. He pointed out two riders coming slowly from the opposite end of town. "That's Eddie Rings and Marshal Campbell."

Before the two had stepped down from their saddles, two other riders appeared from a side street and turned in the direction of the bank. "And here comes Tony Weaver and Earl Duggins."

"Weaver," said Dawson, "that's one I recognize." He turned and gazed searchingly along the boardwalk for a moment, then looked back at Odell. As he spoke, he reached up and unpinned his badge from his chest. "He's the only one who'll recognize me." He slipped the badge into his shirt pocket and removed his wide-brimmed hat from his head. He leaned his hat against the side of a rain barrel, picked up the wool suit coat and shook it out.

"What's that for?" Odell asked, watching him curiously.

"It's to keep everybody from seeing a lawman on the street and bolting away," Dawson said. He put on the suit coat and took a short-brimmed cap from its pocket and pulled it down on his head.

Odell nodded. "Nobody in Walker's gang is going to know who the hell you are." Then he saw Harvey Walker and Dick Hohn ride slowly into sight amid the growing street traffic. "Speaking of a dirty son of a bitch, here he comes, his segundo right beside him."

Dawson studied the two riders.

"Hey!" said Odell. "You better hope there's no townsmen hiding out there! If you bring in townsmen, the woman is dead!"

"None of the townsmen know about this, Clarkson. You have my word," said Dawson, staring coldly into the outlaw's eyes until Odell felt forced to turn his eyes away.

They stood in silence, watching Dick Hohn and Harvey step down from their saddles in front of the bank. The two outlaws stepped unhurriedly onto the boardwalk and into the bank, each carrying their saddlebags slung over their shoulders.

Dawson gazed across the street at his deputy and nodded slowly. Carter gestured toward the street to his right and held up four fingers, letting Dawson know that Turner had pointed out the men to him.

"Get ready, Deputy. I'm counting on you," Dawson said to Carter under his breath, as if his deputy stood right beside him.

Inside the bank, Dick Hohn stayed at the door after closing it behind them. Harvey Blue Walker stepped quickly over to the polished oak handrail separating the manager's office area from the wide lobby. "Well," said the manager, standing, clasping his hands together, "my first customers of the day! Good morning, gentlemen. Gilliam Stuben at your service. How may I help you?"

Harvey sprang over the handrail, drawing his pistol

and slinging his dusty saddlebags onto the manager's desk. Top of the morning, Gilliam Stuben," Walker said in a mock greeting. "Harvey Walker and Dick Hohn here. We're robbing your fine facility this morning." He cocked his pistol an inch from Stuben's bulging eyes. "Get your fat ass over there and open that safe." He snatched his saddlebags and followed the frightened banker.

Dick Hohn turned the sign from open to closed and drew the blind down. "Where's your teller this morning?" he asked, hurrying over, jumping the handrail and accompanying them to the large safe in the rear wall.

"He—he's off today with the grippe, sir," Stuben replied, his pale hand nervous on the safe door handle. Drawing a key from inside his coat, he tried to get it inserted into the lock.

"Hurry up, Mr. Stuben!" Walker demanded.

"Yes, there we are, sirs," the bank manager said, swinging the door wide open, revealing the safe's almost empty interior. "Take it all. Only please don't hurt me, I beseech you."

"Take it all?" Walker turned his shocked gaze from the safe to Stuben. "Are you being funny, you son of a bitch?" he growled, swinging his gun back into the manager's ashen face.

"Oh no, indeed not, sir!" said Stuben, appearing bewildered. "I'm only trying to let you know that I am cooperat—"

"Where's the Gawdamned money?" Walker bellowed, shoving Stuben out of his way and stomping into the safe.

"Right there!" said Stuben, pointing a shaky finger at

a modest row of bills stacked neatly on a wall shelf. "I'm afraid that's everything the bank has, except for a few dollars in the teller's drawer, of course."

"Gawdamn it!" Walker shrieked. "A bank this size? In a town with a big gun like Cray Dawson for sheriff? I don't believe you!"

Opening the teller drawer, Dick Hohn raised a few dollars and let them flutter from his gloved hand. "This is pitiful," he said in disgust.

Stuben tossed his hands up in helplessness. "Somos Santos usually keeps the capital for all the cattle ranchers hereabouts. But this time of year, most of them deposit their money in Abilene near the railheads, to keep from having to carry it on them across the wilds."

Walker lowered his pistol and aimed it at Stuben's crotch.

"Hold on, Harvey!" said Hohn. "Don't pull that trigger! It's bad enough we're not getting paid! Don't bring the town down on us. Remember who's the sheriff here!"

Walker gritted his teeth, but lowered his gun. "You lousy Gawddamn banker!" he growled at Stuben. "You've probably robbed this place yourself!" Shoving the saddlebags into Stuben's stomach, he demanded, "Fill them up!"

"This is bad," said Hohn, stepping over beside Walker while the bank manager quickly stuffed the money into the saddlebags. "But at least we've got the money from the last job. Once something goes this sour, it's best to cut out and not look back."

"I wanted this to be a big one," said Walker. "I wanted to show that I could clean out a bank under a big gunman's nose."

"Next time, Harvey," said Dick Hohn, stepping over and picking up the loose money he'd dropped from the teller's drawer. "We're on to a good thing. We ain't about to stop."

Chapter 26

Odell stood watching with his gun drawn. He liked this setup. Dawson walked along the dirt street, just off the boardwalk, getting ready to meet Walker and Hohn when they came out of the bank. Smiling to himself, Odell practiced aiming his pistol toward Eddie Rings from the cover of the shadowy alley.

"Ka-pow," he whispered, his hand jumping as if he'd really fired a shot. He could shoot anybody he wanted to from that position. But the real shooting, out there in the open, he'd leave to Cray Dawson, right up to the end, right up to where he'd walk up to Harvey, wounded on the ground, and say "So long, pard. It looks like I've won after all."

Walker's men paid no more attention to Dawson in his wool suit coat and soft cap than they did to any other pedestrian walking along the dirt street. Dawson paced himself, hoping his timing would allow him to meet Walker and Hohn straight on as they tried to ride calmly out of town.

Glancing back toward the bank after he passed it, he saw the door open and Walker and Hohn walk to their horses, their saddlebags draped over their shoulders. He hurried his pace just a little, giving a guarded glance toward each of Walker's men, who stood strategically spread out along his exit route.

The last outlaw along the street, Tony Weaver, stood nervously keeping an eye on the sheriff's office. Once Dawson walked past Weaver, he slowed his pace, hearing the two horses draw closer to him in the middle of the street.

"Now!" Dawson told himself, swinging wide to the middle of the street, his Colt coming up cocked and ready in his hand. Without warning, he fired. But Harvey Walker and Dick Hohn, in their highly intense state, managed to react quickly. Dawson's first shot lifted Walker sideways from his saddle and into the dirt; but it didn't render him helpless. With blood gushing from a shoulder wound, he got off a return shot at Dawson.

At the sudden outbreak of gunfire, townsfolk ran for cover. Doors slammed shut; horses and wagons fled in every direction. A large hound appeared out of nowhere, and stood in the middle of the street, barking madly.

"It's Dawson!" Tony Weaver shouted from his position on the boardwalk.

"Kill him!" Dick Hohn shouted out to the other gunmen as he fired at Dawson from atop his spooked and rearing horse. His shot grazed along the band of Dawson's soft cap, spinning it from his head.

Weaver fired one wild shot before retreating out of sight in panic. Hohn got off another shot as he spun his horse quickly into an alley. "Kill the sonsabitch!" he demanded. But his words weren't needed. The rest of Walker's men had already sprung into action. Pistol and rifle shots exploded almost as one from along the street. Bullets sliced through the air all around Dawson's head and chest; dirt exploded upward from the ground at his boots. He fired as he hurried backward, needing cover badly.

From his alley, Carter ran out to the middle of the street, bringing the shotgun to Dawson's defense. Seeing the deputy, Earl Duggins turned toward him, his pistol blazing. But an overpowering blast of nail heads caught Earl Duggins full in the chest and sent him flying backward through a large window in a spray of shattered glass.

Four feet from Duggins, the same blast had also sent Curtis Miggs spinning along the boardwalk until he struck the corner post of the overhang and broke in half. The corner end of the boardwalk sagged dangerously low. Marshal Campbell ducked from under the boardwalk into the street, firing at Carter on his way. The second blast from Carter's shotgun exploded. Campbell's head flew away, leaving a mist of blood and bone matter in its wake.

"Gawdamn it!" shouted Harvey Walker, struggling to his feet and giving his horse a slap on its rump to send it away. "Come out, you lawdog son of a bitch!" He stalked forward, firing steadily toward where Dawson had ducked around the corner of a building for cover. When his Colt ran out of bullets, he flung it to the ground and jerked another from behind his back. In that second, Dawson stepped out, facing him from a distance of thirty feet, his Colt poised and ready to fire.

"Hey!" shouted Dick Hohn, bolting out of an alley on his horse, his rifle coming up and aiming at Dawson.

Carter hurriedly reloaded his shotgun, seeing both Walker and Hohn leveling down on Dawson. But before he could get the shotgun clicked shut, his attention turned quickly to the sound of breaking glass from the second floor of the Somos Santos Hotel.

From a broken hotel window, Paco reached out with a Winchester and fired. Hohn flew from his saddle, his shot going wild, and landed flat on his back in the middle of the dirt street. At the same time, Walker, advancing on Dawson, sent a bullet screaming past his head.

"Shoot him, Sheriff!" Carter shouted, hurrying sideways to get a clearer shot at Walker.

"No! Stay back!" Dawson called out, his right hand extended with his Colt cocked and ready.

"Yeah, Deputy, Walker's all mine!" shouted Odell, running from the alley, afraid one of the lawmen would kill Walker before he got his full taste of revenge.

"Wait!" shouted Dawson, hearing Odell running up the street behind him. Keeping his arm extended and ready, he watched Walker stagger forward, his gun hand drooping, and fall to one knee.

"Why?" Odell said with a dark chuckle. "He's no danger now." He hurried past Dawson. With his gun out and pointed at Walker, he said, "Remember me, you rotten son of a bit—"

From twenty yards away, a shot exploded. The impact of the bullet caused Walker to jerk stiffly upright so hard that his gun fell from his hand. "No!" shouted Dawson, knowing what consequences Walker's death would have for Carmelita. Insantly, Dawson's Colt bucked in his hand, his bullet hitting Eddie Rings, the last of Walker's gunmen, as he ran out of an alley and managed to get off a shot. Now Rings lay flat on his back, dead in the street.

Dawson cut his gaze to Odell, who stood weaving back and forth, a look of disbelief in his eyes, his hands clutching his chest as if trying to stop the flow of blood. "You didn't . . . do what . . . we agreed to," he said haltingly. He dropped to his knees as Dawson hurried to him.

"I told you to wait!" Dawson said. He grabbed Odell by his shirt and shook him, seeing the outlaw's eyes begin to glaze over. "Where is she, Clarkson? Tell me! Tell me!"

"He's not going to tell you," Carter said. "He's dead."

Dawson let go of Odell and stood up, his shoulders slumped. "Now what will become of Carmelita?"

But no sooner had he spoken than, from the broken window on the hotel, Paco called down, "Rider coming, Sheriff! It's a woman."

"Huh?" Dawson turned and saw the rider come into view at a flat-out run, in front of a large cloud of dust. "Carmelita?"

From the window, Paco called down, "More riders coming, Sheriff! It looks like a lot of riders coming! I think it is the posse."

"Edwards," said Dawson. "Come down here, Paco. Give Deputy Carter the rifle. You're still Edwards' prisoner."

Waiting for Paco, Dawson asked Carter, "Where's Turner?"

"He's knocked out cold, handcuffed around a post over in the alley," said Carter. He nodded at Odell's body lying no more than five feet from Walker's. "I figured if something like this happened, we would want to make sure no harm came to Turner until he told us where to find your woman."

"That was good thinking, Deputy," Dawson said, hoping he sounded more pleased than surprised. He continued to watch the approaching rider, certain that it was indeed Carmelita keeping the horse at a hard, fast pace.

A moment later he turned his eyes to Paco. The Mexican walked toward him from the hotel, the rifle hanging loosely in his hands. Along the boardwalk, townsfolk began to reappear, walking cautiously among the dead in the street. Handing the rifle over to Carter, Paco asked Dawson, "Will you put in a word for me, tell Edwards I helped you here?"

"I will," said Dawson. "I'm much obliged to you." To Carter he said, "Take him back to the jail."

Dawson stood in the same spot, watching Carmelita ride into town. He only stepped forward toward her when she stopped her horse twenty feet away and slid down from her saddle. They embraced for a moment. Then each took a short step back. She glanced around at the dead on the street.

"I know what you were willing to do for me, Cray," she said, her eyes tearful. "I will always be grateful to you for that."

Dawson smiled. "Thank God you're all right. How did you get away?"

"Joe Christi saved me," she said. "He killed Freddie Tapp and saved me from those animals." She studied Dawson's eyes and said, "He is not an outlaw, you know—him or Bennie."

"I never figured they were," said Dawson. "I was curious why he was riding with Odell, though."

"It was to watch over me," Carmelita said. "He saw the spot I was in, and he could not leave me alone with Odell and his men." She crossed herself quickly. "God must've sent him to me."

Dawson only nodded, letting her speak her mind.

Carmelita pointed at the riders coming quickly along the trail into Somos Santos. "They started chasing us no sooner than we headed here. I made Joe and Bennie leave me and take the Old Comanche Trail. We must tell Edwards to leave them alone."

"I expect once Edwards gets his bank's money, he'll be satisfied to go on back to Schalene." He nodded toward the saddlebags on Dick Hohn's and Harvey Walker's horses as a townsman led the shaken animals to a hitch rail and tied down their reins. "But I'll tell him Christi and Bennie are both innocent anyway."

"Good," said Carmelita. She folded her dusty hands and looked down at her feet in silence for a moment.

Finally, Dawson said, "So how did Odell come to hold you hostage anyway? You were on the stage, last I knew."

"*Sí,* I was," she replied, "but I saw smoke, I was coming back."

"You were worried," Dawson asked, "about me?"

"Of course, about you," said Caremelita. "Just because we are no longer lovers does not mean I wouldn't worry if I knew you were in danger."

"I understand," said Dawson. "Same here."

They stood for another moment in silence, each of

them realizing that all they had to say had been said the night before she'd left.

"You must be tired," Dawson offered, reaching out for her hand again. "Let's get you over to the hotel."

"No," she said, ignoring his hand. "I cannot stay." She looked past him toward the livery stable. "I must get a fresh horse and ride. I must leave quickly."

"But where will you go? What's your hurry?" Dawson asked, giving her an astonished look.

Carmelita only stared at him until realization came to him.

"Oh, I see." He turned with her and gazed toward the livery barn. "You can have Stony," Dawson said. "He's saddled and ready to ride. He's the fastest horse in town."

"No, I cannot take Stony," Carmelita said quietly. "I know how much that horse means to you."

"Come on." Dawson took the reins to her horse and walked her and the tired horse around the sheriff's office, where Turner and Odell had left their horses earlier. "Take them both," he said. "You might wear one out if you have to travel that fast."

Carter had returned to the street when Dawson walked back around alone. "Here they come," Carter said, nodding toward the posse. Looking back in the direction Dawson had come from, he asked, "What were you doing back there? Where's Carmelita?"

"She's gone," Dawson said, giving no indication that he wanted to say any more.

"Oh," Carter said flatly.

"I've been thinking, Deputy," said Dawson changing the subject, watching the posse draw closer. "That anvil is not a bad idea on a prisoner like Jimmy Shaggs. But maybe you should get one just a little bit lighter."

"I sure will!" said Carter.

"I'll go find one right now and get him out here cleaning the streets!"

"You do that, Deputy." Before Carter turned to walk away, Dawson said, "I must be out of my mind."

"Why's that, Sheriff?" Carter asked.

"I just told the most beautiful woman in the world that she could have the best horse I ever owned so she could ride off into the arms of another man."

Carter gave him a strange look—one that said he wasn't sure if Dawson had spoken for a laugh or for sympathy.

"I have to admit, Sheriff, that does sound pretty peculiar," Carter said, offering only a half smile until he better understood the nature of the conversation.

Dawson looked at him, offering a tired smile. Feeling confident enough now to offer a laugh in return, Carter said, "What say we finish up with Edwards, then go get ourselves a beer and a steak? We'll sit down and have ourselves a rest."

"A beer sounds good, Deputy." Dawson glanced toward the posse coming in faster, and at the townsmen picking up the dead outlaws and carrying them away. "So does a steak." He gazed out at the single lonely line of dust rising in Carmelita's wake. "No rest for you and me, though," Dawson said in a softer voice. "We're the law in Somos Santos."

SIGNET HISTORICAL FICTION

Ralph Cotton

THE BIG IRON SERIES

JURISDICTION

0-451-20547-2

Young Arizona Ranger Sam Burrack has vowed to bring down a posse of murderous outlaws—and save the impressionable young boy they've befriended.

VENGEANCE IS A BULLET

0-451-20799-8

Arizona Ranger Sam Burrack must hunt down a lethal killer whose mind is bent by revenge and won't stop killing until the desert is piled high with the bodies of those who wronged him.

HELL'S RIDERS

0-451-21186-3

While escorting a prisoner to the county seat, Arizona Ranger Sam Burrack comes across the victims of a scalp-hunting party. Once he learns that the brutal outlaws have kidnapped a young girl, he joins the local sheriff in the pursuit—dragging along his reluctant captive.

Available wherever books are sold or at www.penguin.com

SIGNET BOOKS

"A writer in the tradition of Louis L'Amour and Zane Grey!" —*Huntsville Times*

National Bestselling Author

RALPH COMPTON

NOWHERE, TEXAS	**0-451-21132-4**
SHOWDOWN AT TWO-BIT CREEK	**0-451-20854-4**
THE SKELETON LODE	**0-451-19762-3**
DEATH RIDES A CHESNUT MARE	**0-451-19761-5**
WHISKEY RIVER	**0-451-19332-6**
TRAIN TO DURANGO	**0-451-19237-0**
DEVIL'S CANYON	**0-451-19519-1**
SIXGUNS AND DOUBLE EAGLES	**0-451-19331-8**
THE BORDER EMPIRE	**0-451-19209-5**
AUTUMN OF THE GUN	**0-451-19045-9**
THE KILLING SEASON	**0-451-18787-3**
THE DAWN OF FURY	**0-451-18631-1**
DEATH ALONG THE CIMMARON	**0-451-20769-6**
DOOMSDAY RIDER	**0-451-21080-8**
RIDERS OF JUDGMENT	**0-451-20214-7**
DEMON'S PASS	**0-451-19763-1**

Available wherever books are sold or at www.penguin.com

S543